THE REBEL
DA

MILLS
BOON

Published in Great Britain 2015
by Mills & Boon, an imprint of Harlequin (UK) Limited,
Eton House, 18-24 Paradise Road, Richmond, Surrey, TW9 1SR

© 2015 Lauri Robinson

ISBN: 978-0-263-24804-3

Printed and bound in Spain
by CPI, Barcelona

A lover of fairytales and cowboy boots, **Lauri Robinson** can't imagine a better profession than penning happily-ever-after stories about men (and women) who pull on a pair of boots before riding off into the sunset—or kick them off for other reasons. Lauri and her husband raised three sons in their rural Minnesota home, and are now getting their just rewards by spoiling their grandchildren.

Visit: laurirobinson.blogspot.com, facebook.com/lauri. robinson1, twitter.com/LauriR

Books by Lauri Robinson

Mills & Boon® Historical Romance

Daughters of the Roaring Twenties

The Runaway Daughter (Undone!)
The Bootlegger's Daughter
The Rebel Daughter

Stand-Alone Novels

Unclaimed Bride
Inheriting a Bride
The Cowboy Who Caught Her Eye
Christmas Cowboy Kisses
'Christmas with Her Cowboy'
The Major's Wife
The Wrong Cowboy
A Fortune for the Outlaw's Daughter

Mills & Boon® Historical *Undone!* eBooks

Testing the Lawman's Honour
The Sheriff's Last Gamble
What a Cowboy Wants
His Wild West Wife
Dance with the Rancher
Rescued by the Ranger
Snowbound with the Sheriff
Never Tempt a Lawman

**Visit the author profile page
at millsandboon.co.uk for more titles**

To Sara at the White Bear Lake Historical Society.
The information you shared was invaluable!

Chapter One

White Bear Lake, Minnesota, 1925

Twyla Nightingale swore she'd been reborn. Released. Free. Like a bird that had just learned to fly, or a dog that had finally chewed through the rope tying it to the porch. Excitement hummed through her veins. The smile living on her lips was there when she woke up and still there when she went to bed. It was real, too. As genuine as a new bill. At times her cheeks hurt from grinning.

And she loved it.

L-O-V-E-D. It.

Rightfully so.

Just a few weeks ago she'd have been watching out the bedroom window or crouched down peering through the spindles of the staircase that led from the ballroom to the second floor of the resort. But now she was front and center, wearing that cheek-aching grin while greeting guests, as men in neatly pressed three-piece suits and dapper hats escorted their ladies through the double front doors of the resort. The latest fashions these women wore were as elegant as the men escorting them. Floppy hats and feathered headbands matched their fringe-covered flapper dresses and two-piece skirt outfits in the most popular colors. Teal, burgundy, gold and green.

Green.

Now that was a color. Twyla's favorite. The color of money. Lettuce, kale, clams, jack—whatever you wanted to call it, it was all money. Even before tonight she'd loved how money had changed her life. She gave her father the credit for that. A few years ago he'd been a brewery worker, bringing home barely enough money to keep his family clothed and put food on the table. Now she and her sisters were dressed in the height of fashion and Nightingale's resort served finer food than some of the most famous hotels in the world.

Life was so good she wanted to skip instead of walk. Just standing here her feet itched with excitement. She'd imagined, but still couldn't believe how wonderful things had become since she'd stopped living on the sidelines.

In many ways she had her sister to thank for the life-changing transformation. If Norma Rose asked, Twyla would get down and kiss her sister's toes. That's how appreciative she was, and she would do anything and everything to keep things going just as they were this very minute. One of the largest parties of the year was taking place at the resort tonight, and she was the hostess. Well, one of them. Norma Rose and another sister, Josie, were here, too, but in many ways that only made things better.

Smiling brightly, and elegantly waving a hand with brightly painted nails, Twyla greeted another couple and directed them toward the elaborately carved wooden front desk, where Josie would write them a meal receipt. They would then be directed to the ballroom and adjoining dining room, where the celebration of Palooka George's fiftieth birthday would soon begin.

Up until two weeks ago, Josie, younger than Twyla by two years, and Ginger, younger by five years, had also been living on the sidelines. Norma Rose, the oldest at twenty-five, had been the only one permitted downstairs during parties. Mainly because until recently she'd run Nightingale's all by herself, ever since it had been transformed from a dance pavilion to an expansive resort catering to those with wads of cash to spend. Their father, Roger Nightingale, claimed he ran it, but everyone knew that Norma Rose did, while Roger oversaw his bootlegging business. Her father's profession didn't bother Twyla in the least. Without bootlegging, she'd still be wearing Norma Rose's hand-me-downs, which had been someone else's hand-me-downs before Norma Rose had acquired them.

Folks could hate Prohibition all they wanted; Twyla loved it.

She loved the glitzy and glamorous parties, the racy freedom and even the wild and wicked underground world that flourished more every day. No one could have guessed her life could change so fast. Especially not Twyla. It had all happened when Ginger had run away with Brock Ness, and Ty Bradshaw had shown up searching for some gangster. Although everyone thought Ty was a lawyer, Twyla now knew differently, but her lips were sealed and would remain so. He'd caught the hoodlum he was after out in Wisconsin, or so Twyla had heard, but that wasn't what had changed things. Norma Rose had. Shortly after Ty arrived, Norma Rose turned a proverbial corner. Love, that's what had done it. Ever since falling for Ty, Norma Rose wasn't focused on running the resort by herself.

Finally, thank heaven above, she'd asked her sisters to help run the place.

Twyla had jumped at the chance to step up, and so had Josie. Ginger was still in Chicago and Twyla didn't expect her to return home anytime soon, but that opinion she kept mostly to herself—except when she was with Josie, who felt the same way. The two of them had discussed that Ginger had been in love with Brock for some time. Neither Twyla nor Josie were looking for love. They had other seeds to sow.

Josie was the quietest of the sisters and rarely complained, but Twyla knew she had been as tired of Norma Rose ruling them as Twyla had. Before Ty appeared on the scene, Norma Rose had staunchly refused anyone's help—other than to make beds and scrub floors. Those chores she'd passed out like candy at a parade.

There was more to it than the chores. For the past few years, along with their father, Norma Rose had treated them as if they were still the young girls who'd all shared a bedroom in their old farmhouse, where the flu had swooped down one winter as dark and pitiless as any plague. That had been devastating to all of them. Within weeks of each other, their mother, brother, grandparents and several other community members had died.

The epidemic had taken more than lives. It had taken hopes and dreams and promises never meant to be broken. Those were the things Twyla remembered slipping away that cold, dark winter. Those were also the things she was determined to get back.

The deaths of so many in their family had left

holes. Big holes right in the very center of her heart. It had been a painful time to live through, but she had. And so had her father and three sisters. Norma Rose had appointed herself to take on the role left vacant by their mother's death, and life had marched forward much as it had before. It hadn't been until a couple of years later, when another blow shook their family, that things changed immensely. It was also when Norma Rose had taken it upon herself to see that none of the Nightingale sisters became doxies—her words, not Twyla's.

Twyla wasn't overly concerned about being labeled a doxy—people could think what they wanted, she knew the truth—but she was interested in having fun and adventures. That was the part of her life that had completely disappeared. There were no adventures for a girl locked in her bedroom. If you asked her, none of them were likely to become doxies—not with their father. Very few people chose to anger Roger Nightingale, who was known as The Night in some close-knit circles. Even fewer were brave enough to actually show interest in one of his daughters. Not that kind of interest.

That, too, played in Twyla's favor. Now that she had her father's blessing—for he had been very happy she and Josie were helping Norma Rose—she was going to live it up. She was going to dance until the sun came up with as many men as she liked. Have herself some good old-fashioned adventures.

She'd be careful, though; men were a slippery slope. On that particular subject, she was more wise than people realized. Take Norma Rose, for instance. As smart as her sister thought she was, it hadn't taken long for Ty to make Norma Rose turn over a new leaf.

Twyla saw why. The way Ty looked at Norma Rose made her sister melt in her shoes. No one had ever done that to Norma Rose before. Not even…

Twyla stopped her train of thought, or at least rerouted it. Nothing lasted forever. Life had taught her that years ago. Besides, right now she had a lot of living to do, a lot of making up to do. She would admit watching Ty and Norma Rose made her smile. It was time Norma Rose found someone else, something else, other than the resort. Her sister had gone through a bad time a while back, and Twyla was happy to know Norma Rose had finally gotten over it.

The two of them—Ty and Norma Rose—hadn't announced wedding plans or anything, yet Twyla knew that would happen soon. At least she hoped beyond all hope on this green earth that was what would happen, because she had plans. Big plans. All those people who'd teased her about being the little sister who couldn't come out and play would soon be eating their words. By the end of the summer, Nightingale's resort would be known as her playground, and it would be *the place* everyone wanted to play.

"Good evening, Twyla."

Twyla's thoughts were shattered and her spine quivered as if a hairy spider had just zipped up her back. She turned, ever so slowly, to face the one man she'd just refused to think about. The one man who could very well throw a wrench into everything, into all her dreams of stepping into Norma Rose's shoes and running the resort.

That could not happen. Would not happen. She pulled up every evil thought she'd ever had against him, in the hope it would help. "Good evening, Forrest," she said calmly, coldly. "Glad you could make it."

"I'm sure you are," he said dryly.

With immense effort, Twyla held a smile on her face and continued to greet and direct the couples still streaming through the open double doors, as she told Forrest, "Josie will write you a receipt."

"I'll wait for you," he said, smiling and nodding at guests as if he had every right to do so while standing next to her. "Considering neither of us has a date."

He was a smooth one, Forrest Reynolds, always had been. A real charmer, even as a kid, teasing all the girls and pretending to be a hero. In truth, leastwise in Twyla's eyes, Forrest was the reason Norma Rose had become a tyrant over the past few years. Norma Rose had always been bossy, but after Forrest had left, she'd turned gnarly. She'd worn nothing but black and acted like a spinster twice her age. At one time Norma Rose had been in love with Forrest, but then he and his father, Galen Reynolds—an evil man if ever there was one—had broken her heart. Nope, Twyla would not let Forrest spoil her sister's happiness, or ruin the life she was finally getting a chance to live.

"I don't need a date," Twyla muttered out the corner of her mouth. The evil thoughts she'd poured forward were slipping, perhaps because there weren't too many. At one time she'd considered Forrest a friend. Her best friend. She reminded herself she'd been about ten years old back then. That allowed the reason he was standing beside her now to pop forward. "You're only here because with Brock in Chicago, we needed a musician." It was the truth. Brock going to Chicago to play on the radio had left the resort without a top-notch performer, which the guests of Palooka George's party expected. "Norma Rose only agreed to let you come because you wouldn't loan us Slim Johnson if she didn't."

"She didn't put up much of a fight," Forrest said. "Far less than I expected."

Twyla spun to shoot a glare directly into his chocolate-colored eyes. They were such a contrast to his blond hair that she had to suck in a quick breath before she could spout, "You leave my sister alone."

"Norma Rose and I are old friends," Forrest said, curling his lips into a sly smile. "Just like you and I. And I look forward to getting reacquainted with all of you."

She wasn't fool enough to believe that. If he'd wanted to get reacquainted with any of them he could have made an effort months ago, when he'd first returned to town with his convertible roadster and airplane. Her hopes, if she'd had any, of reigniting their friendship had died long ago. "My father put yours in prison," Twyla reminded him. "I don't believe that would lay ground for any of us to be friends. I for one have no desire to get reacquainted with you, and I know Norma Rose feels the same."

"Same old Twyla," he drawled.

She'd give about anything to be able to kick him in the shin.

Glancing around, he added, "I'll let Norma Rose decide that."

Kicking him might be impossible, but she wouldn't allow him to ruin things. Not again.

"Stay away from her, Forrest," Twyla warned. "Test me on this, and I guarantee you won't like the outcome."

He had the gall to laugh right in her face. Then again, he'd always had the gall to laugh at her. Usually she'd laughed with him. Not anymore. She let her glare tell him that.

"Everything's still a challenge to you, isn't it?" He flicked the end of her nose. "When are you going to learn *you* are no match for me, Twyla, and no match for your sister, either?"

That invisible creepy spider moved from her spine to her chest, where it wrapped all eight hairy legs around her heart and squeezed tightly. She was a match for Forrest and would prove it. No one would get in her way. Especially not some flyboy who thought himself a hero because he'd returned home in the nick of time to save his family business, the Plantation nightclub.

"I hope you're hungry," she said, in between greeting guests and wearing the smile that moments ago had started to slip but now returned, rejuvenated. The Plantation would never rival the resort, no matter who ran it. "Because you're about to eat your words."

The glimmer in his eyes was full of challenge. To say Forrest Reynolds was handsome would be an understatement. He'd always been more on the gorgeous side. Besides his contrasting brown eyes and blond hair, he was tall and lean, the type of man who looked good in everything he wore. His navy blue suit was fitted—wide across the shoulders, slender at the hips. He looked ravishing in it, and although she'd never told anyone nor ever would, no one looked as dashing as Forrest when he was wearing his flyboy getup. With brown boots that came up to his knees, his bulky leather jacket and that hat with its floppy ear flaps and round goggles, no man came close to his handsomeness. Her heart fluttered just thinking about it.

Only because she appreciated a handsome man. She always had. Forrest, handsome or not, was no contest for her. Few knew, but Twyla had long ago learned how to charm men into doing just about anything. She'd learned how to be slick, too, in order to sneak away from the resort without being seen by her father's men, the watchmen and guards who surrounded the property twenty-four hours a day. There was, after all, only so many nights a girl could stay locked in her room. She'd met her quota some time ago.

If she was a compassionate woman—which she was not—she might feel a bit sorry for Forrest and his beliefs.

As she only came up to his shoulder, he leaned down slightly, and the warmth of his breath tickled her ear. She'd just pierced the lobes a little over a week ago and was thankful they were no longer sore and throbbing. She sincerely hoped Forrest noticed those were real diamonds dangling on the silver loops. He was not dealing with a poor little girl anymore. She was far from that. In fact, they were on even ground these days. Her family now had as much wealth as his—if not more—and she would gladly use that against him, along with everything else she could come up with.

"Don't forget where I live, Twyla," he said as softly as the wind blew.

Caught off guard between the scent of his cologne and the warmth of his whisper, she stuttered slightly. "Wh-what?"

"Where I live. The Plantation."

She rolled her eyes. "Of course I know you live at your nightclub. Everyone does. So what?"

"It's next to the amusement park."

After greeting another guest, she said, "Everyone knows that, too."

"Where you held your kissing booth."

Her stomach dropped to the floor. There were a few things she wasn't proud of, namely the childish things she'd allowed Mitsy Kemper to talk her into while rebelling against Norma Rose and her father, but she truly didn't believe anyone would have the gall to bring them up, especially to her face. If her father ever heard about some of her antics, things could change. Swiftly.

"Aw, there's your father," Forrest said. "I think I'll go say hello."

Twyla grabbed his arm. Her father knew nothing about the kissing booth and several other things, and if he learned of them, whether she was twenty-three or eighty-three, she'd be back to watching life from the sidelines. "Don't you dare," she growled.

Forrest lifted a brow.

Damn. He knew he had her cornered, just like always. If they were anywhere but the front foyer of the resort, where people continued to file through the door, she'd tell him just what she thought of him. And of the way he always seemed to be one step ahead of her. She wasn't prepared for this. She needed time to think.

That spider was now in her stomach, stinging the dickens out of her.

She bit down on her bottom lip, hard, forcing her mind to come up with something. Anything.

Hadn't she heard something about keeping enemies close? Well, Forrest was enemy number one. Therefore, the closer she kept him, the better. Norma Rose would be furious, but it was the only option. Forcing her lips into a smile, Twyla added, "After all, you are my date."

"Your date?"

"Yes," she said with more confidence than she felt. "My date."

Forrest questioned his sanity. He'd spent years distancing himself from all of the Nightingales—out of necessity—yet here he was, back at square one. What had he been thinking?

That the past wasn't over. That was what he'd been thinking. Requesting to be allowed to attend the parties Norma Rose had asked to hire Slim for had seemed logical at the time. It would give him the chance to talk to Roger Nightingale face-to-face, but now he wondered if he should have spent more time considering the consequences.

Maybe it was just Twyla's obvious disdain toward him that caught him off guard. He hadn't expected that from her, although he should have expected it from her and all the Nightingales, including the new lawyer it was rumored Norma Rose was glued to. He was prepared for the lawyer and Norma Rose, just not Twyla. A million years may not have prepared him for her.

It wasn't her attitude that surprised him. She'd been the one to call him to ask about Slim Johnson filling in for Brock and had been more than a little put out when he wouldn't talk to her. No, it was her that surprised him. The woman she'd become.

Forrest glanced down at the redheaded sister. Seeing her from afar hadn't done her justice. If he'd known then—when he requested attendance—what he knew now, he might have approached this situation a bit differently.

Maybe.

The bottom line was, it had to be done.

Her hair was naturally blond, like all the Nightingale girls, but being the wild one, Twyla had dyed it cherry-red. It had faded since he'd last caught a glimpse of her at the amusement park. Her hair was now more auburn, and the color looked good on her. It brought out the blue of her eyes and made her stand out in a crowd in a best-looking-gal-in-the-room sort of way.

She definitely stood out in a shimmering silver dress that barely covered her knees and a tiny pill hat swathed with silver netting. Twyla had always been the most brazen of the sisters, and Forrest hoped Roger Nightingale knew what he was doing by turning her loose in his resort. Especially tonight. He recognized faces. Lots of them. There were more gangsters filing through the door than roamed the streets of Chicago. That also made him wonder if all the tales he'd heard about Roger Nightingale and his bootlegging business were true.

Things had certainly changed since he'd left town. His return hadn't been overly welcomed, either, but he hadn't expected it to be. The tapping of a toe, along with those glittery blue eyes shooting daggers at him, brought his mind back to the conversation at hand, which had been... Aw, yes, being Twyla's date for the evening.

"I thought you didn't need a date," he said, nodding to another couple he recognized who'd just walked through the front door—the local sheriff and his wife. Nightingale sure knew how to play the game. Galen should have taken lessons.

"I don't *need* a date," Twyla said coyly, gracefully sweeping a hand toward the front desk, indicating that was where the couple could purchase their meal tickets, which included complimentary drinks. No one had to be told that; it was a given. The resort didn't need the lure of a blind pig to bring in drinking customers, or the ploy to make the government think it was all legal. People poured through the doors knowing full well drinks would be flowing all night. Even lawmen.

Twyla was peering back up at him and batting those long lashes. Forrest bit back a grin. She did make a dazzling hostess—a glimpse of the glamour people could expect all evening—however, all the charm she had in that sweet little body wouldn't work on him. He was immune by self-inoculation, if there was such a thing, but he could let her think differently for now. Toying with Twyla, challenging her every word and action, had long been a favorite pastime, and he'd missed it.

Last week, when he'd attended Big Al Imhoff's anniversary party, Norma Rose was the only sister he'd seen. She'd disappeared shortly after it started. So had Roger. Forrest had left early, too, but he couldn't do that tonight, and connecting himself to Twyla would give him more chances to do what had to be done. There were things that needed to be cleared up between their families and it would help if he knew for sure if Roger had orchestrated Galen's arrest.

To his benefit, Twyla had never been able to keep a secret. At least, not from him.

It wasn't Twyla's intake of breath, but the flash of fear that raced across her face that had him shifting his gaze to the hallway that led to the resort's offices. A cold lump formed in his gut. Norma Rose stood in the hallway, in a shimmering purple dress with a single feather poking out of the matching headband that circled short waves of blond hair. She'd fared well, and for a moment the past returned. He wondered how different things could have been. If he hadn't been who he was and the Nightingales hadn't been who they were. Unfortunately he couldn't change any of that back then. He couldn't change it now, either.

Norma Rose wasn't alone. A tall man stood beside her. Oblivious to anyone watching, they were looking at each other and laughing and in truth, looked happy, very happy. The man was obviously the lawyer, and for a moment Forrest wondered if he should leave and telephone Roger to say what he had to say. But he wanted to look the man in the eye when they spoke, so his work was cut out for him. All thanks to Galen Reynolds, the man his mother had married years ago and the reason all the Nightingale sisters hated him.

Norma Rose and the lawyer, who Forrest had heard was called Ty Bradshaw, made a striking couple. Despite the way Norma Rose felt about him, he did hope Ty made her happy.

She reached out and plucked something, a piece of lint perhaps, from the lawyer's shoulder and then kissed his jaw. The man's hand roamed over her side familiarly and Forrest's hands wanted to ball into fists. Galen had ruined so much. It was past time it stopped. For good.

The tapping of a toe snagged Forrest's attention and he turned to the woman at his side. Twyla's lips were pursed and her little nostrils flared as she breathed in and out. He shoved his hands into his pockets. Galen would not win this time. "You may not *need* a date," Forrest told Twyla, "but I do. I hate attending these shindigs by myself."

A softness entered her eyes, but disappeared quickly. "Really?" she asked sarcastically. Her gaze bounced from Norma Rose and the lawyer to him.

Forrest grinned, though it was as false as the floorboards of a bootlegger's truck. "Everything's more fun when you have a partner." That part was true. Twyla had always been fun and adventurous. Then again, they'd only been kids. She could have changed, and might well have, considering the way her blue eyes turned brooding and rather cold.

Yet, to his surprise, she nodded.

"All right, then."

"All right then," he repeated, for no other reason than to get in the last word, knowing that it would irk her. Norma Rose still hadn't noticed him. He was watching out of the corner of his eye, trying to make it look as if he wasn't. She wouldn't be impressed to see him at Twyla's side. From all he'd heard over the years, she'd like to see him six feet under.

Twyla, however, was watching him. She knew exactly what he was doing—and not doing. That much hadn't changed; keeping a secret from

Twyla hadn't ever been any easier than her keeping one from him. Under her unyielding gaze the blue tie that matched his suit, which he'd struggled to tie in an even bow, started to choke him. Forrest reached up and tugged at his shirt collar, but found little relief.

He tugged harder. It didn't help, but the smile that appeared on Twyla's face did. Her eyes had changed, too. They were no longer shooting daggers. Instead they'd softened with something he couldn't quite explain. Sympathy? He didn't want that. Not from her. Not from anyone.

"Here," she said, grasping his hand and pulling it away from his neck. "You're twisting your tie." She straightened it and asked, "Isn't that awfully tight?"

"Yes," he admitted.

With deft fingers, she undid the bow and pushed his chin up when he tried to look down. A moment later she had it retied and he was no longer choking.

"How's that?" she asked.

"Fine, thank you." No one had tied his tie in years and the intimacy of it twisted something inside him. He'd missed that. Intimacy. At one time he'd had a close relationship with all the sisters.

Twyla's smile never faltered as she turned toward the door again, greeting more couples and directing them to her sister at the front desk.

That was Josie at the desk. She was the tomboy of the family. The one who'd dug worms and caught frogs beside him, and together they'd chased Norma Rose and Twyla, even Ginger at times, dangling their latest finds. Being only two years older than Norma Rose, he'd grown up playing with all four sisters. His mother and Rose Nightingale had been the best of friends at one time. Right up until Rose had died. The flu epidemic had taken their baby brother, too, and his. That was the thing Galen had never gotten over. The loss of his only son.

Forrest shoved his hands in his pockets again, where they balled into fists. His gaze went back to Twyla. She was chatting with a woman who, despite the warmth of the June evening, had a fox fur draped around her neck. Twyla's laughter, light and carefree as it was, caused dread to churn in his stomach.

Galen Reynolds, who almost everyone thought was his father—only he, his mother and aunt and uncle, besides Galen, knew it wasn't true—had all but crucified and burned Norma Rose on a stake years ago. She'd overcome that, the entire family had, and Forrest had to wonder if he shouldn't just walk out the door. It was over. He should let sleeping dogs lie, as his mother had told him to do when he'd returned home once a couple of years ago. Even now, every time they talked, she'd ask if he'd seen any of the Nightingales and didn't miss an opportunity to point out it wouldn't be fair to Norma Rose to dredge up the past.

The trouble was, he'd needed the Nightingales as a kid, and he needed them now, in more ways than he cared to admit. For a moment Forrest considered Twyla, how stirring up the past might not be fair to her, either, but if he didn't, Galen would win, and that was what he had to stop.

If things had remained as they'd been, he'd have let it all go. He would have forgotten what Galen had done to Norma Rose, to him, and eventually, perhaps he would have reclaimed his friendship with the Nightingales, but as it was, everything had changed again.

He had to do this.

Twyla was as bold as she was beautiful, and he'd make sure she didn't get hurt. He knew something else, too; her anger toward him, or her dislike, was a ploy. She was just being Twyla. She hated to lose, or to be called out. Their mother had burned plenty of decks of cards and games because of Twyla. She'd pitch a fit every time she lost or got caught cheating, and into the woodstove the games had gone. In truth, she could be a brat when she wanted to be.

Now that he thought about it, Twyla could be the most beneficial to him. She fought to the death but was known to flip sides, and having her on his side would all but guarantee his success in drawing out the information he needed to gain.

Convinced he was doing the right thing, Forrest turned toward the hallway. Norma Rose and Ty were gone. Scanning the open doorway into the ballroom, he took a step to see past the crowd.

"Wandering away already?"

Coming up with the first excuse he thought of, he turned back to Twyla. "Just thinking I should go and see if Slim has everything set up."

Her rather stoic expression said she didn't believe that any more than she believed monkeys could fly. "Well, don't wander too far," she said. "We'll be sitting down for dinner soon. I'll have them add a place for you at the family table."

"I wouldn't miss that for the world," he said. On impulse he flicked the end of her pert little nose. "Not for the world."

Chapter Two

Less than half an hour later, Forrest found himself right there at the family table, sitting directly across from Norma Rose with Twyla on his left and Josie on his right. There were eight of them in total. Roger Nightingale sat at the head of the table and Palooka George sat on the other end. Ty Bradshaw sat on Roger's right, opposite Twyla, with Norma Rose beside him. Palooka George's wife, the woman with the fox fur around her neck and named Dolly, sat on Norma Rose's other side, across from Josie.

"Thought you'd have stopped out before now, Forrest. I've missed seeing you around," Roger said. "I'm glad to have you back in town."

"Thank you, sir. I've been busy," he answered. "But thanks to Twyla, I'm here tonight." Forrest turned to her with a smile that was a bit mocking. "Thank you for inviting me."

"You're welcome," she said demurely. "I've

always been benevolent, and I hate to see anyone eating alone."

The family members at the table reached for their glasses or turned to each other, clearly trying to appear as if they hadn't heard her jibe.

Forrest's smile didn't falter. It had always been this way between the two of them. A competition. There had never been a prize, other than getting the best of each other. "Nice one," he whispered next to her ear.

"I thought it fitting."

"It didn't draw blood," he told her quietly.

"I wasn't attempting to," she said, taking a sip from her wineglass. "You'll know when I am. You'll need a tourniquet."

His laugh drew everyone's attention, including Norma Rose's. He lifted his glass. "May I propose a toast?" Norma Rose's startled look held a frown. He could understand why, as their parting hadn't been pleasant. All the same, Forrest smiled. "For George's birthday."

"Hear! Hear!" Roger said. "To George."

Having been a professional boxer for years, Palooka George was full of stories—animated ones—which entertained everyone at the table while the meal was served. The man was no longer boxing. He was now the leader of a different kind of ring, headquartered in Chicago. Plenty of his cutthroat boys were here tonight, along with several well-known dames who were as hard as the men they clung to. Forrest recognized some faces. These were men who used to visit the Plantation on a regular basis, and Forrest took note of the curious stares generated by his seat at The Night's table.

All five courses of the meal consisted of delicacies that few in the area would ever have tasted if not for the spectacular chefs Nightingale's employed, and each course was paired with an accompanying alcoholic beverage. However, each of the Nightingale women had been served only half a glass of wine at the beginning of the meal. After that, they'd been provided nothing but water.

He'd also noticed how Twyla eyed the glasses the men and Dolly consumed, with an almost longing look. Making sure everyone else was engrossed in one of George's tales, Forrest leaned over. "Remember when we snuck into your grandfather's basement and took sips out of several of his wine casks?"

Her cheeks turned almost as red as her hair had been right after her dye job. "Shush up," she said under her breath.

"We didn't get caught," he reminded her.

"You didn't get caught," she corrected. "Norma Rose found me throwing up after you left. I thought she was going to take a switch to me."

Taking a drink of her water, she added, "Although I doubt I would have felt it."

Forrest was torn between smiling and frowning. He'd never known she'd gotten sick, or been in trouble, yet could remember she'd been very drunk. So had he. He hadn't thought about that for years.

"Are you finished?" he asked, nodding toward her plate.

A good portion of the sugary pastry dessert was still on her plate, but she nodded. "Yes. You?"

His plate was empty. "Yes." There wouldn't be any business discussed at the table, not the kind he wanted to discuss with Roger, yet he couldn't come up with a logical excuse to leave. Instead his mind was dredging up a few other secrets that involved him and Twyla, although none of the others included her grandfather's wine.

"Want to go check on Slim?" she asked. "I've had enough boxing stories."

He grinned. She'd always been honest to a fault. Or blunt. "I'll make our excuses," he said, laying his napkin over his plate. After explaining that he and Twyla were going to see to the music, he thanked Roger for his hospitality, wished George a happy birthday and nodded to the others as he stood to pull out Twyla's chair. He purposefully didn't do more than glance in

Norma Rose's general direction. She seemed sincerely taken with the lawyer, and Forrest wasn't here to cause her any trouble. Reuniting friendships with any of the Nightingales beyond tonight wasn't part of his plan. The repercussions of what he had to do would likely make that impossible.

Loaning Slim Johnson to them had been an excuse to visit when he'd needed one. Plus, Slim deserved the opportunity. He was a good musician and the small weekend crowds at the Plantation were nothing compared to the ones at Nightingale's. Slim was hoping the chance to play here might give him as much luck as it had given Brock Ness.

With his hand resting on the small of Twyla's back, Forrest guided her into the ballroom. Slim had been playing music while folks ate but had left the stage a short time ago, taking a break while he could, before the dancing started. There'd be no resting then.

As they walked, Forrest allowed another thought to cross his mind. "Where's Ginger?"

Twyla's answer was delayed, and she didn't look at him when she said, "In Chicago with a friend."

Both were sure signs she was lying, at least partially. Forrest may have been gone for several years, and many things may have changed, but Twyla's inability to lie to him hadn't. The fact that Roger Nightingale wouldn't allow one of his daughters out of his sight hadn't, either. Forrest may not have had any contact with the family since he'd returned, but the Nightingales were celebrities in these parts, and folks talked. He hadn't heard Ginger was out of town, which meant it was hush-hush.

"Looks like Slim's out on the balcony," Twyla said, directing Forrest in that direction. She had to stay on her toes when it came to him. A moment ago she'd almost let it slip that Ginger was in Chicago with Brock. No one outside the family knew about that and it had to stay that way. Being next to Forrest was affecting her mind.

The setting sun glistened across the lake as she allowed him to escort her outside. She did want to speak with Slim, but getting Forrest away from her family was a priority. Norma Rose didn't appear to be upset by his presence at the family table, which was odd. For years, Norma Rose had blamed Forrest for everything and swore she hated him. Up until the moment Ty appeared. He didn't seem upset, either. Neither did her father. The only one who'd looked at her as if she'd lost her mind when she led Forrest to their table was Josie, and that was who Twyla decided she should steer clear of tonight. Though Josie did somehow seem to know everything that went on, she didn't know *everything*, and keeping it that way would be best.

Slim, a man who wasn't exactly what she'd call slim, was leaning against the railing, looking out over a lawn decorated with manicured flower beds and a water fountain before the ground gradually sloped toward the lake, where a swimming beach and boathouses filled the shoreline. Rather short and pudgy, Slim had pleased the crowd last weekend with his ability to play several instruments. His singing wasn't all bad, either, when it came to the slow ballads that some of the older folks liked dancing to.

"Quite the gala you have going on tonight, Twyla," he said as she and Forrest approached.

"Thank you. Palooka George has been a friend of my father for years, and he expected nothing less than the best." Tossing a glance at Forrest, she added, "I'm sure you won't disappoint any of us."

Forrest grinned, which irked her.

Slim grinned, too, but he sounded sincere when he said, "I hope not."

She stepped forward to rest her arms on the wooden rail, hoping Forrest wouldn't follow. The warmth of his hand on her back had burned her skin. Right through the sequins of her dress. Maybe the tiny bits of metal were the reason why his touch had felt so hot. Then again, it could just be her fury. Keeping him away from Norma Rose was seriously going to interrupt her good time tonight. She'd noticed how his eyes had rested on her sister during the meal. That alone had made her stomach ache. His gaze hinted he wanted to renew the relationship he'd ended when he'd left town years ago. That would not happen. Not on her watch. She'd just gotten her life back and wasn't going to lose it again. Most definitely not over some old flame.

He'd stepped up on the other side of Slim, and the two of them started talking about guitar strings and how Slim had restrung his instrument for tonight. For the most part, Twyla ignored them, still trying to get her mind and body in sync after Forrest's little walk down memory lane. She hadn't needed the reminder about her grandfather's wine cellar. Not now. Not tonight. Back then, when they all used to play together, Forrest had been a part of the family—a mixture of the big brother she'd never had and the boy she'd wanted to grow up and marry. That part— the marrying part—had dissolved when it was clear Norma Rose was the sister he wanted. Having him as a brother-in-law would have been the next best thing to a girl in her early teens. Therefore she'd accepted it readily enough and gone on to search for her own knight in shining armor.

Just when that search should have hit its peak,

Prohibition was introduced. One would have thought that would have increased her opportunities of meeting fascinating and interesting men, but in her case, it threw up a roadblock faster than if she'd been a bootlegger driving an old jalopy in downtown Minneapolis. That city was as dry as an empty bottle. An odd thing, considering all one had to do was cross a bridge into St. Paul to enter a city as wet as the Mississippi River, which separated it from Minneapolis. Prohibition seemed to have separated the two cities far more than anything else ever had.

Like many others, it hadn't taken long for her father to capitalize on the new law. His work at Hamm's Brewery had helped. He knew the ins and outs of the world and those in it, and used all of that to turn Nightingale's into a highfalutin resort that rivaled others nationwide. Men poured into the place like leaves falling off the trees in October, but rather than being able to rake them in, she and her younger sisters had become little more than prisoners, locked in their gilded cages atop the largest speakeasy in the nation, watching all those men come and go.

Forrest was the reason Norma Rose wasn't locked away like her, Josie and Ginger. The two of them, Forrest and Norma Rose, had never really dated, it was just known they'd be together. After finishing the private high school he'd attended, Forrest had gone to college, but by then he had a car, so he was home more often than the previous years. He'd spent a good portion of the days he was home at their house. Back then, her family had still lived in the old farmhouse on the other side of the barn located across the resort's parking lot, and Forrest had always been welcome.

It wasn't until he'd graduated from college that things had changed. He'd been gone for months and her entire family had been looking forward to seeing him. They'd all gone to his graduation party, even her father, which had been unusual. Galen Reynolds and Roger Nightingale had never seen eye-to-eye. Their relationship became worse after that night. The rest of the sisters had already gone home, leaving Norma Rose behind for Forrest to give a ride home.

It had been a scene she'd never forget. The way Galen had hauled Norma Rose into the house that night, cursing and shouting.

Galen had never liked any of them, but after the flu epidemic had taken many lives, including his five-year-old son, August, he'd really started hating all of the Nightingales. He claimed the girls' mother had killed August by exposing him to the flu.

Forrest's mother, Karen, didn't agree with her husband, but she'd never said that in front of him.

No one ever said much in front of him. He was too mean. His evil glares used to put the fear of the devil in all of them.

When Galen had hauled Norma Rose into the house that night, their father had ordered all of the girls upstairs. The walls hadn't prevented them from hearing Galen calling them gold-digging doxies. Twyla had feared for her father's life that night and had been thankful after Galen had left and she'd snuck downstairs to find her father unscathed.

The feud really started then. Galen spread rumors about Norma Rose, calling her all sorts of names. Though things calmed down some over the years, the rivalry hadn't completely stopped until last year, when her father, by then far wealthier than Galen Reynolds ever hoped to be, had seen that the man was run out of town.

The damage had been done to Norma Rose. After that dreadful night, she'd flipped into a tyrant whose goal became proving to the world that none of the Nightingale girls would ever be doxies.

Twyla couldn't say she wanted to be some man's doll, but she couldn't stay locked up any longer. She wanted to live fancy-free. A man wasn't needed to do that, but they did make things more fun. A woman just had to know how to play with them. To Twyla's way of thinking, one never knew what was in someone else's heart. Especially a man's heart. And that's where the problem lay. In a person's heart. That's what made someone who they were. They could think all they wanted, or say all sorts of things, but their actions showed what was in their heart. Who they really were.

Take Forrest, for instance. He'd supposedly been in love with Norma Rose, but he certainly never showed it. Rather than standing up for Norma Rose against his father's blasphemy, he'd left town. Without a word he'd just vanished, and hadn't retuned until last year, after his parents had gone to California. It had been hard to believe. For years Forrest had protected all of them. Not that they'd ever been in real danger, but he'd squashed spiders and shooed away garter snakes.

She snuck a peek his way, where he stood next to Slim.

Rumors, mostly started by those who'd been in cahoots with Galen Reynolds, claimed Galen had gone to California for his health. Others said he'd run away with his latest doxy. Only those close to Twyla's family knew Roger Nightingale had been behind Galen's move. She wondered if Forrest knew that, and what he thought about it. From the tidbits she'd heard—because her father didn't ever let them hear much of anything—the film company Galen bragged about owning in

Hollywood was nothing but a front for something much more illicit.

Exactly what, she didn't know, but considering the mobsters who used to frequent the Plantation, she assumed bootlegging was involved. It was behind most everything that went on anymore. From small towns to big cities, there was rarely a person who wasn't somehow and in some way involved in making, selling or running booze.

Apart from Forrest. Word was there hadn't been any booze served at the Plantation since his return.

He hadn't even bothered to let any of them know when he'd returned home. That would have been enough for her to knock him off the pedestal she'd put him on in her early years if she hadn't already. It was a good lesson to learn. Never trust a man. Never believe anything could last forever.

"Twyla?"

She spun around. The look on Forrest's face suggested he'd said her name more than once. Huffing out a breath, half wondering, half knowing why her mind had wandered so far from the present, she asked, "Where's Slim?"

As soon as the words left her mouth she heard the music, and certainly didn't appreciate the way Forrest lifted his brows and grinned.

"Lost in thought, were you?"

"More like plotting," she answered. It had always been like this with Forrest. The two of them never fought or argued; they just tried to outwit the other one. It was a game she'd missed.

He laughed. "If every woman thought they were as smart as you think you are, this world would be one dangerous place."

Twyla didn't have time to tell him it was dangerous, that she'd grown smarter during his absence, because her father chose that moment to walk out the door and cross the wide balcony.

"Forrest, I want to have a word with you." Dressed as he always was, in a maroon three-piece suit, black shirt and shining black-button shoes, Roger Nightingale's presence was strongly felt. However, as formidable as he might appear to others, her father was the one man Twyla did trust. She knew fully what was in his heart. Not even while being banished to her room as soon as the lights had come on had she ever doubted that her father loved her and her sisters. Sure, he spoiled them, bought them anything they wanted from cars to clothes to cosmetics and all things in between. But none of that assured his love. The way he protected them did. Even when he thought they didn't know that he was doing it.

Forrest used to be like that, always watching over them. Until… She grabbed his arm. Her father would want to talk to Forrest, find out his plans. As wonderful as her father's protection was, it was not what she needed right now. Not when Forrest might squeal about the kissing booth and everything else he knew.

"It'll have to wait, Daddy. Forrest and I are heading for the dance floor. We need to get this party started. George will only turn fifty once, and we want it to be a party he'll remember," she said, hooking Forrest's arm with hers. She tried to tug him toward the door, but his feet were planted firmly and he didn't even wobble.

Twyla cringed inwardly, and when Forrest's gaze left her father and landed on her, she knew her eyes were full of pleading. She was virtually begging him to leave. She really, really didn't want him talking to her father.

Her stomach fell, along with her eyelids when he turned his somewhat regretful gaze back to her father.

A thundering laugh snapped her eyes open. Her father slapped Forrest's shoulder playfully. "You never could say no to my daughters any more than I could."

Forrest chuckled, too. "That was true."

Twyla picked up on the *was* and Forrest's tone.

Her father however, laughed again. "That may be the downfall of us both."

Forrest turned to her again and a glimmer of a smile crossed his lips before he said, "Or it could be a crutch, which—" he turned back to her father "—isn't always a bad thing. A crutch can allow a man to walk when he otherwise couldn't."

Twyla caught a double meaning behind his statement but couldn't fathom what it was.

"Ain't that the truth," her father said. "Go on. You two hit the dance floor. I'll catch up with you later."

"All right," Forrest said. "I do look forward to talking with you."

"But not as much as you look forward to dancing." Her father laughed again as he waved a hand toward the door. He'd become more of his jovial self the past couple of days, and the broad smile on his face was a welcome sight.

That was the other thing Twyla didn't want to see change. Over the past couple of weeks, her father had been overly worried. She assumed Ginger running off to Chicago was a part of it, but believed more of it had to do with the hoodlum Ty had been chasing. She never tried to fool herself into believing that her father's business wasn't a dangerous one. Lucrative, but dangerous. Twyla also understood it could all end, too. The money, the parties. Nothing was forever, but there were things she'd fight tooth and nail to not lose.

"Thanks, Daddy," she said, and meant it. She gave Forrest another hard tug.

He followed this time, and she wasted no time in pulling him through the doorway.

Slim was playing the piano and doing a good job of it. Twyla led Forrest past the few couples already on the dance floor, not stopping until they reached the center. She'd never been nervous around Forrest, yet for the briefest of moments her stomach fluttered and hiccupped as they stood looking at each other. A crazy thought dashed across her mind. What if Norma Rose was still in love with him? Her sister acted as if Ty was the only man she had eyes for, but she'd proclaimed to have loved Forrest at one time. And he was just as handsome as Ty, if not more so.

Keeping Forrest away from Norma Rose would be easier—much easier—than keeping Norma Rose away from Forrest. Dealing with gangsters was easier than dealing with Norma Rose when she set her mind to something.

"Shall we?" Forrest asked, holding out his hands.

Twyla swallowed and cleared her mind. Norma Rose was in love with Ty, not Forrest, but that didn't mean Forrest couldn't ruin everything. That's what she needed to remember.

Reaching out, she pressed one hand against one of his and laid her other on his shoulder.

"We shall," she said. "Lead the way." Eyeing his brown eyes critically, she added, "Unless you'd prefer I lead."

His fingers folded over hers as his other hand grasped her waist firmly and tugged her close. "I prefer to lead."

Catching the breath his touch had momentarily stolen, she followed his side step and backward glide. "Oh? Do you always get what you prefer?"

"Yes, since I took control of my life."

"By becoming a flyboy?" she asked. It had intrigued her that he flew airplanes. It irritated her, too. Thinking about the adventures he'd had while she'd been locked in her bedroom. Yet she kept her thoughts from going there. He'd gone on to become a flyboy after ruining her sister's life, which had now been saved, no thanks to him. Norma Rose deserved every ounce of happiness she found with Ty. They all deserved the happiness they were finding, and the adventures. Oh, yes, the adventures. She'd soon have more of those than him. Airplane or not.

"Among other things," he said, guiding her in a swift twirl beneath their clutched hands. When she ended her spin and faced him, he added,

"Life either bests you, or you best it. That's a lesson you've yet to learn, Twyla, my dear."

"Well, Forrest, *my dear*," she said, spinning again. "I've already learned that."

"Have you?" he asked, pulling her close before shuffling her sideways across the floor in a fast two-step.

"Indeed I have."

He laughed, a sound that tickled her insides. Or perhaps it was the dancing, the gaiety surrounding them, as other dancers sashayed around and across the floor. Then again, it just might be that he thought he was going to win the game of wits they were playing. That was a delusion on his part.

Twyla laughed, too.

Leading her back two steps and then sideways, he said, "Aw, Twyla, indeed you have not."

There was so much more meaning behind his statement, her feet faltered, and if not for Forrest she would have tripped and fallen all the way to the floor. His hold increased, keeping her upright and dancing.

Peeved by both his hold and his attitude, Twyla planted her heels on the dance floor, bringing them both to a stop. To her dismay, the music stopped at that exact same moment. She chose to consider the timing as luck. She'd been about to tell him the game hadn't even started yet, this one that he'd challenged her to, and was thankful she hadn't spoken those words. They'd have carried loudly through the silent room, and she certainly didn't want anyone else to know about the game they'd always secretly played.

Forrest merely lifted a brow.

She repeated the action, but added a glare. It was time for him to realize she had grown up and taken control of her own life.

And she would win. Even if that just meant keeping him from talking to her father tonight.

The music started again and, more determined than ever, Twyla took the lead this time, initiating footsteps that had Forrest hopping to keep up. She loved having the upper hand, being in control, and Forrest had best learn to move a whole heap faster or he'd be trampled in her wake.

Packed with couples, the dance floor vibrated beneath her feet. She laughed again and kicked her heels higher as she pushed Forrest backward and pulled him forward. He was keeping up, and that kept her moving faster and bolder, stepping so close her body almost touched his before they separated again.

Her temperature rose with each step, and her heart thudded, pumping blood that tingled with excitement to every inch of her body. This was Twyla Nightingale in full bloom. The fact she was kicking up her heels with the best-looking man for miles around increased the thrill of it all.

When the music stopped she was slightly winded, but so was Forrest. Still holding both of her hands, he tugged her toward the edge of the wooden floor, where there was a line of tables.

"Oh, no," she said, holding her ground by pressing her feet onto the floor. "We aren't done yet."

"I have to get out of this suit coat," he said.

"Not now, Slim's about to hit the keys again."

She'd no sooner spoken than notes rang through the air. Dancers cheered, recognizing the ragtime tune that would have people dancing fast and wild, exchanging partners after no more than a couple of twirls.

Forrest hooked her waist and danced her to the edge of the floor, where he released her after a twirl that ended when another man grabbed her waist and danced her back in the other direction. Twisting to keep one eye on Forrest, she watched him toss his suit coat and tie over the back of an empty chair and then grab a woman, dancing deep into the crowd.

Twirling from one man to the next, Twyla tried to find Forrest. He was taller than several others and should be easy to spot, but the constant spinning didn't give her vision time to focus. The men all looked alike. Without his blue suit coat his white shirt and suspenders blended in with all the others.

As the music briefly paused, signaling it was time to swap partners again, Twyla was spun into another man's arms. Without noticing who her partner was, she twisted her neck, searching the crowd.

"He's right behind you."

Twyla snapped around.

"Forrest is right behind you," Ty said while shuffling her slightly sideways. "Dancing with Norma Rose."

Twyla's stomach fell.

Forrest willed his hands to rest loosely upon Norma Rose. A part of him wanted to hug her, tell her how deeply sorry he was for what Galen had put her through. Dancing with Twyla had reminded him of all he'd left behind, and how badly things had eaten at him over the years. Especially during those first few months while he'd been incapacitated, healing from the wounds caused by his stepfather.

No one had been safe from Galen.

Forrest had attempted to apologize to Norma Rose a year after he'd left, when he'd been able to walk again, but a car accident had stopped his efforts. Two weeks ago, when Norma Rose called asking to hire Slim for the parties, he'd broached the subject by telling her he'd tried to stop Galen's allegations, but she'd said his sentiments were a little late. She was wrong. They weren't just sentiments, and it was never too late. Not for some things.

"This is some shindig," he said, knowing it wouldn't be long before Slim stopped the music for everyone to switch partners again. "You outdid yourself."

She shook her head. "I can't take any of the credit. This party was all Twyla and Josie."

"You're too modest," he said. "Everyone knows you run Nightingale's."

"Things have changed."

He'd have to be blind not to notice how she twisted to gaze at Ty and the bright smile she flashed at the other man. Forrest didn't have time to react or comment before the music paused. As graceful as a butterfly, Norma Rose fluttered out of his arms and into Ty's. The other man swept her onward without missing a beat.

The woman who landed in Forrest's arms was more like a blue jay—pretty to look at, but loud and ornery.

"I told you to stay away from my sister," Twyla squawked.

"I'm free to dance with whomever I want," he

said, twirling her in the opposite direction from where Ty spun Norma Rose.

"Not Norma Rose," Twyla insisted. "She doesn't want anything to do with you. Hasn't for years. Don't you see that?" With a well-aimed glare, she added, "You aren't welcome here, Forrest."

He didn't react to the sting of her words. There was no reason to. He hadn't expected any of the Nightingales to want anything to do with him. He didn't blame them, nor did he blame Roger for putting Galen behind bars. Galen did, though, and had sworn vengeance. If what his mother claimed was true, Galen might get his chance, and that was what Forrest was here to stop.

They were near the edge of the floor when the music ended. There would be no more switching partners. The song was over.

Forrest used his close proximity to the tables to grab his jacket and tie. Flipping the suit coat over his shoulder, he gave Twyla a wink. "See you around, doll."

She looped an arm through his before he'd taken more than two steps. "You're leaving?"

He had no intention of stopping, but something in her tone stilled his feet. Glancing down, the shimmer in her eyes held a touch of sadness. He felt that, too, deep down where it had settled years ago. Not about to let the emotion show, he grinned. "Are you flipping sides already?"

"Fl-fl—" she stuttered before gathering her tongue. "I'm not flipping anything."

"You aren't?"

"No."

"You just told me I'm not welcome here."

Her mouth opened and closed a couple of times before she pinched her lips together.

The sight was comical and he laughed.

"Fine," she said, pulling her arm out of his. "Leave. But you'll be missing the best party this country has ever known."

Slim was striking up another tune, so Forrest leaned close to Twyla's ear and said, "I hate to tell you this, doll, but your ice sculpture is already melting. The fun will be over before you know it."

With that he marched forward, through the ballroom doors, across the entranceway and out of the double doors that led to the parking lot. He could talk to Roger tomorrow. The man was an integral part of his plan. A plan he was seriously reconsidering. Drawing any of the Nightingales back into his family's trouble wasn't right. It was his fight, not theirs. Trouble was, Galen's pending release wasn't the thing eating at him. Twyla was. He could only handle small doses of her. She'd already gotten under his skin, too deep for comfort.

He was opening the door of his roadster when his name echoed over the parking lot.

Chapter Three

"What'll it be, boy?" Roger Nightingale asked with his booming voice while gesturing toward the mass of bottles and crystal highball glasses set upon the credenza in his office.

Forrest didn't take offense to Roger calling him *boy*; the man always had, and in a sense it brought back good memories. "I'm fine," he said, shaking his head while taking a seat in one of the two red velvet chairs facing Roger's desk. "I've learned to limit myself."

"Limit? You a teetotaler?"

"I guess I am, sir," he answered respectfully. "By choice. After taking the oath for flying, I learned I need my senses alert at all times."

"Aw, yes, your piloting," Roger said, pouring himself a good bump of brandy before walking over to sit down behind his big mahogany desk. The man might look the size of a bear, but he had the stealth of a mountain lion. "Hear tell you've got a lot of hours under your belt."

"That I do," Forrest said. "Flew airmail from Washington to Pennsylvania for six months and then to New York for another six."

"I gotta admit those flying contraptions scare the dickens out of me, but they intrigue me, too. How'd you get involved in that?"

Forrest had no doubt Roger already knew. The man spoke to other people who talked with his mother, and she never shied from making his flying part of her conversations. "Mechanical engineering always interested me. After earning my degree I went down to Nebraska, to Lincoln and the air flight school there." He didn't mention that had been a year after graduation. It had taken him that long to learn to walk again after both his legs had been mangled. "From there I joined the air service reserve corps. The army didn't have much use for pilots since the war had ended, but they used us occasionally for things, and then regularly once airmail started."

"I heard you were one of the pilots that carried mail all the way across the nation," Roger said, appearing to be genuinely interested.

"I was," Forrest answered. "The route includes thirteen stops for fuel, mail exchange and aircrew changes. I flew the section from Chicago to Iowa City and back again. The entire trip, from ocean to ocean, took just a little over seventy hours when we first started."

Roger let out a low whistle.

"Last year we got it down to little more than thirty," he said. "With night flying."

"Night flying? How do you fly a plane in the dark?"

"With navigational instruments," Forrest answered. A familiar longing rose up in him by simply talking about flying. He loved it, and missed it daily. He also knew his flying opportunities would be limited if he couldn't update his plane. Currently, his controls consisted of an oil pressure gauge and a horizontal indicator, not enough for night flying. "Things change," he said, not realizing he was responding to his internal reactions. "In February of this year the government passed a new bill. It took the airmail contracts away from the army and opened it up to private aviation companies. Right now anyone can put a bid on flying a route, especially new ones that connect with the transcontinental route between New York and San Francisco."

"Are you putting in a bid?" Roger asked.

Forrest smiled. Roger had always been able to read between the lines. "I already did. I've surveyed and established a route between Minneapolis and Iowa City. It'll be Minnesota's first opportunity to have airmail. I won't know whether or not I've got the contract until October, but I've already sent in my paperwork along with the fee they required."

Roger guffawed. "The government, they get money from us in every way possible." He leaned back then, folding his thick arms across his chest. "What about the Plantation?"

An undeniable ball of disgust rose in Forrest's stomach. If not for the Plantation, he'd have a new plane, which would guarantee his contract for mail service. Right now, if the government did accept his bid, he wouldn't be able to fulfill it.

"I've heard you made some remarkable changes."

"I wouldn't call them remarkable," Forrest admitted. His goal had been to erase Galen from his mind and life. It still was. "You know Galen never owned the Plantation."

"I do," Roger answered. "Your grandfather willed it to you before he died."

"I wish I'd known him," Forrest said sincerely.

"He was a good man, but hard, and one hell of a master brewer," Roger said with a laugh. "Hans was one of the originals in the brewery business. He knew about the artesian wells over in Swede Hollow and said it would be the perfect spot for a brewery, being that close to St. Paul. That's where they built it, and in no time it was the second-largest brewery in the state. It still is, although right now it's bottling little more than soft drinks. It'll make a comeback, though, once Prohibition is recalled. We all know that."

"That the brewery will make a comeback, or that Prohibition will be recalled?" Forrest asked, interested in the man's opinion. It was well-known that almost every brewery had caves lining the river or back rooms where plenty of illegal beverages were still being brewed, bottled and sold.

"Both," Roger said. "Prohibition isn't working. Not for the government anyway," he added with a laugh. "For me, it's been a gold mine, but I only look for it to last a few more years. So do the brewing companies. They're voicing their objections. They've got legislators writing up repeals one after the other."

Forrest had no desire to get deep into a conversation about Prohibition. It was obvious Roger looked upon the laws governing alcohol as many others did—that they'd been made to be broken. He, on the other hand, held no solid opinion. Though he should, as owner of a nightclub. "How well did you know my grandfather?" he asked, going back to their earlier conversation.

"Very well. Hans Swenson was known and liked by everyone. He got me the job I had at the brewery. He'd already sold out his shares by then, and made a good sum doing so," Roger added with a wink. "He used that money to build the Plantation, which is where he made his wealth. This entire area was a vacation spot for the rich mill owners in the cities, and they loved the idea of a yacht club. Hans had visitors coming all the way from England. They'd haul their little sailboats on ships into Duluth and then down here by train. It was amazing. Those were the days. They'd sail their boats all day at his place and then come over here to my father's dance pavilion and dance the nights away."

Roger sighed as if the memories were turning dark. "A few bad years, and resorts opening up in other places, closer to the cities, made our area wither and dry up like worms left in the sun. Some folks burned their places down. They'd never admit it, but so many insurance claims were made companies stopped insuring resorts in this area. That didn't stop your grandfather. He built the amusement park to keep folks coming to this area. That's why the Plantation survived when everywhere else around here dried up. Because it was unique."

Forrest nodded. He knew a whole lot more than that but couldn't say any of it. Family secrets were ugly contenders at times and had thrown many a wrench in his plans over the years.

"You could make it that way again," Roger

said. "Hans would like that. He was never impressed with your father."

"Was anyone ever impressed with Galen?" Forrest asked sarcastically.

"No," Roger replied swiftly. "No one."

"What about when he first moved here?" Forrest asked, fishing for information. "I know my mother and your wife were friends—were you and Galen ever friendly?"

"No. Even before Rose died, there had been no friendship between Galen and me." Leaning forward, Roger rested both elbows on his desk and tapped the ends of his fingers together. "You didn't answer my question earlier—what about the Plantation? Who's going to run it while you're flying mail across the country every day?"

Forrest nodded, mainly to give himself a moment to respond. Slowly, precisely, he said, "Galen, if he has his way."

Roger's scowl turned darker than his black shirt.

"He's being released," Forrest said.

"Hell!" Roger erupted from his chair, slapping his desk. "That's a lie."

"It's true," Forrest said. "My mother called. Said Galen was getting a new trial and most likely, due to time served, will get out shortly."

"Trials can't happen that fast," Roger insisted. "They can't."

"Well, apparently they can," Forrest replied, without further explanation. That wasn't important. "And Roger," he said seriously, "when Galen gets out, he's going to be gunning for you."

A noise had Twyla spinning, glancing up and down the hallway. The long walkway to the kitchen was empty, as was the shorter distance that led to the entrance of the resort. The coast was still clear. She lifted the glass to the door again and pressed her ear to the other end. So far all she'd heard was her father shout once. Even then the only word she'd heard was *hell*. Her father used the expletive often, so that didn't necessarily mean the conversation he was holding with Forrest was a bad one, but her insides said it couldn't be good. She was also betting the topic was her.

She'd knocked down two dancers and a waitress trying to get out of the ballroom when she'd spied her father and Forrest heading toward his office. By the time she'd helped everyone up and found someone to clean up the mess, the office door was shut tight. Everyone knew you didn't interrupt one of Roger Nightingale's closed-door meetings.

"What are you doing?"

She spun around so fast the glass tumbled to the floor. Seeing Josie, Twyla released a sigh of relief and picked up the glass. "Forrest is in there with father," she whispered.

"So?"

"So?" Grabbing her sister's arm, Twyla dragged Josie down the hall toward the kitchen. "You know what that could mean, don't you?"

"What *what* could mean?"

Twyla wanted to shake her sister. "Forrest," she hissed. "He's still in love with Norma Rose."

Josie shook her head as if Twyla had just said the sky was falling, as if what she'd said was an impossibility.

Twyla crossed her arms. She was right. Josie had to know that.

Her sister made no move at first, but then Josie straightened the buckle on the gold belt she had around her waist. Her red-and-gold outfit was gorgeous and she looked fabulous, which was strange. Josie normally wore pants and loose-fitting shirts, claiming she went for comfort long before fashion. Twyla couldn't understand that. Fashion was everything. She'd walk around with blisters on her feet before wearing a pair of shoes that didn't match her dress.

Pulling her attention away from her sister's outfit, Twyla repeated, "Forrest is still in love with Norma Rose."

"I doubt that," Josie said.

"I don't," Twyla insisted.

Josie shook her head. "Forrest caring about Norma Rose is a moot point. She's in love with Ty."

"Forrest could make her question that," Twyla replied. "Maybe cause her and Ty to break up, and turn everything back to how it was."

"You really believe that?"

"Yes," Twyla said. "I don't want things to go back to how they were. And you shouldn't, either."

"I don't, and they won't," Josie said confidently. "Norma Rose and Ty will soon be married. Which means we'll both be needed more than ever to keep this place running." Taking the glass from Twyla's hand, Josie added, "Now stop being silly. We have over three hundred people here tonight. You need to be in the ballroom ensuring they are having a good time."

Twyla wanted to insist she wasn't being silly. She was being serious. Josie needed to take her blinders off. Things changed in little more than a heartbeat. They'd all seen that. Josie, though, wasn't one for bickering. Or idle talk. "What are you doing?" Twyla asked, and then followed up by asking, "I mean, aren't *you* making sure the guests are having a good time?"

"I am," Josie said. "But the ice sculpture is melting and water is dripping onto the floor. I'm

on my way for a mop to clean it up before someone slips."

"I have to know what they're talking about,"
Twyla said, reaching for the glass her sister had
confiscated.

Josie hid it behind her back. "No, you don't.
Stop worrying about Forrest and go see to the
guests, or I'll tell father and Norma Rose you're
resorting to your childish ways."

Twyla growled, but Josie had already spun
around and was marching down the hallway toward the kitchen and storeroom, where she'd find
a mop.

Balling her hands into fists, Twyla spun
around and walked the other way. Passing her
father's office was torture. Not knowing what
was being said behind that door would haunt
her all night. Forrest was thwarting her. If he
told her father all about her escapades, and Josie
told him about her listening at the door with a
water glass, she'd be banished to her room until
she turned thirty.

It wasn't fair. Surely wasn't. The world was
at her fingertips and it was as if Forrest had
stomped on her freshly painted nails right before she'd been able to grasp it all.

Music and laughter caught her attention as
the hallway gave way to the front entrance. The
doors to the ballroom and dining room were

open, and she paused to survey the scene. People dancing, drinking, smoking and having a good time were laid out before her. This was the world she wanted. She gave a slow, lingering glance down the hallway. Forrest might be telling her father all he knew, but that wouldn't stop tonight.

A smile formed on Twyla's lips. Tonight she'd prove who was the most spectacular hostess of the family. Her father couldn't banish her to her room then. Not after she ensured Palooka George had the best birthday bash ever. She entered the ballroom with all the persistence of a bee buzzing toward a fresh-blooming flower. She knew how to gather nectar when needed.

Twyla headed straight for the bar, where she downed two shots of Minnesota's finest corn whiskey. Then, with the whiskey burning her throat and belly—even though Reggie had watered it down as he always did with her shots—she made a beeline for the guest of honor. The show she made of pulling Palooka George onto the dance floor got the crowd rolling with laughter and she didn't let it die down.

Not once.

Not even when she noticed her father leading Ty and Norma Rose out of the dining room.

Forrest kept himself concealed among a group of men on the balcony smoking and sipping tall

bottles of beer while he watched Twyla single-
handedly entertain the crowd. She did so naturally, with her smile and outrageous yet charming
behavior. Nightingale's hadn't needed Slim. They
could have just set Twyla loose. She was the real
draw and the reason people filled the dance floor.
There wasn't a man at the shindig who wasn't
captivated by her, including several he'd recognized from here and there. A man didn't do the
amount of traveling he'd done without hearing
the latest news. These days that news included
gangsters. From small-time mobsters to big-time
bosses. A good number of them were here tonight.

Loose Lenny, Mumbles and Knuckles Page,
Gorgeous Gordy and Fire Iron Frank were all sitting along the bar, eyeing one another as if they
weren't sure who was going to pull out a piece
first. Sylvester the Sly and Point Blank Luigi
were at a table playing poker in the dining room
along with a few others.

Forrest couldn't say he was too worried about
any of the mobsters causing trouble tonight.
Roger had his own entourage. Bronco Mitchell,
Tuck Andrews, Duane Luck, Tad McCullough,
Danny Trevino and Walter Storms. They'd all
been with Roger for years and were stationed
throughout the property, inside and out. Bronco
was around Forrest's age. The man's uncle, Jacob

Wertheimer, worked for Forrest, had worked for the Plantation for years. Although Bronco was devoted to Roger, he stopped at the Plantation now and again to see his uncle, which was how Forrest had learned about Twyla's escapades. Just last month Bronco had swung by while looking for her and admitted she'd escaped their watchful eyes once again.

He grinned. She was still a brat. In a sense, Forrest felt sorry for Bronco, and he would never admit the man had told him anything, not even under fire. Dealing with the Nightingale women was more than Forrest could ever have handled, and he'd assured Bronco his secrets were safe with him. Every man needed to vent now and again. Besides, Forrest enjoyed hearing about her escapades. It proved she hadn't changed.

As if he could read his mind, Bronco caught Forrest's eye and gave a friendly nod as he continued to weave his way through the crowd, making sure everyone was behaving. The man paused behind two rather rowdy fellows being a bit brash when it came to encouraging Twyla to dance with them. With nothing more than a meaty hand laid upon each one's shoulder, Bronco mellowed the two men. They took their seats, nodding at something the watchman said.

Forrest shook his head. Though well over six feet of muscle and brawn, Bronco had his work cut out for him. That was for sure. Forrest held up the bottle of beer he'd been nursing all night, in a silent salute to his friend, and then turned around to once again gaze over the lake reflecting starlight back into the heavens. He set the bottle on the rail beside him, but then picked it up and spun it around. No label. That didn't surprise him. Beer was harder to find during Prohibition than whiskey, but he had a good idea where it came from.

His grandfather may have found Roger a job at the brewery, but Roger had worked his way through the ranks all on his own. By the time Prohibition hit, Roger had made some very tight connections, and from the looks of things, he was still using them.

That had sliced Galen deeper than any knife. He'd thought by taking over the Plantation and the amusement park he'd become the big man in town. It hadn't worked that way. Galen didn't have the personality it took, nor did he have a savvy business mind. A man with no past or family, at least not any that he'd claim, Galen had arrived in White Bear Lake with nothing but the clothes on his back. A month later he'd married the girl of the richest man in town. Forrest had to wonder what people had thought about that but figured, because his mother and Galen had immediately left for a honeymoon abroad that lasted over a year, no one had given it much thought.

When they'd arrived back in town, he'd been with them as a tiny infant, and his grandfather had died a couple months later. Most folks, just like Roger, knew Hans Swenson had left the Plantation to Forrest, but what most of them didn't know was Hans had never given Forrest's mother guardianship of the holdings. His mother's sister—Aunt Shirley—had been given that duty. That, too, had goaded Galen to no end. Not that it had stopped Galen from finding a way to weasel away the money. From the time Forrest was old enough to pen his name, Galen was making him write letters to Aunt Shirley, telling her his tuition fee had been raised or he needed new clothes. Shirley thwarted Galen whenever she could, by sending clothes instead of money or mailing the fee directly to the school. If not for her, he might never have attended either the private boys' academy or college.

Forrest turned back around and his gaze landed on a familiar face that made his skin crawl. The scar that slashed the man's cheek from temple to chin was impossible to miss and unforgettable. Nasty Nick Ludwig. The man raised an eyebrow and one corner of his mouth; the other side of his face was fixed in a permanent frown due to the scar.

Forrest lifted his chin, his only acknowledgement of recognition. Nasty Nick was the kind of mobster he hadn't expected to see here. There were gangsters and then there were lowlifes, the kind of men Galen always associated with. Ludwig was a lowlife. He'd been in jail with Galen just last month out in California. Forrest's gut churned. Although he hadn't needed the confirmation, Ludwig's release proved Galen would soon be out, too.

There was no telling who could get hurt. His aunt and uncle swore the fact Forrest could still walk was nothing shy of a miracle. All Forrest had at this moment was hope that Roger would act, and fast. The man had connections Forrest didn't. He should have come over here before tonight, but up until the phone call from his mother, there hadn't been a need. He still couldn't be sure she was telling the truth. She always seemed to have one eye covered when it came to Galen.

Ludwig moved slowly through the crowd, not talking to anyone, simply observing like a rat on the prowl. He was exactly the type of person Galen chose to have in his employ. Someone who wouldn't think twice about beating up another person—man, woman or child.

Galen claimed Roger had run him out of town to take over his business, and he wasn't talking about the Plantation. Roger hadn't become known as The Night by mistake. He was ruthless, but his dealings didn't stink like those of some others. Roger's goal was money. Galen's had always been power. There was a big difference.

Forrest understood that, yet he couldn't deny Roger had come a long way in the past few years.

"I thought you'd left."

Despite the darkness and gloom filling his thoughts, Forrest grinned. He shifted slightly to meet the glimmer of the shimmering blue eyes looking up at him. "You thought wrong." He'd been set to leave after talking to Roger, but the man had asked him not to. Said he wanted to talk to a few people and then they'd talk again.

Twyla glanced left and right before she grabbed his elbow. "Come on."

"I'm not dancing again," Forrest said, although he let her pull him away from the rail. He shouldn't have. Just talking to her could be as dangerous as dancing. That sweet, sparkling dress she had on was lighting a flame in places he didn't need a fire built.

"Neither am I," she said. "My feet are killing me. Palooka George has to weigh three hundred pounds and I swear he thought my toes were part of the dance floor." She led him toward the long set of wooden stairs that descended to the grass beneath the balcony. "I thought boxers were supposed to be sure-footed, hopping around the ring like they do."

As if his feet couldn't be stopped, he walked down the steps beside her. "When have you been to a boxing match?"

She opened and closed her mouth before huffing out a breath. "I didn't say I'd seen one, I said I thought."

"Aw-w-w," he said, drawing it out. "So you weren't at the boxing match last month at the Rafters in St. Paul?"

She stumbled slightly. Forrest reacted quickly, catching her by the waist before she tumbled headfirst down the remaining steps. His actions were for naught, considering the way she shoved his hands aside. Which was just as well. He wanted to irritate her. An angry Twyla wouldn't be the threat a sweet, worn-out Twyla would be.

"Of course I wasn't at the Rafters," she insisted, bounding down the last few steps.

"My mistake," he answered dryly. She'd been there. He'd heard it from more than one person. He grinned, too, at her delusions. She truly had no idea how many people watched her every move. Nothing she'd done was a secret.

After glancing up at the still crowded balcony, she grabbed his hand. "Come on."

Folding his fingers around hers was as natural as a sunrise. "Where are we going?"

"Some place we can talk."

He continued walking beside her, but said loud enough to be heard, "Your father's men are stationed everywhere, and I will not be caught in the bushes with you."

"Hush up," she hissed. "We aren't going to the bushes, but we need to talk."

"As long as we stay out in the open."

"Chicken?" she asked smartly.

"Smart," he answered smoothly.

She led him to the water fountain and continued around its circular cement base to where the splaying water would hide their location from the resort's patrons, but not from any of Roger's men, who walked the paths and the perimeter of the yard. Lowering herself onto the ground, she sat with her legs stretched out before her and her back against the fountain's concrete wall.

She patted the ground beside her. "Have a seat."

Fires licking at very specific parts of his body said he shouldn't, but when it came to Twyla his common sense and judgment were compromised. He'd always been able to control himself, though, and still could. Lowering himself to the ground, he appreciated the coolness of the water shooting into the air and the concrete against his back. He could use more salvation, but would take what he could get. "So what do you want to talk about?"

"Not want," she said. "Need."

"So what do you *need* to talk about?"

"What did you tell my father?"

Forrest had figured that was what it was. Letting his gaze wander to the lake, he held his silence. Keeping her on edge was enjoyable, but that wasn't why he couldn't say anything. Even as a kid, he'd never told anyone about the backdoor dealings and cruelty that took place behind the papered walls of the Plantation. He'd feared that if he ever did tell someone, they'd be hurt. It was still that way.

Twyla had the patience of a gnat. It hadn't been more than fifteen seconds before she asked, "Well? What did you talk to my father about?"

"About flying for the army and delivering airmail."

"What else?"

The mixture of white starlight and yellow moonbeams caught in her eyes and he chuckled at how the mixture softened her glare, making her look about as fierce as a poodle.

"It's not funny," she said. "Now, what did you tell him?"

"Let's see," Forrest said, tapping one index finger against another. "I didn't tell him about the boxing match at the Rafters."

"I was never—"

"I didn't tell him," Forrest interrupted, while

tapping his next finger as if counting down, "about the kissing booth, or about the Yellow Moon speakeasy in Minneapolis, or the Pour House in—"

"How do you know—"

"Or how you told him you were spending the night at Mitsy's and she told her father she was spending the night out here, when in truth both of you spent the night in a boxcar in St. Paul because you missed the last train back to White Bear Lake."

Lips pursed, she snapped her head forward. With the moonlight glistening against her profile, her eyelashes looked two inches long. He had to swallow.

"It's impossible for you to know any of that," she said.

"It can't be impossible." From the moment he'd hit town, he'd made it his job to know how she was doing. How all of the Nightingales were doing. Not doing so would have been impossible. The urge to protect Twyla and her sisters from Galen was even stronger now than it had been way back when.

She turned to look at him. "Yes, it is. You weren't even around town when— You must be lying."

"When they took place?" He shook his head.

"The kissing booth was just a couple weeks ago. The boxing match last month."

She folded her arms and beneath the sparkling dress, her breasts rose and fell as she sighed heavily. "Did you tell him any of that or not?"

Forrest picked a blade of grass and stuck it in his mouth, attempting to look thoughtful as she peered up at him. He was thoughtful, but he was attempting to *not* think about how she'd grown into the beautiful woman he'd merely caught glimpses of years ago. He recognized something else, too. The weariness in her eyes. She was far more tired than anyone could possibly know. He could understand why; her dancing alone would have exhausted most people. Tossing the blade of grass aside, he answered, "Not."

She sat up straighter, and looked rather startled. "Why?"

"I said *not*," he clarified.

"I know what you said. Why didn't you tell him?"

Chapter Four

Twyla couldn't believe Forrest hadn't told her father everything. For a moment. Then it dawned on her as bright and unstoppable as a new day. Of course he hadn't said anything. If he was in love with Norma Rose, he wouldn't want to alienate her father by saying anything bad about any of the Nightingale girls. The fact he hadn't said anything should make her happy.

Well, it didn't. Instead a hard knot had formed in her stomach. One she didn't appreciate, but one that also reminded her that Forrest being in love with Norma Rose had always been a problem. The fact it still was, was no surprise.

"I didn't tell him," Forrest said, "but that's not to say I won't."

"And who's to say I won't tell him what you're up to?" she asked, mainly out of spite.

"Which is?"

She rolled her eyes and turned to settle her

gaze on a yellow shaft of moonlight shimmering against the water. The sight was familiar; her bedroom window faced the lake and she'd spent many nights staring out at the water, listening to the music below and dreaming of the time she could be a part of all the fun. Like it had many times in the past, the soothing and tranquil image made her lids heavy. She had a reason to be tired. The sun had barely risen when she'd crawled out of bed this morning to finalize the preparations for Palooka George's party. The party was still going strong, and therefore she needed to be, too. It was what she'd always wanted, and she wasn't about to complain now that she had it. Exhausted or not.

Twyla seemed to catch her second wind right then, a little internal blast of energy that told her the party wasn't over. She wasn't done. The chef best leave the oven on because there'd be no poking a fork in her. She wouldn't be done for hours. Her spine grew stiff and firm as she deliberately turned her head slowly to deliver her best I-dare-you-to-deny-it gaze. It was time for Forrest to know that she knew the real reason he was here. "Which is," she repeated, "that you are still in love with Norma Rose."

Forrest lifted a brow and the smile that appeared on his lips grew slowly, methodically.

Twyla felt her shoulders sinking and she held her breath as she tried to decipher his reaction.

"Still in love with Norma Rose?" he said.

It sounded like a question, and she responded, "Yes, you're still in love with Norma Rose and you're trying to break her and Ty apart." For good measure, she added, "It won't work."

A full smile curled his lips as he turned toward the lake. It remained there, his grin, at least from what she could see by staring at the side of his face. He had a dimple in his cheek, a tiny one that was a mere a fraction of his handsomeness. She liked dimples, but no matter how hard she tried or how long she stood before the mirror twisting smiles and frowns in all directions, she couldn't make one form in her cheeks. In all the years Forrest had been gone, she'd never forgotten his dimple. That hard lump in her stomach twisted into a double knot.

"That's why you told me to stay away from your sister," he said, more a declaration than a question.

Snapping her attention away from his dimple, Twyla sighed. There wasn't anything she could do about the knot. "Yes."

"And that's why you agreed to be my date tonight."

She nodded, yet inwardly wanted to shout that a meal and a dance didn't constitute a date. Not a real date. The kind she'd always dreamed of. One that included hours of fun and adventure. Maybe a kiss or two.

"Aw, Twyla," he said slowly. "I assure you, I'm not in love with Norma Rose."

A blank formed in the space occupied by her brain. It was a moment or two before she could speak. "Yes, you are. Why else would you be here?"

He stared at her for several long and rather intense moments, before saying, "Maybe because I'm set on the Plantation becoming a rival to your resort."

Her mind kicked in fully. He was attempting to fool her. That wouldn't happen ever again. She let out a snicker. "The Plantation hasn't rivaled Nightingale's for years, even before your father went to jail. He practically ran that place into the ground with his Hollywood prostitutes and button men."

"Yet Galen was never busted, was he? No federal agents ever came sniffing around his door."

Twyla thought it odd that he called his father by his given name. She didn't remember him doing that in the past. His tone was notable, too. Almost as if he was disgusted his father had never been caught. "Because his button men had machine guns at every entrance," she said. "Sheriff Withers may be growing older, but he's not stupid." Recalling something she'd once overheard, she added, "Besides, it was all a show for your father. He wasn't involved with real gangsters. They'd have planted him five feet under the first time he cheated them, and everyone knows your father wasn't an honest man. My father proved yours wasn't invincible."

"Or, maybe your father wanted to keep him alive. Sometimes that's worth more."

Twyla could have sworn that hairy, creepy spider was back and crawling its way slowly up her spine this time. The conversation had taken on a completely different tone. She leaned forward to peer around the side of Forrest's face and look him in the eye. In the darkness, his eyes looked black instead of brown, but not even the night sky could hide the dullness they now held.

"Why do you say that?" she asked. "Like that?" she added, withholding a shiver. Surely he didn't believe her father was in cahoots with his. That would be insane. They hated each other. Forrest hadn't been around when things had been really bad. When Galen had bad-mouthed all of the Nightingales, claiming they were gold diggers. No, Forrest had already up and left. Vanished without a word to anyone. That had been before Prohibition, before her father started making money, but that was also when her father started refusing to let them leave the house. The exact time her world had turned into a dark and lonely place.

Forrest shifted slightly, turning her way, and she held her breath, sensing he was about to answer. When a smile slowly curved his lips, her breath stalled in her lungs.

"I am not in love with Norma Rose, Twyla."

She leaned back against the fountain's concrete wall and huffed out a breath, totally flustered he'd brought the conversation back to that. "Yes, you are," she insisted. He'd always been in love with Norma Rose and probably always would be. There was no mystery there, but there was something behind his other comment— about her father keeping his alive. He knew something. A deep, dark secret he wasn't prepared to share. If she knew what that was, she'd have some real power to hold over him, perhaps enough to make him stay this time. Inside her head she pinched herself, a reminder that she needed to get rid of him, not make him stay.

"Why would you care if I was?" he asked.

She took a moment to contemplate how she wanted to answer that. This was Forrest, a man she'd known all her life, and despite what she told herself, a single day hadn't gone by when she hadn't missed him. Missed the fun they used to have. Swimming and fishing, playing hide-and-seek, and card games when it was raining. He'd been a permanent fixture at their house in the summertime. He'd been someone she believed would always be there. Right up until his disappearance. That's when she learned nothing was forever.

At first she hadn't believed it and refused to listen when Galen spouted that it was Norma Rose's fault that Forrest had left town. As time went on and no one heard a word from him, Twyla had to start believing, especially when Norma Rose voiced her hatred of Forrest.

A flicker of hope had been lit inside Twyla when she'd heard he'd returned to town last fall. For weeks she'd stared out the window, waiting for him to visit, but he never had. He'd refused to talk to her, too, when she'd called about hiring Slim. Last weekend, when he'd come out for Big Al's anniversary party, she'd purposefully stayed clear of him.

Hating him had been much easier when he'd been gone. The thrill of spying him from afar at the amusement park or seeing his airplane overhead, soaring around like an eagle in the sky, did something unique to her insides.

Flying had to be the ultimate freedom. Up there, you weren't attached to anything. The closest she'd ever come to that would have been years ago, when they used to go swimming. Forrest had tied a rope to a tree branch hanging over the water, and she'd loved those few seconds that occurred between the time she let go of the rope and when she landed in the water.

She'd told him that once, when it was just the two of them jumping off the rope—her sisters had been afraid of it, even Josie—and Forrest had agreed with her. Maybe that was why he took up flying.

Her mind had gone full-circle. Turning to look at him again, she asked, "Why do I care?"

He nodded.

Her stomach tightened and her throat grew a bit thick. Her answer had to be about her. That way, Forrest would believe her. It also was the truth, even if it didn't feel as important as it had before. "Because I want more excitement than hosting a kissing booth out of the back of the cotton candy shed. While you've been out seeing the world, flying planes, I've been stuck here." Pushing off the ground, she rose to her feet and waved a hand toward the resort on the other side of the water fountain. "I live at the biggest, most fabulous speakeasy in the nation, but I've never been able to enjoy it."

"Why?"

"Because of Norma Rose," she snapped.

"Why are you blaming Norma Rose for that?"

"Why?" Twyla planted both hands on her hips. She had her reasons, and was sticking to them. "Because of what you did. Because of the way your father acted and the things he said, Norma Rose became fixated on making sure that none of us would become doxies."

"It's all my fault."

It *was* all his fault. He'd left when she couldn't stand losing something else. Yet, with the way he said it, with such meaning and implication, something jabbed at Twyla. Something invisible, but with as much power and pain as anything real could ever have.

Forrest climbed to his feet and used one hand to push aside the wayward hair that had flopped over his forehead. "Is that what you want, Twyla? To be a speakeasy doxy?"

He made that sound immoral, which added to the sting inside her. Twyla spun around, not liking the hint of disgust in his eyes. "No, and I'm not a doxy." Twisting back around, she added, "But I am twenty-three. Too old to be told what to do and when to do it."

He stepped forward, and for a moment Twyla couldn't move, was barely able to breathe. There was a glimmer in his eyes, a faint, enticing shimmer that held her attention. When he took her hand and squeezed it gently, her knees quivered. Years ago he'd looked at her like that once, and it had frightened her. Not tonight. This time it made other things happen inside her. She felt anticipation. Excitement. All the things she'd longed for, and still did.

"I have a feeling, Twyla," he whispered, "age has nothing to do with it."

A knot formed in her throat, preventing her from responding. Not that she had a reply. Her mind had gone uncommonly empty. Because she knew what was about to happen.

He was going to kiss her.

Forrest was going to kiss her.

Her.

The knot in her stomach disappeared as a great sense of exuberance rose up. Her heart started racing and she had to part her lips in order to breathe.

Her lips quivered as Forrest leaned down. He tugged on her hand, forcing her to lean toward him. For a split second Twyla feared toppling to the ground.

That couldn't happen.

Could.

Not.

Happen.

Not when she was this close to experiencing paradise.

It didn't.

She didn't topple.

But as relieved as she was, Twyla was so overly disappointed her shoulders slumped clear to her elbows.

Forrest's lips had barely brushed against her forehead.

"Thanks for the party, doll," he said, letting loose her hand.

Never one to give up easily, Twyla's wits returned, at least partially, before he was completely out of arm's reach. She stopped herself from grabbing his arm, but did ask, "You're just going to leave me out here?"

That wasn't the question she wanted to ask, but she couldn't very well beg him to kiss her. Not when he'd always been in love with her sister.

Turning to glance over his shoulder, Forrest said, "You're in your own front yard."

Inhaling through her nose, she insisted, "I know." Pulling up a bit of charm that never failed when she wanted her way, she tilted her head and twirled an earring with one finger. "But it's dark."

He laughed. A joyful trill that echoed in the night air.

She dropped her hand and cast him a glare.

"I don't remember you being afraid of the dark."

"I'm not." A great desire to pout rose up in

her and she wanted to ask if he remembered how years ago, he'd always chosen her to be on his hide-and-seek team for that very reason. She certainly remembered.

With little more than a nod, he turned and started walking again. "Walter's standing next to the first boathouse. He'll make sure you get back inside safely."

Twyla let out a growl instead of screaming as she really wanted to do, and kicked at the grass, now slick and damp with dew. One shoe went flying. She barely caught herself before going down. As Twyla stood there wobbling, to her utter dismay, her shoe landed in the water fountain. How Forrest knew that—he hadn't turned around so he hadn't seen it—she wasn't sure, but his laughter said he knew her shoe was submerged in the bubbling water.

She stomped—well, hobbled—to the fountain, retrieved her shoe and, wet or not, stuck it back on her foot. Forrest disappeared around the side of the resort, and Twyla instinctively knew this time he was leaving for sure. She also knew she was no closer to—and perhaps even further away from—hating him than ever.

Forrest stopped in the shadows on the side of the massive three-story resort building and watched to make sure Twyla did indeed make her way back to the balcony stairs. The plunk of her shoe hitting the water had left a grin on his face, and despite all, it felt good. Her temper hadn't lessened over the years. Considering there were no rocks on the highly manicured lawn, he'd assumed the plunk and splash he'd heard was her shoe. She wasn't wearing anything else heavy enough to throw. He should be glad she hadn't thrown it at him. Maybe she had.

He should be glad, too, that he'd seen Walter, one of Roger's night watchmen, standing in the darkness next to the boathouse. Otherwise, he might have kissed Twyla in a bit less of a brotherly way.

Once she had made her way up the stairs, Forrest turned and walked along the building to the front parking lot. In love with Norma Rose. He never had been in love with Norma Rose, but he had been fond of all of the Nightingales, and had been diligent about keeping Galen away from them.

He climbed in his roadster and sat there, staring through the windshield at the building. It never used to look anything like this. No bricks. No second or third stories. No fancy lights framing the double front doors. No manicured lawn, little concrete statues or big water fountain. The dance pavilion had been a white wooden structure with doors on all four sides to let the air in and out. He and the girls had played tag inside it, their laughter echoing off the walls as they raced across the floor, which was slick and shiny from years of people dancing on it.

The old pavilion was gone, and he had to wonder if, had it still been there, it would be as large as he remembered. A child's mind did that. Inflated things.

He used to leave here and go home to his bed, where he'd pretend he didn't belong. He'd plot there, too, in his bed, trying to find ways to make his presence at the Nightingale household permanent. A child's mind also imagined things could become different just with hope. He'd grown out of that belief, but would never grow out of trying to protect the Nightingale girls from Galen's corruption.

The entire time he'd been at his aunt's house, he'd kept in touch with Scooter Wilson. Scooter had assured him that Roger had all of his daughters well protected, and kept them far away from Galen. Forrest had seen that for himself when he'd returned home after learning to walk again.

He pulled his eyes away from the resort and started the car. After that one visit, he'd had no intention of ever returning. Not even when his mother called, telling him about Galen's "move," as she put it, to California to appear in court in order to clear up the charges brought against the film company.

Shifting into first, Forrest eased his car forward and then steered around and between the rows of vehicles of every shape, color and size. As he started down the long driveway, he glanced in the review mirror mounted on the spare tire next to the hood. Golden light shined from windows on all three floors and he turned his eyes back to the road ahead of him. He'd returned to far more than he'd bargained on.

Several things, mainly the changes he'd witnessed, crossed Forrest's mind as he drove the four miles from Bald Eagle Lake to the city of White Bear Lake. Including how the town had changed during his absence. Besides new businesses, it was thriving in ways it hadn't for years.

Employment was up. Everyone seemed to have a job and money to spend. It hadn't been that way when he'd left. The people he'd met since returning were jovial, happy, content and satisfied with the lives they had. In the nine months he'd been here, he'd concluded Roger Nightingale had a lot to do with that. The man said Prohibition had been a gold mine to him, and he was right. Roger had made plenty of money the past few years, but he hadn't kept it all to himself. He'd poured a goodly sum into the resort, and in doing so was sharing his wealth. The grocers, the gas stations, the clothing stores and pharmacies, even the amusement park, all benefitted from the success of the resort.

Understanding that fact increased the heavy troubles weighing on Forrest's shoulders. The Nightingales' wealth was everywhere you looked. He hadn't had to see Twyla's glittering outfit or tasted the delicacies their chef set on the table to know that. He'd heard about it, long before returning home.

The tables had certainly turned.

He ambled along the quiet main drag of the city. This late, everything was dark as folks were already settled in their beds. The town council had passed a noise ordinance last year, along with a ten-o'clock curfew. Forrest could only assume, but he was about ninety percent sure that Galen was the reason the ordinance had been passed. Twyla had been right. Galen was not an honest man and had made a plethora of enemies because of it. She'd been wrong, too, in her statement about Galen never associating with real mobsters. He had. The mobsters that visited the Plantation years ago had been the lowest of the low and the greediest of the greedy. Prohibition hadn't hit yet, but it was on its way, and gangsters that had found success with extortion and theft had been making plans to increase their activities and make the most of the amendment.

Galen had been involved with the Eastman crew from New York, one of the first non-Irish street gangs, who'd formed a prominent underworld empire in the late 1800s. They'd profited from prostitution rings, illegal gambling and hired thugs, but peddling opium had been where they'd really made their money and gained notoriety. From the information Forrest had gathered over the years, Galen had been ousted from the gang, but had been able to reconnect himself after marrying Forrest's mother, and had squandered almost every dime his grandfather had amassed to maintain his affiliation.

The depth of Galen's corruption had eluded Forrest until he'd been recuperating at his aunt's house in southern Minnesota after his graduation party. Uncle Silas—Aunt Shirley's husband—felt he was old enough to know.

Gravel crunched beneath the tires of his roadster as he drove through the Plantation's front lot and around to the back. There he cut the engine, and like he'd done at Nightingale's, he stared at the building before him. When his grandfather had built it, the large four-story white building, with its huge, gracefully carved pillars and wraparound porch, had been the most stunning and elaborate structure in White Bear Lake. His grandmother, who'd died long before Forrest had been born, had been from the South, a plantation owner's daughter. Wanting to please his wife, Hans had aptly built and named the building in honor of her roots.

It still glistened brightly in the moonlight like the shrine that it was, but, as he'd noted when he'd returned last fall, all the shine was only on the surface. *Neglect* wasn't the word he'd used to describe what he'd discovered, for parts of the building had been kept up and even modernized. *Illusion* was a better description. The building had the illusion of being magnificent, whereas underneath, upon closer inspection, the wear and tear that was slowly eroding the splendor had been covered up.

The first thing he'd noticed had been that lightbulbs were only in every other, or every third, socket and the heavy drapes were nailed closed, giving the interior a shadowy atmosphere that also hid how threadbare the carpets were, how grimy the wallpaper was after years of smoke and how the ceiling paint had cracked and chipped.

A heaviness settled over Forrest as he continued to gaze at the building. He'd gone over his options several times in the past few months, even while pouring the few funds he did have into the Plantation. His plan when he'd first arrived had been to sell it, to get rid of any reason for his family to remain here, but as his mother pointed out, his grandfather's will held a clause stating the Plantation couldn't be sold. She also reminded him that Hans had left it all to him so it would continue into the next generation. Forrest figured a wily, fast-talking lawyer could make a case to override the clause, but he also imagined that if that was the case, Galen would have found a way for it to happen years ago.

He'd warned Roger of Galen's pending release, but that wouldn't be enough. A dozen watchmen may have stopped Galen before, but not after his arrest. The devil wasn't as evil as Galen Reynolds. After months in jail, he'd be out for blood and would go straight for Roger's heart—his daughters.

Galen had threatened to harm the girls for years, whenever he'd wanted Forrest to ask Shirley for money. Willing to do anything to keep the girls safe, Forrest had always given in. There was nothing left for Galen to take from him now, and they both knew that.

Letting out a sigh, Forrest glanced to the sky. The stars still shone brightly. Normally, at least since he'd removed the heavy and cumbersome car roof, he garaged the roadster at night, but right now, the simple act of restarting it and driving it across the back lot to the garage seemed like more effort than he had energy for. That wasn't like him. He respected his vehicles—the roadster and his airplane—and the engineering beneath them, and he certainly didn't have the money to replace them if they became weather damaged. Although in truth, a car didn't matter much when all was said and done.

Concluding it wasn't going to rain and one night outside the garage wasn't going to hurt the roadster, he pulled the key from the ignition and opened the door.

The waves of White Bear Lake a few yards away washed up on the shore with a steady swish, echoing gently through the otherwise still silence. Waves had washed ashore out at Bald Eagle Lake, too, while he and Twyla had been sitting near the splashing fountain. At the resort, music had accompanied the waves, as had the sound of the gaiety of the partygoers.

None of those sounds accompanied Forrest now and the emptiness of that left him feeling more tired, more alone, than ever.

Jacob, the one and only employee who'd remained after Galen had left town, opened the back door before Forrest had finished climbing the steps to the porch.

"I was wondering if you were gonna sit out there all night," the elderly man said.

"Quiet night?" Forrest asked, rather than explaining what he'd been doing.

"Of course," Jacob answered. "Anybody who's

anyone was at Nightingale's tonight. We had a few bowlers, but Martha and her brood took care of them."

Forrest nodded as he entered the building. Martha McMillan was a gem. Having fourteen children, the woman knew how to organize and manage most anything that came her way. When he'd first approached her about working at the Plantation, she'd had her doubts, claiming she was a respectable woman and wouldn't work at a place the likes of the Plantation. Forrest had promised there would be no more gangsters, no more drunken brawls that, come morning, left the place in shambles. And above all, no more prostitution and gaudy dancers.

He'd made no mention of the other activities. If it was illegal, Galen had been involved in it. Trafficking young girls and trading them for opium had been his specialty, and something he'd always used as a threat. He'd claimed one of the Nightingale girls would be worth more than a dozen of the others.

"You hear me?" Jacob asked.

Forrest nodded, and changed the route of his thoughts back to his employees. He'd persuaded Martha and hired her, along with the three children she still had at home—two teenage sons who liked being pin boys for the bowling lanes and a daughter who enjoyed serving soda pop and popcorn to her friends during the weekends. Martha had also managed to find other staff—cooks who served a modest menu, waiters to carry plates and wash dishes and general maintenance workers.

"How was the party?" Jacob asked, having closed and locked the back door.

"How are all of the parties out at Nightingale's?" Forrest answered, a bit more harshly than he'd intended. "The place was packed to the rafters and the food and drinks were flowing."

"You questioning the decision you made here?" Jacob asked.

In his midfifties, Jacob Wertheimer wasn't old, but he'd been around the Plantation a long time and had seen a lot. His father had managed the Plantation under Hans, and Jacob had taken over shortly before Galen had arrived on the scene. During Galen's reign, Jacob had been demoted to a groundskeeper, but his commitment and dedication to what Hans and his father, Joseph Wertheimer, had created never faltered. In fact, Jacob had been the one who had saved Forrest's life the night of his graduation. He had no recollection of how the man had stopped Galen's henchmen from beating him to death, but he did recall Jacob driving him to Rochester. All the way to Aunt Shirley's house the man kept saying, "Don't you die on me, boy. Don't you die on me."

"No," Forrest answered. "I'm not questioning my decision about the Plantation." Shortly after he'd received the phone call from his mother, insisting he come home to run the place while she and Galen moved to California—to take care of the few minor allegations against Galen— he'd decided this could be his chance to change things. By then, he'd heard Galen could end up serving serious time, and his airmail contract had ended due to the new legislation then still in discussion.

A pilot friend, Isaac Hammer, gave him the idea of changing the nightclub into a bowling alley. Bowling had become a rave on the east coast. Some alleys were merely covers for speakeasies, but others were legitimate businesses that people flocked to, especially during the winter months. He'd capitalized on that idea, placing an order for bowling pins and balls to be sent to Minnesota, and envisioned his remodeling plans while flying his last few routes. However, what he'd discovered upon arriving home had made him wonder if any of it was possible.

"You talk to Roger?" Jacob asked.

"Yeah," Forrest answered, following the shorter, bald man down the long hallway that led to the front foyer and the staircase leading to the second and third floors, where only he and Jacob resided. When he was a kid the entire third floor had been occupied by prostitutes. Originally, while the second floor had always been the family living quarters, the third floor had been the hotel section. Forrest had considered reinstating guest rooms, but his funds had run out before the renovations had finished.

Although he'd arrived only a week after his mother and Galen had left, others had been here before him. Those who'd had money owed to them had taken anything of value. Even old beds and chests of drawers. In almost every room, what they hadn't taken they'd left too damaged to use.

Jacob said it had all happened in one night. Everything had been fine when he'd left one evening and then it was either gone or destroyed the next morning. The man had been living in the back of the garage then, in the small room he'd been forced into under Galen's ownership, and suggested it must have been frustrated employees. Jacob swore the doors had been locked that night, and he hadn't heard a thing, yet come morning, the damage had all been done. The odd part was that the building hadn't been broken into; someone had had a key.

The staff, including Jacob, hadn't been paid for several months. Forrest had taken care of that issue first. He had used a good portion of his savings to find all the disgruntled workers and pay them their wages, but it had been money well spent. Whether he had anything to do with it or not, those people deserved to be paid for their time rendered. People seemed to appreciate his honesty, although none had jumped at the chance to renew their employment. Then he'd changed the locks.

"What did he say?" Jacob asked.

"He's checking into Galen's pending release."

"I'm sure he is," Jacob said, climbing the curved stairway of the front entrance.

Still following, Forrest said, "He's done well for himself, Roger has. I know you told me that, but until really seeing it all for the first time tonight, I didn't know how well."

"Yes, he has," Jacob agreed. "But don't be fooled. They don't call him The Night for no reason."

"You don't think he's involved in the opium trade, do you?"

"Nope, and never have."

"I wish I didn't," Forrest said honestly. "But after seeing what I saw tonight—the money spent on that place—I have to wonder." He stopped his mind from taking another path. One that was filled with a shimmering dress and blue eyes. "If Roger was the one who blew the lid off Galen's cover, he had to know about the opium."

"I'm sure he did." Jacob shrugged. "But that doesn't mean Roger was involved, then or now."

"I know, but it's the only thing that makes sense. If Roger just wanted to take Galen down, why didn't he just have him busted? Here?" Forrest shook his head. "All of Galen's charges were from California. Serious charges. Federal agents extradited him there. It doesn't make sense."

Scratching his tingling scalp, Forrest added, "Roger has the backing of big men. I saw them at the resort tonight. They're men who own Chicago. He could have had Galen taken down here. Taken out. But he didn't. Why?"

Jacob shook his head "I don't know. I admit, it doesn't make sense, but let me tell you, don't be fooled. Galen had people behind him, too. And he's ruthless and mean, but he's smart when it comes to protecting his own hide. If what your mother says is true, that they are coming back here when he's released, he won't return to Minnesota unless he has the backing he needs to go up against Roger Nightingale." Pausing at the landing on the second floor, Jacob glanced up with eyes full of sincerity. "The fact he got a second trial tells you he has some firepower behind him."

"But who?" Forrest asked, sincerely wanting to know. "Galen burnt every bridge he ever crossed. The way this place was wiped clean tells us that. We're lucky it wasn't burned to the ground."

"Yes, we are," Jacob agreed, "and you're going to need firepower behind you to save what you've invested in this place. If you are serious about saving what your grandfather built."

Forrest had no intention of revealing that wasn't the driving force behind his actions. Not to anyone. Gesturing toward Jacob with one hand, he said, "I'm not convinced that should be Roger."

"You really think he was involved in the opium business?"

Forrest's stomach knotted. "I don't know what to think." What he did know was that Galen's determination and hatred would only be increased if he learned Forrest had asked for Roger's assistance in preventing his release. Although there was a list of charges against both Galen and his Hollywood film company, his mother claimed only one was the cause of his incarceration, and was tight-lipped about it. Even to him. "Galen was arrested for money laundering. What he was selling has never been revealed."

"Maybe Roger didn't know what it was," Jacob suggested. "Just that Galen was using his Hollywood film company to do it."

"It had to be the opium," Forrest said. "The authorities have cracked down on that."

"Well, then," Jacob said thoughtfully. "Maybe whoever was behind the opium has stepped forward and wants to reciprocate for Galen taking the fall."

An uncomfortable twinge crossed Forrest's shoulders. "What do you know that you're not saying?"

"Nothing," Jacob answered earnestly. "I was just thinking aloud. I made it my business not to know anything back then. It was hard enough working here. I certainly never put myself in the position some gangster would want to beat information out of me."

Forrest believed that. "Do you have any theories?"

"No new ones. I don't believe Roger has anything to do with the opium trade, but I do believe you need his help to keep Galen behind bars. Where he belongs." Jacob started walking down the hall, to where both his and Forrest's rooms were. "I saw how evil that man is. I kept the lawns mowed and the snow shoveled, all the while keeping my ears closed and my nose clean. The only time I interfered in anything was that night, with you. No one ever discovered it was me, and I'm thankful for that. Other than the fact Galen thought it was your mother."

Forrest refrained from replying. Even before he'd discovered Galen wasn't his father he'd questioned why his mother was so devoted to her husband. Galen hadn't been any more pleasant to her than he'd been to anyone else. His aunt and uncle hadn't had the answer to that. Upon his return home, Forrest had asked his mother. Sternly and rather harshly she'd informed him she'd done it all for him. To make sure he wasn't born a bastard.

Being born one and being one were two different things in his eyes, and when he'd voiced that, she'd raised her hand to him. The one and only time. She'd apologized afterward and told him how his real father, a man she'd met and fallen in love with while she'd been attending school in New York, had been robbed and killed while escorting her home after a Broadway play. She claimed to have returned to Minnesota, shattered and heartbroken, only to discover a short time later she was pregnant. Galen arrived then and gallantly swept her off her feet, promising to raise the child as his own. They were married within a few weeks.

Forrest hadn't been impressed with her tale. That was also when he'd left for Nebraska. He'd come home once, after he'd paid to have the hangar built north of town, where his plane was stored. Until nine months ago, he'd only used that hangar once. That had been enough.

He was here now, and had poured every bit of

his savings into refurbishing the Plantation. For the first few months he'd completely closed the doors and worked right alongside the men he'd hired, installing the bowling lanes and the billiards room and repairing things that had been neglected for too long. By February, he'd reopened, and although it had taken time for people to enter the doors, skeptical of what was behind them, the novelty of the bowling alley finally won them over. There was only one other alley in the state, in a hotel in St. Paul that was also known to host one of the state's largest gambling rings and therefore didn't allow the average person much of a chance to visit.

For the most part, his investment was paying off. The Plantation was now making enough money to pay its employees and utilities, but it would be years before Forrest saw a return on his money, which left him in a predicament—even without Galen's release.

They'd stopped near Jacob's bedroom door and as the man opened it, he asked, "You are going to talk to Roger, aren't you?"

"Yes," Forrest replied. Having to involve the Nightingales tore at him, but Galen's pending release didn't give him much choice. All the ground he'd gained since coming home would wash away faster than a mudslide once Galen hit town. Whether he was peddling opium or not,

Roger Nightingale's influence was his only hope for keeping Galen where he belonged.

"Make it soon," Jacob said. "Your mother called tonight. She wants you to call her back in the morning."

Chapter Five

Up until today, Twyla had never realized why Norma Rose had cherished Sundays. Today she'd determined it was because Norma Rose had been tired and needed a slow day to recuperate. Twyla had a throbbing blister on one heel, caused by her shoe, a bruise on her hip from when Palooka George knocked her over on the dance floor after he'd had a few too many highballs, and a headache that said she'd do about anything to not have to get out of bed this morning. It had only been a few hours since she'd collapsed upon the mattress.

She had hauled herself up because this was what she wanted, and she wouldn't complain. There was no large party to worry about today, but the resort was full of overnight guests and it was part of her job to oversee everything ran as smoothly today as it had last night.

That, however, was a remarkably easy feat. All

the time and effort Norma Rose had put in over the past few years had paid off. Housekeeping staff already had the resort as sparkling clean as ever, including the guest rooms and cabins that needed attention. The cooks had meals filling the dining room tables or being carted off to rooms and cabins—room service was just one of the luxuries people bragged about after staying here—and the phone, as it was Sunday, was quiet.

After making her rounds and discovering Josie had already taken care of the few small incidents that had appeared, Twyla retreated to the balcony, where tables had been set up for anyone wanting to enjoy the lake view while partaking of their breakfast.

In the serenity of the warm sun, with the quiet murmuring of the few people inside the dining room and the fresh scent of the lake flowing on a cooling breeze, she consumed a bowl of oatmeal with cream and brown sugar and a full glass of freshly squeezed orange juice. Not the most elaborate of breakfasts, but her very favorite.

The food helped her headache. The loose-fitting yellow-and-white polka-dot dress covered the bruise on her hip without any chafing, and she'd pushed the back of her shoe down to prevent further irritation to the blister. The day was looking up, and she was going to appreciate it being Sunday, too. A bit of downtime never hurt anyone.

Her gaze swept down the hill to the lake, where a couple walked along one of the docks. A boat tied to the end bounced lazily upon the water and Twyla watched as Ty assisted Norma Rose into the craft after he'd climbed in himself. Norma Rose untied the boat while Ty took an oar handle in each hand and started paddling away from the dock. The rowboat gradually swung around and Ty started paddling forward, toward the big island in the center of Bald Eagle Lake.

Twyla closed her eyes. Although she looked at it every day, it had been years since she'd been on the island. She hadn't set foot there since the days when Forrest used to row them all over to the shore. In their youth, they'd spent hours looking for treasure buried by some ancient and quite imaginary pirates.

Under the table, where no one walking by might notice, she lifted her legs and rested her feet upon the chair across from her. Life had been fun back then. Every day had been an adventure. From searching for pirate treasures to playing tag in the echoing old pavilion. A portion of the dance floor was all that was left of the old building. With Norma Rose's vision and father's money, the entire resort had been remodeled over the past few years, turning it into the showy place it was today.

For a split second, Twyla wondered how different things might be if Norma Rose and Forrest hadn't been caught kissing in his car that night of his graduation. If Forrest hadn't left and if the two of them, Norma Rose and Forrest, had gotten married.

Her mind didn't have time to wander down that road because her sense of tranquility was rudely interrupted.

"Sleeping on the job?"

The sound of Forrest's voice not only tore her lids open, but it also sent her heart careening across her chest like a rowboat in a windstorm. "You're back," she said coldly, although an inner flash of heat left her almost feverish.

"I'm back," he said, grasping the back of the chair her feet were on with both hands.

Challenging him to move the chair with a single glare, she didn't remove her feet. She still didn't believe he wasn't in love with Norma Rose. There could be no other reason for him to be here. "You're too late," she said, gesturing toward the water. "Norma Rose and Ty are rowing to the island."

He turned to look and that irritated her more.

"I haven't been to the island in years," he said.

Her eyes wandered down the length of him.

He didn't have on his flyboy getup, but looked almost as good in the brown pants and cream-and-brown-striped shirt.

"Remember when we stole the boards out of the hayloft and rowed them over to the island to build a tree fort?"

Her heart sprouted wings, fluttering at yet another happy memory. Twyla lifted her gaze to meet his. "Yes, I remember." She searched her brain for a minute, but was unable to recall and asked, "Did we ever build it?"

His smile was rather contagious. "No, Josie stepped on a nail and we had to haul her home."

"That's right," she agreed. "You had to carry her all the way to the boat and then she lay around for weeks, making us all wait on her."

"Yes, she did, and then school started again, so we never got back out to work on it."

His tone had turned solemn. She could relate. They'd all hated fall. Forrest hadn't attended school around here like her and her sisters. He'd gone to a private boys' school down in the city. Other than during the Christmas and Easter breaks, he hadn't returned home until late spring. Twyla, along with her sisters, had eagerly awaited his return, for it had always seemed like a part of their family had been missing.

"And," she added, looking for something to erase the heaviness settling around them,

"Father explained to all of us that we didn't own the island and couldn't just go building on someone else's property."

Forrest's gaze had gone back to the island, and she wondered if the sense of longing hanging in the air was coming from him or her.

"He bought it," Twyla said when Forrest remained silent. "My father bought the island for the taxes owed on it a few years ago."

"I didn't know that," Forrest replied. "Our wood is probably still sitting in a pile out there, rotting away."

She laughed. "It was probably well-rotted when we stole it out of the barn. The hayloft was refurbished when…" She let her voice trail off, not meaning to have gone that far.

"When your father started running shine?" Forrest suggested.

It was no secret, but Twyla understood the importance of not sharing certain things openly. Her father's business was the reason she had the life she did, but she wasn't fool enough to believe it would last forever. Nothing did. Even here. In the past few weeks, Ginger had run away and Norma Rose had made a complete turnaround. Even Josie was more secretive than usual. Her father also understood the way things could change so quickly. He'd signed over the resort to his daughters, and Twyla, by herself if need be, would make sure Nightingale's continued to be a success. Until Forrest had up and left town, she hadn't realized how poor they'd been. She did now, and keeping things as they were was her sole purpose.

Norma Rose and Ty were now little more than a dot on the lake. Gesturing at a gull flying over the water, Twyla said, "I bet you wish you were in your airplane, flying over their boat like that bird so you could see what they're doing."

Forrest turned slowly and looked at her quizzically for several moments before asking, "Do you have the day off?"

For a second she'd thought he was going to say something much more worthwhile. Exactly what, she wasn't sure, but his thoughtfulness had reminded her of years ago when he'd been contemplating an adventure for all of them. Letting go of her whimsical thoughts, Twyla shrugged. "It's a Sunday. They're always slow. People are recovering from Friday and Saturday nights."

"Can you leave if you want?"

Curiosity, or perhaps hope, leaped inside her. Yet, trying not to show any reaction, she asked, "Why?"

"So I can give you a ride in my airplane."

Twyla's heart nearly jumped out of her chest. Unable to control the excitement flaring inside she bounded to her feet so fast the chairs and table wobbled. She very well could have been ten years old again, responding to an escapade he'd suggested. Forrest had always come up with the best ideas. "You mean it?"

"Yes, I mean it. If you want to."

His smile captured her heart as fast as his answer. "I want to," she agreed immediately. "I surely do."

He grabbed her hand. "Well, come on, then."

Her excitement doubled, and she squeezed his hand on impulse. His grin was far more intoxicating than a double shot of whiskey. As they entered the dining room through the double doorway, Twyla's excitement calmed enough for her mind to snag. "Why did you come out here today?"

"To talk to your father," Forrest said. "Josie told me he and Palooka George went someplace and won't be back until this afternoon. That'll give us plenty of time for a flyby."

"A flyby?"

He nodded. "That's a short flight just for fun."

"Where'd you see Josie?" Twyla asked. The thrill of riding in an airplane overtook her again. She could discover what he wanted to talk to her father about anytime, but the chance to have a ride in an airplane might never happen again. The thought was so thrilling she was practically trembling. "I have to tell her I'm leaving."

"In the office," Forrest said.

They exited the dining room side by side and turned the corner to the hallway leading to both Norma Rose's and her father's offices. "Do I need to change?" Twyla asked. "It would only take me a minute."

"Not unless you want to," Forrest answered. "I have an extra flight jacket at the hangar."

A flight jacket! She'd dreamed of wearing one of those leather coats with the fur collars. She hoped he had an extra hat, too. The one she'd seen him wearing was cherries. Just cherries. Her feet barely touched the floor as she made her way down the hall. Life just kept getting better and better, despite Forrest's reappearance. In fact, in this instance he was the reason for the improvement.

Josie was in Norma Rose's office, talking on the phone, which she hung up abruptly when Forrest pushed open the door. She most likely had been talking with one of the women from her Ladies Aid Society. Twyla had no idea what went on at all those meetings, having only attended the few Josie dragged her and Norma Rose to a couple of times a year, but she did know they weren't as innocent as they appeared. Yet she couldn't imagine some of the old women who hosted the meetings doing a lot more than crocheting doilies and watering roses.

"I'm going to town with Forrest," Twyla said. "We'll be gone a couple of hours."

Josie cast a curious glance between her and Forrest, but then nodded. "All right, but just so you know, I have a meeting on Tuesday, a long one. I'll be gone most of the day."

"All right," Twyla replied. This, too, was working out wonderfully, the way she and Josie could swap time at work in order to see to personal things. She'd covered when Josie had attended a meeting last Tuesday, too, and on Thursday Josie had covered for her while she'd spent the day shopping for the outfit she'd worn last night and the polka-dot dress she had on today. Pulling the door closed, she asked Forrest, "You sure I don't need to change?"

"Not unless you want to," he said again.

She didn't want to waste the time, and she also needed to get away before someone stopped her. With her father gone and Norma Rose on the island, it wasn't likely, but one never knew. Then again, she was so used to sneaking out that not rushing was impossible.

Forrest stopped on the front porch to tell Bronco, "Twyla's going with me, so there's no need for you to go looking for her."

Bronco laughed. "Thanks."

Twyla pinched her lips against a sense of chagrin. She liked Bronco, he was a nice man. She just didn't like him being her tail all the time, and, in all fairness, she had led him on more than one wild-goose chase.

"I'll have her back in a couple of hours," Forrest said.

"Good enough," Bronco replied, leaning back in the chair he often settled upon near the front door.

Twyla understood her father paid his watchmen well, as he did all his employees. Even she made a nice salary, but she did feel a pinch of sympathy for Bronco and the others. Their jobs had to be so boring. "Oh, goodness," she said, while crossing the parking lot and the realization hit that she was leaving the resort. "I didn't even fetch my purse."

"You aren't going to need it," Forrest said, opening the passenger door of his roadster. "I'm not going to charge you for the ride."

She laughed, feeling freer than she had even in the past two weeks. "Well, that's good to know."

Forrest chuckled. He shut the passenger door after she'd climbed in, then walked around the hood of the car. Twyla leaned over to check if she could catch her reflection in the chrome framing the windshield. Her image was a bit distorted, but she could see well enough to double-knot the yellow scarf around her neck so it wouldn't come loose while they were driving.

Or flying.

Applesauce and horsefeathers! She was going flying!

Little old Twyla Nightingale flying. It just couldn't get much better than this. Just couldn't. Twisting, she checked her hair and earrings and then wished she had grabbed her purse so she could reapply the lipstick that had rubbed off during breakfast.

Forrest climbed behind the wheel, amused at the way Twyla was using the windshield frame as a mirror. When she'd finished and sat back, he asked, "Are you ready?"

"Indeed I am," she answered with a full smile. "Indeed I am."

He started the engine and drove slowly across the parking lot, not wanting to stir up dust. Her yellow-and-white dress looked brand-new and he wondered if he should have told her to go and change. Once the thought of taking her flying had formed, excitement had filled his blood. He hadn't been up in his airplane for weeks and missed it. There'd been a time when he'd flown every day, and even then, he couldn't wait to get back in the cockpit.

Currently his money was so limited he couldn't squander it on fuel just for fun. This might be his only chance to take Twyla on a short flight.

Practically every time he got in the cockpit, he'd found himself thinking about her, and how much she'd enjoy flying.

Forrest kept his speed low while driving along the curvy road that went from the resort to the main highway, and they had to stop to wait for the morning train at the tracks near the Bald Eagle depot. It was an oddity for a township to have its own depot when it didn't have a town, but Bald Eagle was the exception. Jacob claimed Roger had a lot to do with that, and Forrest didn't doubt it. Trains hauled as much moonshine as runners.

Once on the highway, Forrest increased the speed of the roadster. Even though the road was dirt, it was firmly packed and didn't stir up dust like some of the side roads. Laughter had him glancing over to the passenger seat. Twyla had her head back and her arms in the air. Her yellow scarf flayed behind her in the wind.

"Haven't you ever ridden in a convertible?" he asked.

"No," she said. "Father claims breezers are dangerous. He only buys cars with tops. This is wonderful."

He laughed. "If you think this is wonderful, you're going to love flying."

"I know," she said.

Forrest had to drag his eyes back to the road.

She was a looker, with her yellow scarf flapping behind her. All the Nightingale girls had been cute, but the years had turned Twyla into a more-than-beautiful woman. Her tease-me attitude took her one notch above her sisters. She'd always had that quality, but now she knew how to use it.

A few miles later, Forrest turned off the highway and once again slowed his speed to accommodate the gravel road. He was still pondering Twyla's attitude and beauty. Two things he'd never overlooked in the past—and two things he couldn't get beyond right now.

"Isn't this Dac Lester's dad's farm?" she asked.

Lester had a large dairy operation that kept the area, as well as most of St. Paul, supplied with milk. "No," Forrest answered, "it runs alongside Lester's land and he runs his cattle on it, but my grandfather owned it. It was part of my inheritance. I had a hangar and runway built on it a while back."

"When? I never heard about it."

"Not too many people know," he said. "That's how I wanted it."

"Why?"

This was Twyla, the most inquisitive of the sisters. Forrest shrugged, hoping she'd stop probing if he didn't make much of it. "I was just out of flight school and was considering coming home to stay."

"Why didn't you?"

He should have known she wouldn't stop. He certainly couldn't tell her it was because after he'd had the building built, Galen had informed him how his flying could assist the family business. Becoming a drug smuggler had never been on his to-do list. "I joined the air service reserve corps instead," Forrest told her. Knowing she'd come up with more questions, he continued, "Within a few years I was flying regular airmail routes and didn't have time to come back home until last fall."

"When your father went to jail and you had to come home to run the family business," she offered.

There was compassion in her tone, and Forrest wasn't sure he liked it. "Something like that," he said, while turning off the gravel and onto a field road that wasn't used enough to wear out the grass. It was mostly weeds, and short enough he didn't need to worry about it catching fire from the engine, here or on the runway.

"There you go again," Twyla said. "Saying something I know has double meanings, but I can't fathom what they are. You did it last night, too, when you kept calling your father 'Galen.'"

Forrest held the wheel tight, for the road was

more rutted than he liked, but also because he'd come to hate people thinking Galen was his father. "Because he's not my father."

Twyla's gasp confirmed he'd said it aloud, when he truly hadn't meant to. Forrest bit his lip, cursing himself and wishing he could retract his words.

"He's not?" Twyla asked, looking more than slightly flabbergasted.

Forrest wanted to grin at her animated expression, but sighed instead. Then he recalled their wine-sampling incident and how she'd never told. If she had, her father wouldn't have thought twice about punishing him. Roger had been like that; he'd been welcoming in having Forrest around but had laid down the law with him as readily and sternly as he had with his daughters. "Only a few people know," Forrest said. "Mainly my mother, Galen and me."

"Mum's the word," she whispered. "I won't tell anyone, I promise."

That would be impossible. Her keeping a secret like that. Yet he was tickled by the heartfelt smile on her face. Actually, he wouldn't mind if she spread the word. It might help his reputation.

"How can that be?" she asked, now frowning. "I've never heard so much as a whisper on that subject."

"Oh?" he asked. "Do you know everyone's secrets?"

"I make it a point to," she said smugly. "I know things about people they don't even know themselves."

One little grin from those lips was enough to turn the sky from dark to light. He shook his head at an internal reaction that kick-started his heart into a faster beat.

"And what do you do with all those secrets?" he asked.

"Nothing," she said. "I won't tell anyone, Forrest. I promise."

Maneuvering the car around an old fence line, he concluded that Twyla learning his true parentage was the least of his worries. "My mother was pregnant when she and Galen got married. My real father had died in New York, unfortunately for my mother, before they were able to get married." That was his mother's story, and the only one he had.

Twyla had been quiet for less than a second before she said, "Well, that certainly explains a lot."

"It does?"

"Yes, your—Galen Reynolds, I mean, is not a very handsome man and is as ornery as the devil."

Forrest laughed, but then asked, "Are you

saying I'm handsome and not as ornery as the devil?"

"Yes," she said, with a pink hue on her cheeks. "You are a rather handsome man and can be very nice, when you want to be."

Due to the fact her cheeks were now bright red, Forrest chose to not comment. She was making him feel things he hadn't felt in some time. Bringing the car to a stop, he pointed at the squat shed built against a backdrop of pine trees. "We're here."

She glanced around and frowned. "Where's your airplane?"

"Inside there."

"There? That building doesn't look very big."

"It's called a hangar, and it's big enough," he said.

She turned to look at him with those questioning blue eyes, which were still shimmering with the delight that had sprung out of them back at the resort when he'd asked her to go flying with him. Laughing, he lightly chucked her beneath the chin. "Trust me."

"Do I have a choice?" she asked.

That was Twyla, and he'd missed her. Missed the adventures they used to have. The fun and excitement and the companionship. Though Josie had been the tomboy, interested in frogs, worms, bugs and animals, Twyla had been the most adventurous. There'd been little she wouldn't do for a dare, and even less if there was a reward included. She'd fight tooth and nail for a promised dime out of his pocket, or the last cookie out of one of the tins his mother always sent with him when he went to visit the Nightingales.

Forrest climbed out of the driver's door and walked around to open her door before going to the back of the car. There he opened the trunk and pulled out his flight jacket and goggles. He always kept them in the roadster, just in case. He also had his boots and heavy canvas pants. Pulling those out, he glanced at Twyla's legs.

With her sheer stockings glistening in the sun, her long legs were a feast for any man's eyes. His mouth almost went dry. "I should have had you change," he said. "It's cold up there."

She pointed to the sky. "Up there? How can that be? It's closer to the sun."

He shook his head at her logic. "It's cold, trust me, and windy. I have an extra flight jacket in the hangar, and goggles and a hat. I'm sure they'll fit you, but these are the only extra pants. They'll be big, but it'll be better than getting cold."

She took the pants. "They'll be fine."

Stepping out of her shoes, she stuck one leg in the pants and then the other. When she started to pull them up, Forrest forced his gaze to turn back to the trunk. He gathered up his boots and switched his shoes for them, tucking his pant legs into the boots to keep them out of the way. After gathering his jacket, hat and goggles, he closed the trunk lid.

By then, Twyla had pulled the canvas pants up and the lower half of her polka-dot dress was tucked into the waistband. She looked as fetching as she had before, perhaps even more so.

"I look like I'm pregnant," she said, tucking her dress in deeper to flatten the area surrounding her stomach.

"No, you don't," he said. "You look good. I never looked that good in those pants, I'll tell you that."

She laughed. "Don't bet on it."

The undercurrent running between them was heating up his bloodstream. Although he was enjoying the sensation and wouldn't mind exploring it a bit deeper, he understood that he couldn't. That had been something he'd never been able to do. Forrest gestured toward the building. "Come on. I'll find you a piece of rope to hold those pants up."

"That's all right," she said, hooking the suspenders over her shoulders. "The suspenders will hold them up. It's not like I'll be walking around."

She was right, and once again he was glad he'd asked her to go flying. Spending the number of hours he had in the cockpit, his mind had often wandered. He'd imagined this very moment more than once. She was going to love flying, and he was going to love watching her experience it. At the hangar, he handed her his jacket, hat and goggles, so he could pull open the two large doors.

"It's huge!" she said as his plane came into view. "I'd never have imagined an entire plane could fit in this little shed."

"It takes up every inch," he said, a bit in awe himself. His plane never failed to do that to him. It always filled him with pride, too.

Twyla had already walked inside and was running a hand over the shiny yellow frame. "It's the color of a goldfinch."

"Yes, it is," he answered, chuckling at how she'd chosen the bird he'd named the plane after. "That's what I call her," he said. *"The Goldfinch."*

"That's fitting."

Her gaze was still on the plane, and she appeared completely mesmerized. "Haven't you ever seen a plane before?"

"Not up close," she said quietly.

"Not even at a fair?"

The blue eyes she turned at him had grown dim. "Father doesn't allow us to go to fairs anymore." Sighing heavily, she added, "A lot of things changed after you left."

He knew that very well, yet for Twyla's sake he chose to see the positive side. "Well, it's time for another change, then, isn't it?"

Her grin returned like a golden sunrise. "Yes, it is. How do I climb in?"

"Hold on," he said. "I have to get the rest of your gear, and do an inspection, and remove the wheel blocks, and—"

Her laugher interrupted him. "Okay already, tell me what I can do to help."

She made herself useful, following each of his instructions to the *T*. When they had little more to do except put on their gear and climb in, he held up the extra jacket he'd retrieved. She shrugged it on and he zipped it up. Then he covered her golden-red hair with the leather hat while she arranged the scarf still tied around her neck above the coat's collar.

"It's going to be loud," he said, pushing up her chin to fasten the hat's strap. "When I first start the plane inside the building, and the entire time we're flying, so keep the flaps over your ears at all times. Don't unhook the chin strap or you may lose the hat completely."

"Roger wilco," she said saucily.

He shook his head, but smiled, all the while captivated by her gaze. He hadn't forgotten her beauty, but was amazed by how intense it truly was. She was even more beautiful than he remembered, and seeing her up close was like examining the petals of a flower and the spectacular perfection that put it all together. His lips quivered slightly. He'd never kissed Twyla, except for last night, but he wanted to, and not in a brotherly way.

"Don't take these off, either," he said, grabbing the goggles and sliding them over her head. After adjusting the strap and making sure they were snug, he made her turn around, inspecting her from top to bottom. "I wish I had a different pair of shoes for you to wear."

"These will be fine," she assured him.

"At least pull the backs up so they won't fall off," he said.

"That's all right," she answered, spinning to the plane. "They won't fall off. Now, how do I get up there?"

After he put on his own gear, he grasped her waist. "You climb." Hoisting her upward, he instructed, "Grab that bar, now put this foot here…" He guided her the entire way into the front hollowed-out area that contained little more than a seat. Forrest climbed up and then strapped her in firmly before he climbed into the area behind her.

"Shouldn't I be in the backseat?" she asked over one shoulder.

"No," he said. "This is the cockpit, and it's for the pilot."

"But how will you see around me?"

"I'll see around you just fine," he assured her. "Normally, bags of mail are piled in that area."

Twisting about as much as the straps allowed, she frowned. "Mail?"

"Yep, up to five hundred pounds," he said, settling into his seat and strapping himself in. Taking the opportunity to tease her, he said, "You don't weigh more than five hundred pounds, do you?"

"Very funny," she replied sarcastically, turning forward. A moment later, she spun back around. "Wait. Shouldn't we have pulled it out of the garage first or something?"

"Nope, we'll drive out and head straight down the runway," he said, checking his instrument panel, which was little more than a horizon indicator and oil pressure gauge. If he were to fly a regular mail route, he'd need an updated plane, especially for night flying. Ignoring that thought, he asked, "Ready?"

She nodded, but before turning around, asked, "Don't we need parachutes, in case we go down?"

"We aren't going to go down," he said. "I've never crashed yet."

"Well, just in case…" Her voice faded as she cringed slightly.

He shook his head. "Sorry, I don't have an extra parachute."

"Oh." Her frown increased. "But you do have one?"

"I do have one." Taking account of her nervousness, he said, "And I'll share it with you if needed."

"But I won't know—"

"Twyla," he interrupted.

The blue of her eyes shimmered even through the thick goggles. "What?"

"Shut up."

She stuck her tongue out at him.

He laughed and hit the ignition switch.

Twyla grabbed the edges of the curved wood around her. The rumble of the plane reverberated through her, making her shake, and the noise made her ears ring. The wooden propeller in front of her started turning slowly, then faster and faster. So did her excitement. Twisting, she glanced back at Forrest. Son of a gun, but he was handsome in his flyboy getup. Especially up close. His lips moved, and she assumed he was asking if she was ready. She knew for sure when he held up a thumb.

She copied the action, but quickly grabbed the side of the plane again and turned forward.

The wheels started rolling, and slowly they

eased out of the building into the bright sunshine. A hint of fear tickled her spine, but anticipation overrode it. She'd always felt safe with Forrest years ago, and now wasn't any different. He'd never let her get hurt back then, and she trusted him as much as ever.

The speed of the plane increased. Soon the field zipped past faster than she'd ever seen, and with a bump that made her stomach drop, they started skyward.

Even though her teeth were clenched, she emitted a squeal that kept slipping out the entire time the plane flew upward. The pitch of her squeal went higher, too, stealing her breath until all she could do was let it all out. She could feel her scream, but couldn't hear it over the roar of the engine.

The thrill of it all made her laugh. She eased her tight grip on the side, gave Forrest another thumbs-up and then let go with the other hand to stick both arms high over her head. The air wanted to push her arms back, but she held them straight up and let out another full-blown bout of laughter. The wind was a force like she'd never felt against her face; it tugged at her hat and her yellow scarf pressed firmly against her neck as the ends flapped behind her. All in all, it felt marvelous.

Amazing!

The air, the speed, the freedom!

She twisted left and right, to see all she could around the propeller moving so fast it was a solid circle in front of her. Blue sky and white fluffy cotton-puff clouds filled her vision, and she laughed once again. Glancing over the edge, she saw Lester's farm. That, too, was amazing. How the distance made everything look like miniature toys, even the cows standing in the barnyard. She could see Bald Eagle Lake, too, off to the side, and she was reminded of the snow globe Norma Rose had containing a miniature version of Niagara Falls. Ty had won it for her at the amusement park.

This was better than any old snow globe. This was the real thing.

Nothing on earth could ever compare to this. Not the beauty, the thrill, the freedom. Not even all night dances at the world's largest speakeasy.

Something jostled, and one wing tipped. Twyla grabbed the edge of the plane as her stomach plummeted to her toes.

Chapter Six

Relaxing a touch, and realizing Forrest was merely turning a corner, so to speak, in midair, Twyla eased her hold on the side of the plane and once again examined the ground far below them.

She could see for miles. Trees and fields, homes and roads, cars and several more of Lester's dairy cows. Forrest had turned the plane all the way around so they were now flying toward the resort, and far ahead she could make out the buildings of White Bear Lake.

The most spectacular thing was how Bald Eagle Lake looked. She'd lived near it her entire life, but hadn't realized how large it was. From up here, it looked like a huge tadpole, with a long tail that snaked north. Her home was on the south side, the head of the tadpole, and the island was smack-dab in the center of the big oval. It also amazed her that there was more than the one big island. Several smaller ones created a line that went almost to the very tip of the tadpole tail. There were houses and roads, the depot and highway, and everything appeared mere inches apart rather than the miles she knew them to be.

In no time, the resort was below them. She could even see the hidden back road the runners used to transport shine off the railroad cars to the barn, as well as the road that ran parallel to the main highway. On the ground it was well hidden by trees, but up here, it was as noticeable as a run in a stocking, even where it trailed along the long and narrow northern edges of the lake. She could see the cabins, too, all twenty of them, and the summer kitchens, and outhouses, the boathouses and docks.

Forrest waved a hand, pointing downward.

Standing on the shore of the island, she could see Norma Rose and Ty, although she couldn't see their faces. It had to be them. No one else had rowed out to the island. Twyla waved, and she assumed it was Ty who waved back before they were out of view due to the trees that covered the small chunk of land. Soon the lake was beneath them again, with water so clear and blue she thought she could see the bottom in places.

They flew to the far tip of the tadpole tail before Forrest skillfully glided the plane around and in the other direction. It all seemed so effortless, and was so very amazing that Twyla was totally in awe. They flew all the way to town, where she saw the streets laid out between houses and other buildings—White Bear, Goose and Gem Lakes, the Plantation and the amusement park. She'd never imagined this was what it all looked like, and could only envision all that Forrest had seen, flying as much as he had. To so many places, too. All along the east coast, down south, out west. Mitsy claimed Forrest had flown all the way across the United States, and Twyla could only wish that someday she'd be able to say she had, too.

He flew toward the cities of Minneapolis and St. Paul. The size of them amazed her, as did the twisting, turning Mississippi River. He turned the direction of their flight before they reached the cities, and the farm fields caught her attention then. They looked like squares on a quilt.

Time seemed to go by as fast as they were flying. Before she knew it, she could see Lester's farm again. Disappointment threatened to overtake the joy filling her, but she refused to give it room to grow. She was too happy for that. Furthermore, she had no idea how much work it must be for Forrest to keep the plane flying. It must take a lot of concentration. His intelligence had always amazed her, and that amazement had just increased tenfold.

As smoothly as a bird swoops to the ground,

the plane eased downward, and with little more than a couple of bumps, they were on the ground, rolling toward the building. Unable to stop herself, Twyla squeezed her eyes shut, afraid they might run right into the wooden structure. She opened them as she felt the plane turn.

When the plane came to a complete stop, the building was straight behind them. That, too, astounded her. Forrest certainly knew how to maneuver the plane, both in the air and on the ground.

Her ears were still ringing, and it took a moment before she realized the noise of the engine had stopped. Twisting about, she grinned and held up one thumb.

He smiled and pushed his goggles up onto his forehead.

"So?" was all he said.

"So?" Twyla tried to shove up her goggles, but all she managed to do was pinch the skin at her temples. The strap was so tight they wouldn't budge. Forrest had climbed out of his cockpit and stood on the frame of the lower wing as he had when he'd helped her climb in. Reaching over, he pulled the goggles off her eyes and pushed them onto her forehead.

"That," she said, grabbing his forearms, "was the most amazing thing ever. Ever. When can we do it again?"

"You didn't get sick?" he asked.

"Sick?"

"Yes, a lot of people get sick to their stomach or light-headed the first time they go up."

Twyla shook her head. "My stomach fell clear to my toes a couple of times, but I never got sick." She stared deeper into his luminescent brown eyes. "You remember that about me, don't you, Forrest? How I never got sick on amusement park rides or swings, or when the waves would get so high the rowboat would list."

Goodness, but he was so very handsome. The way he stared back made her heart speed as out of control as the little wooden boat they'd once used to row out over the lake.

"Yes," he said. "I remember."

Twyla didn't realize she was holding her breath until Forrest removed his hands from her goggles. She emptied her lungs, but wasn't disappointed, not in the least. She then attempted to release the straps he'd secured around her waist and over her shoulders, but seemed to be all thumbs.

"I'll get it," Forrest said, pushing her hands aside.

"When can we go up again?" she asked.

Still grinning, he winked one eye, an adorable action that made her heart skip a beat. She'd forgotten how much he'd always filled her with something a bit unnerving. That feeling was unique, no matter how hard she'd tried to find it again—and she had tried. She could spot a handsome man at one hundred yards, and make sure they noticed her, too. Yet not one of them had made her feel the way Forrest could. No other man had ever been of his caliber, either in looks or the way he made her heart and stomach flutter.

"Here, climb out," Forrest said, reaching out to assist her.

She held on to his shoulder with one hand while lifting one leg and then the other over the edge of the plane. The pants were big and cumbersome, but eventually she managed, and then followed Forrest's directions as to where to step. Once he'd jumped to the ground, he reached up and grasped her waist.

Setting both hands on his shoulders, she held on while he lifted her down. Her legs wobbled slightly when her feet touched the ground.

"Give yourself a moment to get your sea legs back," he said.

"We weren't on a boat," she needlessly pointed out, while not letting go of his shoulders.

"I know," he said. "But it's similar. Give yourself a moment for your equilibrium to return."

Flying had nothing to do with her unsteadiness. It didn't have anything to do with the way her mouth went dry when their gazes met, either.

She bit into her bottom lip. Hard.

Time stopped. Her mind went blank, and for some unexplainable reason, she felt rather dizzy. This was Forrest. Her old best friend. Her sister's ex-boyfriend. The man Norma Rose insisted they all had to hate and whom she'd claimed was as much their enemy as his father had been. Twyla closed her eyes against the idea.

The brief and teasing sensation of his lips touching hers filled her with an entirely new thrill. She'd waited her entire life for this, and despite all she knew, or thought she knew, she had to make the most of it.

Their lips brushed against one another's, several times, in tiny light kisses that didn't last long enough for her to react. Unable to stand the teasing, she grasped his face with both hands and caught his lips with hers.

Having hosted a kissing booth, Twyla knew a lot about kissing. Not that she wanted to remember it all. As a matter of fact, she'd recently told Norma Rose she'd rather vomit in her mouth than kiss some of the men she'd kissed again.

That certainly was not the case with Forrest. His lips were warm and moist and heavenly sweet, and they fit against hers with such perfection she stretched onto her tiptoes to increase the pressure.

The kiss was like a dream she never wanted to wake up from, until her mind tried to turn it into a nightmare by pointing out this was Forrest she was kissing. The one man she could never love. He'd broken her heart. He'd flipped her entire world upside down, and there was nothing to say he wouldn't do that again. That he wouldn't just up and vanish some night without a word to anyone.

She'd grown up since he'd disappeared the first time, and this time around she was too smart to be fooled. Forrest was attempting to rekindle their childhood, when they'd been friends, not enemies. Taking her flying, kissing her—he was trying to manipulate her onto his side. She just didn't know why, but she soon would.

Two could play at his game.

She wrapped her arms around his neck and slanted her face, so her lips gave room for her tongue to teasingly lick the seam between his lips, enticing them to part. They did, but just as she thought she'd gained the upper hand, his tongue snagged hers in a wrestling match that had her gasping for air.

Not about to give in, she held on tighter and met each swirl, each taste, with one just as bold and hot as his. They were once again in competition, a game of cat and mouse that went deeper than ever before, and Twyla found herself fighting internal sensations that could very well flip things around and make her the mouse instead of the cat.

Elation flared when Forrest was the one to break the kiss, breathing heavily. However, as the elation of knowing she'd won rose, so did something else. The look in his eyes held an odd bewilderment, and she knew what it was. He was questioning where she'd learned to kiss like that.

Once again Twyla found herself in the midst of an internal battle. This time against a rush of shame. There was nothing to be ashamed of. It was the 1920s. Women could kiss men all they wanted. After all, as she'd said more than once, men were like shoes and a woman had to try on several pairs before she found the one that fit perfectly. Comfortably.

Right now, though, she didn't believe her own sayings quite as strongly as she had in the past, especially when Forrest turned around, without saying a word, and started walking back toward the building.

Her heart was still hammering in her chest, and her breathing was not as controlled as she'd like, so Twyla turned about to give herself a moment to gain control before she spoke. Her gaze landed on the plane, and the adventure she'd just experienced rejuvenated her. Oh, yes, two could play at this game Forrest had challenged her to, and there was nothing that said she couldn't have the time of her life while playing. After all, that was what she was all about. Having the time of her life, and making sure Forrest didn't disrupt that again, remained her goal.

After tugging the goggles off her head, and unfastening and removing the hat, Twyla spun around. "So how do we get this plane back in that shed?"

Forrest had removed his goggles, hat and flight jacket. They were lying on the ground near the back of the plane, but he seemed to have disappeared.

Yelling toward the shadows inside the building, she repeated, "How do we get this plane back in there?"

Forrest appeared in the doorway. "We push it."

Attempting to act as nonchalant as he, she unzipped the jacket he'd loaned her. "Push it?"

"Yep. Push it."

Creating a pile next to his, she removed the jacket and then slid the suspenders holding up the pants off her shoulders. Once the pants were on the ground, she smoothed her skirt, admitting to herself that she was thankful the material hadn't wrinkled. After readjusting her scarf, she rubbed her hands together. "All right, then, let's get to pushing."

"Not so quick," Forrest said. "I have a post-flight inspection to do first."

"You inspected everything before we left," she pointed out.

"Yes, that was called the preflight inspection."

Considering he was on the other side of the plane, and she couldn't see his face, Twyla made no comment. Knowing Forrest, he was likely completely serious. Safety, even when they'd just been playing, had always been first on his mind. That did seem odd. Someone who'd always been cautious and careful was now flying around in the air. Then again, maybe that's why he was flying and had never crashed.

He was soon done with his inspection, and Twyla helped—although she didn't do much—maneuver the plane backward until it was once again parked inside the shed he called a hangar. Then she put wooden blocks up against the wheels while he rolled a big barrel over and cranked a hand pump to put fuel into the plane.

"Why are you putting fuel in now?" she asked.

"So it's ready to fly the next time I want to take her up."

"How do you get gas out here?" she asked.

"Scooter delivers it when I call and ask him to," Forrest answered.

Scooter Wilson ran the fueling station up on the highway between the resort and White Bear Lake, and had been a friend of all of theirs for years. "That's nice of him," she said, for lack of anything better to say. Her mind was still plotting, and wondering, and recalling just how closely connected Forrest had once been to her life.

Before she gave herself time to consider the consequences, she asked, "Why'd you leave town like that, Forrest? After that night with Norma Rose."

He didn't answer right away, acting instead as if fueling the plane took all his concentration. That was fine. She could wait out a snail.

Twyla spent a fair amount of time retying her scarf while she waited. When Forrest let out a sigh, she held in a grin, knowing his answer was coming.

"I didn't leave," he said, hooking the gas nozzle inside the barrel. "Not on my own, as everyone thinks."

Twyla wasn't sure if hope or disbelief flared inside her. "You didn't?"

"No." He pushed the barrel back through the wide front doors.

She followed him around the building to where he secured the barrel on a cement block platform near a tree. "What happened?"

He looked around and then wiggled the barrel as if making sure it wouldn't tip over before covering it with a tarp. "After Galen returned home from taking Norma Rose to your place, he and I got in an argument. I left, planning on going to check on Norma Rose, but a few of Galen's men stopped me in the back parking lot of the Plantation."

Twyla understood just how some men stopped people and her hands started to shake. "Did they hurt you?"

Forrest hadn't planned on telling her. Hadn't planned on a lot of things. His mind was still spinning from kissing her. Twyla Nightingale knew how to kiss. Her lips could turn a man inside out. He hadn't expected that to happen to him. Flyboys were used to kissing women, and some would say he'd kissed more than his fair share over the years. Not a single one—short peck or long kiss—had knocked his socks off.

Before today.

As the cat was out of the bag and he couldn't put it back in, he shrugged. "You could say that."

"I don't want to say that."

She'd stepped up beside him and was looking at him with more sympathy than he ever wanted to see.

"Then don't ask questions you don't want the answers to," he said, shouldering around her.

"I wouldn't have to ask if you'd just tell me," she answered, following on his heels.

"Why would I tell you?"

She grabbed his arm. "Because we're friends."

He stopped, but his mind kept flying around faster than his plane.

"We're old friends, Forrest," she said. "Childhood friends who never had secrets from one another." She'd taken a hold of his arm with her other hand, too. "How badly did they hurt you?"

"Bad enough," he answered, trying to sound vague although it was useless. He'd rarely, if ever, been able to keep a secret from her. One way or another, she'd always found a way to wrangle information out of him. That certainly hadn't changed.

He was surprised when she didn't persist.

Instead, she asked, "Where'd you go? After they hurt you?"

"To my aunt Shirley's in Rochester," he said.

"For how long?"

He sighed. She was as relentless as ever. But sincere, too, which was the part he couldn't overlook. The compassion on her face made him care too much about her. Knowing she wouldn't quit until she had her answers, he gave in completely. "Over a year. It took that long for me to learn to walk again." Saving her from another set of questions, he added, "My legs were broken in several places, as were my arms. Uncle Silas, Shirley's husband, is a doctor. He oversaw my healing and wouldn't let me leave until I was as good as new."

"That bastard," Twyla hissed.

Forrest knew she wasn't talking about his uncle.

"I always knew your fath— Galen Reynolds was the devil." She let go of his arm and stomped around in a small circle. "I hope he rots in prison. I tell you what, Forrest, if my father hadn't seen him sent away, I would have once I'd discovered this."

Forrest knew he didn't want her to know about Galen's pending release. It was hard to say what Twyla might do, but she was sure to get herself hurt doing it.

"It's in the past now," he said, "and my injuries have never bothered me. Never stopped me from doing what I wanted to do." He gestured toward the hangar. "That's when I decided to become a pilot, while at my aunt and uncle's. I met Charles Lindbergh while I was staying with them. He's a pilot and he's going to be world famous some day, mark my words."

"I'll mark your words," Twyla said, still acting madder than a hornet whose nest had just been knocked down. "But you mark mine. If I ever lay eyes on Galen Reynolds, there will be hell to pay. I'll knock the spots right out of him."

Forrest's stomach sank. What had he started? Choosing to change the subject, he asked, "Does your father know you swear like that?"

She glared at him.

"Does he?"

"It's the 1920s, Forrest, women can curse." She spun around and started walking toward the hangar. "We can drink and smoke, too, not to mention vote."

"Just because you can, doesn't mean you need to," he pointed out, knowing that would get her feathers more ruffled, but also hoping it would set her mind on a different track.

"Nonetheless," she said, sticking her nose in the air, "I appreciate the new generation and embrace it fully." Giving him a quick head-to-toe appraisal over her shoulder, she added, "Women can even have sex without worrying about getting pregnant."

He shot forward and grabbed her arm before she took another step. "That's the second time you've mentioned pregnancy today," he said, noting inwardly how it twisted his guts worse than flying through stormy weather. "Why?"

"Why what?"

"Why have you mentioned it twice?" He grew cold at the thought. "Are you pregnant?"

"Of course I'm not pregnant. How dare you suggest such a thing?"

Her cheeks had turned bright red. "Are you sure?"

"Of course I'm sure, and I don't appreciate you

thinking otherwise." Frowning, she persisted, "Why would you say such a thing?"

Her huffiness had fizzled out, which he assumed meant she was just being Twyla. In some cases, she liked to sound much more adventurous than she was—at least he hoped that was still the case, especially in this instance. He let go of her arm and walked over to shut the big doors on the hangar. "You did run a kissing booth."

"You can't get pregnant by just kissing," she said. Having followed him, she was now swinging the other door closed.

"But it can lead to it," he said as they met in the middle.

"I only ran that booth for two weekends before I got—" She pinched her lips together.

"Caught?" he inquired. "Two weekends before Norma Rose learned about it?" Bronco had told him that last week. The man had been greatly relieved.

Twyla rolled her eyes and sighed. She moved away then and he secured the door.

"Wait, I forgot to put your extra jacket and hat away," she said.

"We can put them in the trunk with mine," he answered, hoping that was the end of both conversations.

She gathered together the things she'd worn, while he picked up his, and silently they walked to the car, where he opened the trunk. As he swapped his boots for his loafers, she folded the pants and coats and set them carefully in the trunk. After adding his boots, he closed the lid and gestured toward the passenger side of the car.

"Why didn't you ever tell us—I mean, tell Norma Rose—that you hadn't just left town?" she asked as he opened the car door.

"By the time I could have, it was already too late," he said. Norma Rose had said as much when he'd tried apologizing during their phone call.

"It's never too late for some things, Forrest," Twyla said, climbing in the roadster.

"Yes, it is." He was no longer thinking about Norma Rose—he was thinking about Twyla, and what she now knew. It was too late for him to take it back. Now he had to figure out what it wasn't too late for, like how he could guarantee her safety and keep Galen away from her and her family. The consequences of telling her all he knew were sinking in. These were things he should have considered before now, but since the moment taking her flying had crossed his mind, all else had fallen to the wayside.

It shouldn't have. Galen's pending release was a real danger and had just become even more serious. Which meant Forrest had to talk to Twyla's father. Jacob was right. He needed Roger's help in discovering who was backing Galen. Time was not on his side, either.

Although his mother claimed it wasn't, he was still convinced the opium was the reason behind Galen's arrest. There was nothing else it could be. Even though it appeared as if Galen's drug-dealing shenanigans had been swept under the rug, it was the only thing that tied everything together, the only thing that made sense. The rest of Galen's activities, although they were all illegal, wouldn't have merited having him extradited to California—other than laundering the money he made from the drug deals. Where else would the money have come from?

They'd driven along the grassy field road, onto the gravel one, and were almost to the highway when she asked, "What do you want to talk to my father about?"

Evidently, that hadn't changed, either—the way she could practically read his mind. A part of him wanted to tell her everything, for if she knew something, she might help him come up with a solution. Flying with her had brought forth his other dilemma. The problem of keeping the Plantation open while operating an air-mail route…if the government accepted his bid. He had no reason to believe they wouldn't, but the money in his coffers said he couldn't do both. Flying was in his blood and was what he wanted to do, but the Plantation was his heritage. He'd spent years trying to prevent people from learning about the ugliness he went home to every night. Protecting those he cared about from getting hurt was still his main concern.

Twyla would have an opinion on all that, as she did on everything, and in this case it could be worthwhile for him to listen to it, if it wasn't for the fact her couldn't tell her. The less she knew—the less anyone knew—the better. That hadn't changed. If he couldn't find a way to keep Galen behind bars, it never would change.

"The Plantation," he finally said. It was a half truth, but she'd simply repeat herself if he didn't respond soon.

"What about it?" she asked.

His plan could end up with more holes in it than a fighter plane that had been shot down if he didn't get away from her soon. Twyla was making him wish he'd never come home. She was too intuitive and too impulsive. She was also too beautiful and meant far too much to him.

They turned onto the highway and, glancing toward Twyla with her yellow scarf flaying behind her as it had in the plane, Forrest shrugged. "I just need some advice, and Roger seemed like the perfect man to ask."

"What sort of advice?"

She was relentless. "Business advice."

"Well, if it's about running shine, yes, then talk to my father, but if it's about running a nightclub, Norma Rose is who you need to talk to."

A chilling silence filled the car, even though the roadster had no top and the wind was still whipping his hair and her scarf about. Forrest considered once again telling her he wasn't in love with Norma Rose, as Twyla seemed to think, but, in all reality, it made no difference. Twyla was Twyla, and she was going to think whatever she wanted no matter what he said. That hadn't changed, and neither had his goal— to never bring any of the girls any closer to him than necessary. Never to expose them to the corruption embedded in his family.

As he turned the car off the highway and onto the road that led to the resort, Twyla let out a loud sigh. Forrest held his in.

After the car rumbled over the railroad tracks, she said, "I wish we were still up in the air, flying around like we had no worries in the world."

"I do, too," he admitted.

"Will you take me up again someday?" she asked.

"Sure," he lied.

Twyla was fighting hard to find some of the excitement that had lived inside her just a short time ago, but it wasn't to be found. A dark, heavy dread had settled where her excitement had resided. There were several things she could attribute it to, but she couldn't pinpoint which one weighed more heavily. They all made her head hurt, and her heart. Forrest hadn't left years ago on purpose. She knew that now as soundly as she knew her last name was Nightingale. He'd been hurt. Badly. She'd seen that in his eyes.

Once Norma Rose learned that fact, she was sure to forgive him. Although her sister might consider herself in love with Ty, the truth could change her mind.

No one was more handsome than Forrest, and who wouldn't want to be married to a man who could take you on airplane rides? Forrest had money, too, left to him by his grandfather, and owning a plane said he still had all that money. Norma Rose would like that, too. Money meant as much to her as it did to Twyla.

The more she thought about it, the heavier her heart grew. Even though her sister swore for years that she hated Forrest, Norma Rose was sure to choose him over Ty. Any woman with a lick of sense would, and Norma Rose was far from senseless. Twyla couldn't help but think of Ty. She understood the pain of loving someone who hadn't loved her back in return. Her gaze settled briefly on Forrest as she told herself that would never happen again.

Forrest pulled the roadster into the resort parking lot and hadn't even turned the car off before the front door of the resort flew open.

Norma Rose, looking as furious as a caged dog being poked with a stick, flew toward them shouting, "Who do you think you are?"

Chapter Seven

$\infty\!\!\!\infty\!\!\!\infty$

It took Twyla all of ten seconds to figure out Norma Rose was shouting at Forrest and that lit a fire in her belly.

"Don't yell at him," she shouted back, wrenching open the car door.

"I certainly will yell at him," Norma Rose bellowed. "And I'll yell at you. What were you thinking, going up in an airplane with him?"

"I was thinking it would be fun," Twyla responded just as loud, meeting her sister toe-to-toe in the parking lot. "And it was."

"Get inside," Norma Rose barked. "I'll deal with you in a minute."

"No," Twyla argued. "You can't tell me what to do."

"Oh, yes, I can, and I will, as soon as I send Forrest home." Norma Rose flayed a finger toward Forrest, who'd also climbed out of the car. "Get back in your car and get out of here."

"You can't tell him what to do, either," Twyla shouted.

Forrest, arriving at her side, told them both to be quiet. Ty, who'd arrived at Norma Rose's side, did the same, but Twyla couldn't care less who said what. She wasn't exactly sure what Norma Rose had replied with, but just the movement of her sister's lips increased the fury in her belly. Twyla shouted back whatever came to mind, and struggled against a powerful force that held her from stomping forward.

Norma Rose responded in turn. Their shouting continued loud and unbroken, and the grip on Twyla's arms grew so tight she could barely move. Nothing was clear until an ear-splitting whistle sliced the air with a shattering effect.

As the silence settled, Twyla noted how Ty had a hold of Norma Rose's arms from behind, as if keeping her from storming forward. A tingling sensation had Twyla looking over her shoulder. Sure enough, Forrest held her in pretty much the same manner that Ty held her sister. Their father was there, too, standing between them, and Josie, who still had her index finger and thumb in her mouth, was nearby. Twyla should have known that. Josie was the only one who'd ever mastered whistling. Other than Forrest, of course, whose hold Twyla attempted to twist out of, with no luck.

"You," her father said, pointing at her. "Inside. I'll talk with you in a few minutes."

The smirk on Norma Rose's face almost forced Twyla to respond. Forrest's hold tightened a bit, but it was her father's voice sounding out again that kept her mouth shut.

"Norma Rose," he said, more sternly than Twyla had heard him speak in years. "Inside with your sister. And no more bickering." Her father then shifted his stance to point at Forrest and Ty at the same time. "You two, I want in my office, now."

Her father spun around then, gesturing toward the house.

Norma Rose and Ty moved first, and Josie scooted ahead to hold open the door.

"Good grief," Twyla grumbled. "You'd think we were all ten."

"What do you expect?" Forrest asked. "When you act like you are ten, you're treated like you're ten."

"She started it," Twyla insisted.

"Twyla," he half groaned, half scolded.

"Go ahead, stick up for her."

"I'm not sticking up for her," Forrest said.

Twyla refrained from voicing her doubt. He'd always taken Norma Rose's side. Huffing out a breath, she warned, "You're in as much trouble as the rest of us."

"No, I'm not," he said. "I came here to meet with your father, and I'm going to do that."

"Well, you'd best be prepared for a good talking-to."

As they entered the resort, he pulled her to the side of the entranceway, near the long and narrow room where people hung their coats on winter nights. Before she could protest, Forrest spun her about and backed her into the tiny room.

"If you don't want to be treated like a child," he said, "don't act like one."

"She started it, I—" His raised eyebrows made her stop. A hint of humiliation made her stomach sink. "Fine. But she had no right to yell at you like that. You can take me flying if you want to. I'm old enough—"

"Then prove it."

"Prove what?"

"That you are old enough to do as you wish." He tapped her temple. "That you're smart enough to know right from wrong." Forrest then lifted her chin with one knuckle. "Respond to her like an adult instead of like her little sister."

A tingling sensation circled her spine all the way to her neck before the air left her sails in a whoosh. He was right. She was an adult, and would prove it. To everyone. Including him. She may have been a poor schoolgirl when he'd left, but she was now a rich woman. The lessons she'd learned during that transition had changed her. She'd found the one thing a person could control—money. It never turned its back on you. She'd learned that if a person worked hard enough, for long enough, they'd never be without money. Bootlegged whiskey hadn't made the resort a destination point of the rich and famous. The spectacular parties had, and she was just the hostess to make sure they continued to be the best. Now that she had her freedom, the rest would be easy.

"Twyla?"

Glancing up, she nodded. "You're right."

He frowned, as if skeptical that she was agreeing with him.

"It's time I stop letting Norma Rose make me feel like a child." The statement was as much directed at herself as it was to him.

"Good," he said with a nod. "Good. Norma Rose always had a superior attitude, even before your mother died."

Shocked that he, of all people, would say such a thing, Twyla whispered, "That's not a very flattering thing to say."

"I'm not insulting her, I'm just telling you how it is, how it always was. I can't remember a single time the two of you saw eye-to-eye."

Twyla let that remark settle for a minute. "That's true." His other statement had been true, too. Norma Rose's superior attitude was what had always set her above the rest of the sisters.

Forrest's grin was showing his dimples again, and Twyla had to smile in return, even as her cheeks grew warm and a splattering of shame gurgled in her stomach. She hadn't meant to act so childishly, but no one else seemed to understand all that was at risk. Nothing, absolutely nothing, lasted forever.

"Isn't it time you show her you've always had a superior attitude, too?" he asked playfully. "Show her that you're a grown woman who can curse and drink and smoke and vote."

Now he was teasing. Twyla withheld a giggle, but flinched at the heat consuming her cheeks. She duly noted he didn't add that she could have sex without worrying about getting pregnant, but wasn't about to remind him. The twinkle in his eyes said he'd purposefully left that out. He was simply pointing out her attitude, encouraging her. That had been one of the things she'd really missed after he'd left.

"I don't know that I'll remind her of all that," Twyla said. "It might sound childish."

"Now we're getting somewhere," he whispered. "Just treat her like you want to be treated—she'll respect that more than anything."

Twyla nodded, fully understanding more at this moment than she'd understood for a long time. "I've missed you, Forrest." She hadn't meant for that to come out, but couldn't do much about it. He'd always had a knack for making her see things differently. "Missed you a lot," she repeated under her breath. The past five years certainly would have been different if he'd been around.

"I've missed you, too." He planted a simple kiss on her forehead, much like he had last night. "Now behave while I go and talk to your father, or I won't take you flying again."

Despite how dismal everything seemed, her heart fluttered. "Do you mean it?" she asked. "That you will take me flying again?"

His smile grew slightly, giving way to a dimple or two. "Yes, I mean it. But only if you behave."

She bit down on her bottom lip and pressed her heels against the floor to keep from jumping up and hugging him. Oh, yes, she'd behave, and she'd prove to everyone just who Twyla Nightingale really was.

He chuckled and led her away. At her father's office door, which was open, she saw her father sitting behind his desk and Ty in one of the chairs in front of it. Forrest squeezed her hand before he let it go.

"Behave," he whispered.

Twyla nodded and waited for Forrest to close

the door. She'd then move down the hall to Norma Rose's office, which was where she was sure to find her sisters. Both of them would no doubt be ganging up against her.

Something snagged her attention and she leaned sideways, in an attempt to glance around the closing door. The door clicked shut and she frowned. In the background, over Forrest's shoulder, she could have sworn she'd witnessed her father grin and wink at her. She tried her best to recall that very moment. Even closed her eyes briefly. Yes, it had happened. She wouldn't have dreamed that up.

A smile tickled the corners of her mouth and she gave it free will to appear. Her father was proud of her for all she'd done lately, had told her so more than once. Smiling fully, she nodded to herself, happy there was one less person she had to prove herself to.

With Forrest's advice and her father's silent, simple encouragement, Twyla entered Norma Rose's office with more confidence than ever before.

"What were you thinking?" Norma Rose asked as soon as Twyla pushed open the door.

"About what?" Twyla asked calmly while closing the door behind her.

"Don't be smart with me," Norma Rose

snapped. "Do you have any idea how dangerous flying is?"

Twyla refrained from saying she wasn't being
smart, not in the way Norma Rose implied, and
that her sister knew nothing—absolutely nothing—about flying. Instead she sighed. "I know
how marvelous it is. How freeing and utterly fan-
tastic. You should try it someday."

"I will not," Norma Rose said.

"Suit yourself." Twyla sat down in the chair at
the table near the window, where Josie sat in the
opposite chair. Norma Rose was behind her desk,
making herself as superior as ever. Biting back
a smile, Twyla said, "But Forrest is an excellent
pilot. He's never crashed. Not once."

"There's always a first," Norma Rose said. Her
attitude had calmed considerably. "And Forrest
should have known better than to take you flying without my permission."

"I don't need your permission, Norma Rose,"
Twyla answered. "Just like Josie doesn't need
your permission to attend her Ladies Aid meetings."

"Don't bring me in on this," Josie said, holding up both hands.

"I'm not bringing you in on anything," Twyla
said. "I'm merely making a point. None of us
need to ask permission from one another." Twyla
held up her hands. "I'm not saying we shouldn't

talk about things and get each other's opinions, especially when it comes to running the resort." She pointed to the snow globe sitting on Norma Rose's desk. "But when it comes to going to the amusement park with a man, or flying with an old friend, we don't need to ask for permission. None of us are children anymore." For added weight, she said, "Not even Ginger, who's younger than all of us."

Norma Rose's gaze had settled on the snow globe. "I guess you're right."

"Thank you," Twyla said sincerely, shocked as she was that Norma Rose had given in so quickly. Not about to lose the opportunity, she continued, "I want us to be more than sisters. I want us to be partners. We need to be, in order to keep the resort in tip-top shape with all the changes happening." Lifting her chin, she added, "In order for that to happen, we need to treat each other like the adults we are."

Josie, always the most quiet, nodded as she glanced between Twyla and Norma Rose. "Most of the time." Glancing back and forth again, she added, "Most of the time we act like adults."

Twyla had to agree with that.

Norma Rose nodded, too, but then she lifted her gaze, which was very somber and sincere. "Speaking of resorts, did Forrest tell you his father is being paroled?"

Twyla felt as if she'd been hit with a ten-pound hammer. "No," she whispered, more in protest than in answer. "No, he can't be."

"He is," Norma Rose said. "Forrest told Father last night. Father asked Ty to investigate, make a few phone calls. Father talked to people, too, and it appears as if Galen will be given a new trial if the repeal his lawyer submitted is accepted. The lawyer claims to have new evidence."

Twyla pressed a hand to her forehead and then to her mouth. She fought a silent battle as the room turned eerily quiet. Under most circumstances, she'd never share a secret, as she had many of them herself, but in this case, when it came to Forrest's safety, she had to tell her sisters.

A huge, burning lump formed in her throat, one she couldn't swallow around, and she had to blink at the sting in her eyes. She sniffled, too, more affected by the news than she would have imagined. The image of Forrest injured, broken and bruised by a man who proclaimed to be his father had her hands balling into fists.

"There's more," Norma Rose said gravely.

Twyla wrung her hands but the shaking wouldn't stop.

"The new evidence implicates Father," Norma Rose revealed.

Quiet and rational, Josie said, "Of course

it would. Father is the one who sent Galen to prison."

"Exactly," Norma Rose said, "and perhaps Forrest only returned home in order to—"

Unwilling to let Norma Rose finish what she was about to say, Twyla jumped to her feet. "Forrest wouldn't do that." Her sister's insistence that they all should hate Forrest had gone on long enough. "And he's not his father."

"Who?" Josie asked. "Who's not whose father?"

"Galen Reynolds isn't Forrest's father," Twyla said quietly, and repeated the short explanation Forrest had given her. While that was settling in for both of her sisters, she added, "And Forrest never left town by choice."

"What do you mean?"

She briefly shared what Forrest had told her. A tale that made her insides burn all over again.

"Oh, dear heavens," Josie whispered. "Did Forrest tell you that, too?"

"Yes," Twyla answered. The need to protect Forrest grew stronger inside her. "But please don't act like you know. I said I wouldn't tell anyone." Turning to Norma Rose, Twyla paused. Her sister looked rather ashamed.

"You knew, didn't you?" Twyla asked.

Norma Rose shook her head. "No, but Father

always insisted there were things I didn't know about."

"Father knew?" Twyla asked, a bit shocked.

"What doesn't Father know?" Josie responded.

The room grew silent. Mostly because, just like her, her sisters were probably contemplating a few things they hoped their father didn't know about.

Josie was the first to speak. "Remember how mean Galen Reynolds was when Mother died?"

"Who could forget," Twyla said, her stomach churning. "I thought he was the devil reincarnated."

"And now he's being paroled," Norma Rose said.

Twyla's backbone shivered, and she straightened her spine against it. That filled her with something else, a sense of power perhaps, because she let her gaze roam between her sisters. "But this time, we aren't children, and he can't frighten us with his evil glares."

Norma Rose lifted her chin. "And we have ten times more money than he ever hoped to have."

As Twyla and Norma Rose's gazes met, Twyla felt her newfound power growing. In unison they turned to Josie.

With a somewhat frightened look, Josie swallowed visibly. "What are you two thinking?"

"I don't know yet," Twyla said. "But there

has to be something we can do." She turned to Norma Rose, hoping this once they could stand together. "Right?"

Norma Rose was chewing on a fingernail, but nodded.

"But Galen Reynolds is evil," Josie said. "He truly is."

Twyla sensed there was more behind her sister's statement. "What do you know that we don't?"

Gnawing on her bottom lip, Josie once again glanced between sisters. With a sigh, she said, "I'm sworn to secrecy, so it can't leave this room."

"What can't?" Twyla demanded.

"Galen Reynolds never had a film company. Not a real one."

"We know that," Twyla said, disappointed.

"It was a front for shipping girls to California—those he promised movie deals to. And most of those girls that he took to Hollywood disappeared."

A shiver rippled down Twyla's spine. "Disappeared?"

Josie nodded. "Disappeared. Never have been seen or heard from again."

"How do you know that?" Norma Rose asked.

"I just do," Josie answered.

Twyla didn't want to sound cold, but her insides had turned to ice thinking about Ginger and how she'd talked about going to Hollywood. "I thought they were prostitutes he hired to work at the Plantation."

"He's the one that turned them into prostitutes," Josie said. "It wasn't what they'd been promised."

"How do you know that?" Norma Rose asked.

"I can't tell you," Josie said. "But it's true. And there's more."

"What more?" Twyla asked.

"Some that didn't disappear," Josie said, "were found dead."

Twyla believed her sister fully. Goose bumps covered her arms as she turned to Norma Rose. "What are we going to do?"

"I don't know yet," Norma Rose answered. "I need to talk to Ty, and Father—"

"But he'll stop us." Desperation crept up Twyla's spine.

Norma Rose nodded. "They all will. Father, Ty, even Forrest. None of them will want us involved. However, on the other hand," she continued, "we can't come up with a plan if we don't know what's happening. Let me gather a bit more information, and then we can decide what we can do."

Twyla wasn't impressed with that plan, but

considering she didn't have one of her own, she nodded.

"Sometimes," Norma Rose said thoughtfully, "when you make your bed, you have to lie in it."

Twyla's insides jittered. She had no idea exactly to whom Norma Rose was referring.

Forrest had sat down in the extra chair and without protest accepted the glass of brandy Roger had poured for each of them. The alcohol might do him some good, and it wasn't as if he was going to go flying again today.

Roger had climbed out of his chair as soon as Forrest had closed the door, and had been making small talk ever since. About driving around with Palooka George, looking at land the man might be interested in buying, how swell the party had been last night, even how successful businesses in the area were.

Having finished his drink, Forrest leaned over to set the glass on the table between him and Ty—at the same time Ty did—and they locked eyes. Forrest took it that Ty was just as perplexed by Roger's behavior as he was.

Roger picked up his glass then, having been too busy talking to drink much of it, and finished it in one long swallow. He set the empty glass on his desk and included both Forrest and Ty in a long, somewhat scrutinizing stare. Sitting down in his chair, he let out a sigh. "I wanted to give both of you a chance to get over that little scene outside. I know my girls can be a handful, but you two handled it quite well, keeping those girls apart."

Forrest glanced toward Ty, curious to know how the other man was reacting to that compliment.

Once again, Ty met his gaze. "I don't know about you," Ty said, "but I was hiding behind Norma Rose for protection."

The ice that could have been filling the room cracked, and the laughter Roger let out melted any frost that may have been lingering behind. Forrest grinned at Ty in agreement. "I was sure it was going to break out into a full-blown boxing match."

"Without gloves," Ty added.

"I haven't seen those two go at it like that in years," Roger said.

"Really?" Forrest asked dryly. "I remember them fighting fairly regularly."

Roger shook his head. "Things have changed since you left, Forrest. Norma Rose was always full of herself, but she lost a bit of it for a while. I figured giving her charge over her sisters would bring it back. It wasn't the trick I'd hoped it would be. She turned into a tyrant. I still wasn't too concerned, figured when the younger ones got tired of it, they'd give her what for." Roger sighed again. "I was right, while also being wrong. Norma Rose's iron hand kept the girls at home, where they needed to be…protected, but it also made them stir-crazy. They started sneaking out. Running away." He ran a hand through his silvery white hair. "Ginger ran away to Chicago, you know. I'm heading down there tomorrow to get her, something I almost don't want to do."

Forrest attempted to keep his surprise hidden, both at hearing Ginger had run away and Roger's statement, yet he had to ask, "You don't?"

Roger shook his head. "Oh, I want her home, but I'm glad she took a stand. The others haven't. Josie's buried herself in that cumbersome Ladies Aid Society, throwing birthday parties for women four times her age, and Twyla, well, up until lately, she'd reverted back to being ten. Which drove half the men in my employ, as well as her sister, crazy. I couldn't even punish her when she snuck out to the Pour House or the boxing match down in St. Paul." Settling his gaze on Forrest he added, "Or when I found out about her kissing booth."

"I wondered if you knew about all that," Forrest admitted.

"How could I not?" Roger asked. "My men tell me everything. I also know a man can't keep his children under his thumb forever. My girls have been cooped up like a brood of chicks for years. But that's how it had to be." Roger paused briefly to glance at Ty. "Until Galen went to prison."

"I'm not blaming you, Forrest," Roger said, turning his way. "I know what happened. I know if Bronco and Jacob hadn't stepped in when they did, you'd have been killed. And I know Galen hated me more for that. Which I never minded."

Forrest wasn't surprised Roger knew what had happened. He was, however, surprised to learn it had been Bronco who helped Jacob save his life that night. Remorse settled deep at the way he'd turned his back on those men, on his inheritance and on the only people he'd ever cared about for so many years.

"I did mind," Roger said, leaning forward and lifting both brows, "how Galen threatened my daughters, and I did mind how he prevented you from returning home."

Forrest's hands balled into fists. He'd wished a million times things had turned out differently, but never more so than right now. "That will never happen again. Galen threatening your daughters."

"I know it won't," Roger said. "So let's get down to business. Besides being a lawyer, Ty's a private investigator and has learned your father may get a new trial."

Forrest was more than ready to get down

to business and knew where he had to start. Whether he wanted Roger to be involved or not was no longer an issue. Protecting Twyla and her sisters meant he'd take all the help he could get. But blood, in Roger's eyes, ran thicker than water. It was time he knew the truth. "Galen Reynolds isn't my father."

Roger's sigh seemed full of relief. "Karen finally told you."

Taken aback, Forrest asked, "You knew?"

"My wife, Rose, knew, and she told me," Roger said. "I've never told a soul, but I wanted to tell you more often than not."

"My uncle Silas told me while I was staying at their house," Forrest explained, "and my mother confirmed it when I returned home before going to Nebraska."

Roger waited as if he expected Forrest to say more, but Forrest figured he'd said enough. Turning to Ty, he said, "I know a new trial has been requested—I want to know who requested it." He turned toward Roger and asked, "And why."

Roger answered. "Ty hasn't figured out who's behind it, but he will. He's the best of the best."

That was fitting, and explained plenty. Roger only hired the best of the best, so for Ty to be so readily included in the Nightingale family, he had to be top-notch. Yet Forrest questioned exactly what type of private investigator Ty might be. However, either way—gangster or federal agent—the man could uncover the answers he hadn't been able to find. "You were behind Galen's arrest," Forrest said to Roger. "Why California? Why not here?"

"Because I wanted him as far away from my daughters as I could get him," Roger said. "And from you and your mother, too."

Forrest needed a more definite answer than that, and he let his gaze say so.

Roger shook his head as if in dismay. "As hard as it may be to believe, I don't know everything. But I do know your mother held the purse strings."

Forrest had no idea what that had to do with anything. "There was no money," he said. It wasn't something he was bitter about.

"There had been at first," Roger said. "Probably more than anyone knew."

Forrest didn't need another story about how much money his grandfather used to have, so he asked, "What was your involvement?"

By the way Roger leaned back and rubbed his chin, Forrest became concerned his instincts had been right, and he wasn't certain what his response would be if Roger admitted his involvement in the opium trade.

"You know the reason Galen was arrested, don't you?" Roger asked.

"The stories or the truth?" Forrest asked, growing exasperated. He now knew where Twyla got her antics from. "Or the fact the mastermind behind Galen's opium trade was never implicated."

Roger lifted a brow. "You think it's me?"

It was a bit strange, the way Forrest had no problem ascertaining that Galen, the man everyone thought was his flesh and blood, was guilty, yet he didn't want to believe that Roger, the biggest bootlegger in the state, wasn't innocent.

Roger pushed away from his desk and stood, filling the room with a formidable presence that had endowed him with the nickname The Night. He walked around his desk, to the front, where he looked down upon Forrest and Ty, who were still seated. "I'll never admit to some of the dealings I've been in that have got me to where I am, but, when comes it to having any dealings with Galen Reynolds, I'll sing louder than a canary behind iron bars. I won't be a fall guy for any of his monkeyshines." He leaned a hip against the edge of his desk. "From the moment Galen took over the Plantation, it became little more than an opium den. The locals didn't like it, but there wasn't a lot to be done. At the time, opium wasn't illegal, and our proximity to the multimodal hub of international cargo in Duluth and Superior gave easy access for the drug to enter the States. Especially once Congress passed a law that banned the import of all opium. Agents weren't assigned to the Port of Duluth-Superior like they were along the coasts."

Unfolding his arms, Roger pushed off his desk and walked to the window, where he stood silently for a moment, hands on his hips, as he gazed out the window. "That was fifteen years ago. I was working at the brewery, pinching pennies to feed my family and watching Galen throw money around like he was growing it in the basement. I'm not ashamed to say it ate at me, because it also gave me the drive to make changes to my own financial situation." Turning from the window, he added, "But I never became involved in the drug trade. Not then and not now."

"But you know who was, or is," Forrest suggested.

"Unfortunately, or perhaps, fortunately, I don't," Roger said, walking back toward his desk. "I won't lie, I looked down that road, especially after Rose died and Galen accused her of killing his son. But in truth, there wasn't anything I could have done. Not back then. The country was at war—someone peddling drugs wasn't a big deal. I was ready to put a bullet in him again when he threatened Norma Rose and when I heard what he'd done to you, but death would be too good for him. Instead I put my ear to every wall he was behind, and when Ginger became obsessed with Hollywood, I knew it was time to act." With a menacing scowl, he growled, "When she came up missing, all sorts of awful things crossed my mind."

The look the other two men shared told Forrest there was more, a lot more, behind Ginger's running away. He had to ask… "Galen was already in jail then. He wasn't behind it, was he?"

"No," Roger said. "Thank goodness. There were a few years where Galen thought I'd forgotten all about him and his acquisitions, which irritated him, and he tried to goad me into a confrontation. I never let him.It served me better to let him think I was focused on my own business adventure, but I assure you I knew every step he took. The past few years, when he started parading young girls around town claiming they were the new stars of his Hollywood film company, I took advantage of the Achilles' heel he left wide open. I figured those girls were his way of transporting the opium to the west coast, and though I had no desire to get involved in the drug trade, I did make it a point to drop seeds. By then, I had more than enough money, and after ousting the local authorities he'd paid off, I found a few willing to prove they were doing their jobs."

"And?" Forrest asked.

"And," Roger said, "there wasn't any opium."

Forrest couldn't believe that. Not only had Galen boasted about his drug trade, but just last week his mother had also suggested it was part of the evidence being submitted.

"From what I've already discovered," Ty said, "Galen's tracks go way back, to ruthless thugs out of the slums of New York. They aren't just gangsters. They're worse than that. They're outlaws. Thieves. Murders. Drug runners. Traffickers. They thrive on corruption, and don't let anything or anyone get in their way. Galen's been their patsy for a long time, including in their opium trade. He did little more than oversee its transportation off the ships to the Plantation, where it was picked up."

"By whom?" Forrest asked.

"Doesn't matter," Roger said. "Once Prohibition hit, there were so many federal agents assigned to the Port of Duluth, the opium shipments went elsewhere. That's when Galen increased the one trade he had been involved in, that of young women. He used mostly foreign girls, claiming they were part of his Hollywood studio. Gloria Kasper can tell you all about it," Roger said, once again taking a seat behind his desk.

Forrest remembered Gloria Kasper, the doctor who now resided at the resort. She had lived there ever since her house in town had mysteriously burned to the ground.

Roger opened a drawer near his side and reached down to pull something out. "I knew Galen couldn't make the kind of money he tossed around town trafficking women, and I knew the authorities wouldn't chase him down over it, either, but this—" He tossed a wad of bills on his desk. "This caught the attention of the law here and in California."

Forrest was more confused than ever. "Money? What about it?"

"It's counterfeit," Roger said.

"Counterfeit?" He hadn't heard a word about that. Stretching forward, Forrest lifted several bills for inspection. "California banknotes."

"Which stopped being printed fifteen years ago. Every time Galen went to California, he'd return with money, and lots of it. It wasn't until an acquaintance of his came looking for some whiskey that I discovered it was counterfeit. I knew the man was working for Galen, but I sold him the whiskey, and turned the money over to Sheriff Withers. Some of it," Roger added. "I saved some in case further evidence was needed. It wasn't long before a trail was discovered, or several trails, considering Galen would take a different route each time he came home from California. He was passing off these bills all across the states. Paying for a pack of gum with a twenty and getting real money in exchange."

"My mother never mentioned counterfeiting," Forrest admitted. The girls, he'd known all about. Even though he'd been gone from home before Galen's trips to California had started, there had always been a steady flow of young women through the doors of the nightclub.

"This counterfeit money was what he was laundering," Roger said. "Withers found enough on Galen to choke a horse, and the bank was happy to press charges against him. Since it was a California bank, they sent state marshals out here to escort him out there to stand trial. They had enough evidence to put him behind bars. However, his counterpart, the person who was actually printing the money, hasn't been found. That might be who has stepped forward now and is petitioning his release. They haven't found where it was being printed, either," Roger explained.

Which is the reason Galen's so set upon returning to Minnesota. Forrest stopped shy of saying that aloud. More things were making sense than ever before. As much as he didn't want to admit it, his gut told him his mother was involved. Whoever had broken into the Plantation had been looking for something specific and his mother's nonchalant concern over that event told him more than he wanted to know.

"We'll know who and where very soon," Ty said. "The Federal Reserve is now involved."

"Federal Reserve or not," Roger said, "we'll make sure Galen Reynolds never returns to Minnesota."

Forrest stood. "That's where you're wrong. *We* won't make sure Galen doesn't return. *I* will."

"Now, son—"

"I mean it, Roger," Forrest said sternly. "I don't want you involved in this."

"Want or not," Roger said, "we're involved."

Forrest turned and met the man's gaze with one just as stony, just as cold. "Then back out. You may think you know how evil Galen is, but believe me when I say you don't. Only someone who's lived with him can know that." Spinning around, he headed for the door, stopping prior to opening it. "And believe me, this time around, a dozen watchmen won't be enough to keep your girls safe."

A ball of raging fury was trapped inside Forrest as he exited the resort, and burned hotter when he sensed he was being watched. The curtain was pulled aside on the first window and there, not attempting to hide, was Twyla.

Their gazes locked and for a split second, Forrest was torn between heading for his car and going back inside to see how Twyla had fared against her sister. The fire in his guts burned all the way to his heels. Norma Rose may have gotten bruised by Galen all those years ago, but the stakes were higher this time. Twyla couldn't keep her nose clean. She loved hidden treasures, and if she caught wind of counterfeiting…

This was one secret he'd keep from her. If it killed him, he'd keep it from her. Forrest lifted a hand and gave her a salute before spinning around and heading for his car.

Chapter Eight

During his drive home, Forrest forced his mind to shift away from Twyla and back to last fall. He had to focus in order to keep her safe. While remodeling the Plantation, he'd been in every room, every nook, cranny and alcove. There hadn't been anything to indicate counterfeiting. No press or paper or ink, yet they had to be there, and finding the evidence was his only hope of keeping Galen behind bars.

He rehashed every conversation he'd had with his mother and became more convinced he was barking up the right tree. The only remark she'd made about the break-in was that there was no need to report it, that it must have been someone Galen had done business with. That said she knew more. If he only understood how and why. She didn't love Galen, but she'd never left his side, either. Even now, she insisted upon living in California to be near him.

Questions continued to twist his mind as he parked and climbed out of the roadster behind the Plantation.

Unlike Nightingale's resort, the Plantation was busy on Sundays. Entire families came to bowl a few games, and parents found a bit of solitude and respite in the coolness of the building while their children ran half-wild through the amusement park next door. Others rented the few sailboats Forrest had restored and spent the day on the water.

Jacob and Martha were more than capable of running the place, but Forrest rarely left them alone. An instinctual sense always had him on guard, as if he knew someone from Galen's past was lurking nearby. All that had faded today, in the instant he'd considered taking Twyla flying. He hadn't let his guard down since he'd arrived home last fall, and he wasn't impressed he'd allowed it to happen today.

As Forrest sat down at his desk, just off the front entranceway of the Plantation, he offhandedly spun the propeller of the model plane sitting near the phone, watching the little wooden flaps go around and around. Taking Twyla flying had been a definite mistake. Even years ago, Twyla had been the sister he'd loved.

A knock sounded and the door opened at almost the same time. Jacob poked his head in and, seeing Forrest was alone, walked in and closed the door. "Did you talk to Roger?"

Forrest stopped the little propeller from turning. "Yes."

"And?"

"You were right. He's not involved in the opium trade."

"I told you," Jacob said. "What about the other thing?"

Forrest drew a blank. "The other?"

"Your airmail contract?"

Forrest shook his head. That had slipped further and further from his mind.

"You didn't talk to him about that, did you?" Jacob said. "I'm sure he'd loan you the money to buy a new plane and once you got that government contract you—"

"I'm not asking Roger to loan me the money to buy a new plane," Forrest said. "I've told you that." A new plane was the least of his concerns right now.

"How else will you get that government contract?"

"I won't." Forrest stood and made his way to the window. There wasn't much to look at, just the parking lot. "Did you know Galen was arrested for passing off counterfeit bills?"

"Counterfeiting? Is that what money laundering means? People kept saying money laundering and I didn't know what it meant."

Forrest turned around. "Don't, Jacob—don't pretend to be a simpleton around me. It may have worked on Galen, but I know better."

Jacob sat down in an armchair near the desk. "All right. So I know what money laundering is, but I never heard so much as a whisper around here about counterfeiting."

Forrest rubbed his head. "You made it your business not to."

"Yes, I did."

"Why'd you stay here all these years?" Forrest asked. "You were never treated fairly, never appreciated."

"I am now," Jacob answered.

Forrest slapped the edge of the windowsill behind him. "I'm so tired of secrets. So tired of—"

"Because of you," Jacob said.

"Me?"

Jacob nodded. "Your grandfather did something he wished he could take back, but it was too late. He was sick and knew his days were numbered. He asked me to watch out for you. To be here for the day when this place would become yours." Then the man shook his head. "That's not completely true, either."

Forrest's stomach sank, and he silently pleaded Jacob wouldn't say he was in love with his mother. It was the only explanation Forrest had been able to come up with for years.

"Your grandfather paid me to be here for when this place became yours. Paid me very well, and in order to make sure I remained here, I've stayed on the sidelines, but never got directly involved." Jacob shrugged. "It was selfish, too. I never wanted your mother to know how much money I have sitting in the bank. I know she's your mother, and I won't talk bad about her, but I will tell you, if she'd known, she'd have tried to swindle me out of it."

Forrest rubbed his aching temples. This was certainly turning into a day of revelations.

"I told you when you started remodeling this place that I could help, and I told you I'd buy you a new plane, but you said no."

"I figured you were talking about a loan from Roger Nightingale," Forrest said.

"I know," Jacob said.

Forrest turned back to the window as questions once again started gathering in his mind. "What did my grandfather do?" he asked. "That he wished he could undo?"

"I've said enough," Jacob answered. "Your mother knows, ask her. She called again while you were gone."

"I tried calling her before I left," Forrest said. "There was no answer." Glancing over his shoulder, he decided he wanted one more question answered. "Are you in love with her?"

Jacob shook his head. "No, but I do love her. Just like I love you. You're the only family I've ever had."

"She needs money," Forrest said. "That's why she's calling."

"Do you have any to send her?" Jacob asked.

Forrest clamped his teeth together. The only thing he had left to sell was his plane, and that galled him. Telling his mother to ask whoever was bailing out Galen for money occurred to him, but he knew he'd never resort to those measures. His mother was as much a pawn as anyone else in Galen's life of schemes. She always had been, however it irritated him that she never saw it that way, or never tried to do something about it. "No, but I'll think of something."

"My offer to loan you some is as open as ever," Jacob said.

The door clicked shut, but Forrest never turned from the window. A red coupe was pulling in the parking lot, and he certainly didn't need to see the driver, or her yellow polka-dot dress, to know who was behind the wheel.

Not a single Nightingale had set foot on his property since he'd returned home. They'd visited the amusement park, Twyla in particular, but until they'd needed Slim, they hadn't attempted to renew the friendship they'd shared all those years ago. He hadn't expected it, not after all that had happened, and he'd known it would be up to him to make the first move.

Yet in the end he hadn't made the first move, and now he knew why. If it had been Twyla that Galen had said all those things about, Forrest would have been back in town as soon as he'd been able to hobble. Actually, if it had been Twyla with him in his car that night, he'd have driven for the state line. Tried to get as far away as possible. But she'd been just been a kid. In truth, he'd broken things off with Norma Rose that night, told her he was leaving to attend Harvard. That had been another letdown. While recuperating at his aunt's house he'd learned there was no money for Harvard, or any other college for that matter.

That was when Shirley had given him the deed to the Plantation and the several hundred acres where he'd built the hangar, but she'd told him that most of the actual money he'd inherited had gone to pay for his private schooling and college over the years. Shirley told him about numerous times his mother had come to her needing money for one thing or another, and she'd apologized for not overseeing his inheritance with more caution. His mother was her little sister, and despite everything, she'd felt responsible for her, up until that moment when Forrest's injuries had broken the bond between his mother and aunt. He knew they hadn't spoken in years. He'd used the last of his money for aviation school in Nebraska.

It was funny how the disparity between the money his family supposedly had and the amount the Nightingale family once hadn't had played such a part in his life. Until he'd found himself with very limited funds, he hadn't realized just how badly money could consume a person's thinking.

Norma Rose had certainly wanted out of her life back then and had been furious with him for putting up a roadblock to her well-laid plans of a wealthy marriage.

His gaze went back to the red coupe. Twyla, on the other hand, had taken life as it came back then, and though he understood she now loved her life of influence as much as her sister, she still had her love of adventure. Nothing, not even the lack of money, had suppressed that in Twyla. He'd loved that about her back then, and still did.

He was a fool. He should never have taken her flying, never should have danced with her. Never should have kissed her.

The knock on his office door was no surprise, since he'd watched her walk all the way to the front door less than a minute ago. He turned around and leaned against the windowsill as the door opened and Twyla walked in. She was still wearing her yellow polka-dot dress. Still wearing her yellow scarf tied around her neck. Still the most beautiful women he'd ever laid eyes upon.

"You can run, but you can't hide," she said saucily, kicking the door shut with one perfectly placed heel.

"I'm not running or hiding," Forrest responded, although internally he knew he was doing a little of both, and had been for some time.

"Why didn't you tell me Galen was being paroled?"

He shrugged, watching as she crossed the room. Just like he'd done earlier, she paused near his desk to flick the propeller of his model plane. "It's none of your business," he said.

"None of my business?" she repeated as a question. "We're friends, Forrest, almost family."

"We are not almost family."

A slight frown tugged at her finely shaped brows. "We could have been," she said. "If you'd married Norma Rose."

"I would never have married Norma Rose," he said, moving from the window to sit down on the long couch that sat against one wall. "I'd never have married anyone from around here."

She trailed one finger along his desk as she walked to the far corner of it before turning around to face him. "Why not?"

"Because it would have been like the prince marrying a commoner," he said, purposely trying to sound snide. There were some secrets he'd never let out. He couldn't if he wanted to make sure Twyla didn't get caught up in all that was going on.

"Now you sound like your— Galen. Why?"

"Maybe I'm more like him than you know," he said. "More like him than anyone knows."

She laughed. It wasn't a sarcastic giggle, but a genuinely tickled sound. He had to bite his teeth together to combat just how thoroughly it affected him.

"As I said, Forrest, you can run, but you can't hide. Not from me."

Afraid she might see through his facade, Forrest rose to his feet. If anyone could see through him, it would be Twyla. "What are you doing here?"

She'd moved to the wall where he'd hung several pictures. "You know Babe Ruth?" she asked, a bit in awe.

"I gave him a ride in my airplane a couple of years ago."

"So you know him," she persisted.

"Sort of, I guess." He kept his distance. His lips had started twitching and his heart thudded as he remembered how it had felt kissing her back at the hangar. "Why? Actually, how do you know that's Babe Ruth?"

"Everyone knows who Babe Ruth is." She took a couple steps before pausing to gaze out the window.

Across the street from the parking lot was the city park. About the same time the council had put the noise ordinance and curfew law into effect, they'd turned the lot where an old hotel had once stood into a park, including ball fields.

"Look out there," she said, "at those kids playing ball. I bet every one of them knows who Babe Ruth is, and they probably dream of meeting him."

"Could be," he said, not overly interested in the kids or Babe Ruth. Her silhouette was caught in the sunlight and even when he closed his eyes, he could see the breathtaking and shimmering outline of her curves. Disgusted by how easily he could be distracted, Forrest marched to his desk. "I have work to do, Twyla."

She spun around. "Tell me about your airmail contract."

"Who told you about that, and about Galen's release? Your father?" Forrest had been home little more than an hour, and assumed he'd been the topic of conversation back at the resort. Still, things must have changed out there. He'd have expected Roger to be a bit more tight-lipped.

"My father mentioned your contract while telling me I couldn't go flying with you again for the next five days," she said. "But Norma Rose told me about Galen's release."

His mind snagged on one thing. "For the next five days?"

She nodded. "He's going to Chicago in the morning, to get Ginger, and said I couldn't go flying with you again until he returns home. He also said he'd like to go up in your plane someday. I told him how magnificent it was."

"You did? He did?" Forrest shook his head, trying to find a lick of sense, or perhaps shake aside how adorable she looked when her eyes lit up as she spoke about flying.

"Yes, I did, and yes, he did." Twyla continued her little jaunt around his office and ended up near the couch, where she gracefully lowered herself onto the cushions.

He'd found the sofa in one of the boarded-off rooms upstairs, and because it looked relatively new, he'd wondered why no one had taken it—other than the fact it was cumbersome and a rather eye-stinging shade of lime-green. However, right now, next to Twyla's white-and-yellow dress and faded red hair, the couch didn't look nearly as bad.

"So," she said, looking up at him earnestly, "what are we going to do about Galen?"

Forrest crossed the room to his desk and leaned against the edge. Seeing her look up at him with such trust and expectancy stirred a powerful protectiveness inside him. "*We* are not going to do anything," he said. "*You* are going to go back home where you belong."

She grinned coyly.

"Immediately," he added.

She glanced around the room, and Forrest wished he knew what was happening inside that adorable head of hers. Her thoughts included him, of that he had no doubt, and it only increased the reasons why he should send her back home.

"I like the changes you've made here." She rose to her feet. "Will you show me the bowling alley? I've never seen one."

Just as she was able to see through him, he could see through her. The bowling lanes were not her interest right now. However, if it got her out of here, he'd indulge her.

He gestured for her to precede him across the room, but neither of them had taken more than a step when the door opened.

Nasty Nick Ludwig strolled in the room, flipping a wooden bowling pin with one hand. "I see you built yourself a nice little playground for you and your friends," Nick said, "but that's what's to be expected from a little rich boy."

Forrest stepped in front of Twyla. "What do you want, Ludwig?"

"So you do recognize me."

Forrest refrained from admitting anything with Twyla near.

Lifting one corner of his mouth, Ludwig flipped the pin again. "Just thought I'd knock over a few pins. See what fun folks find in it."

Forrest snatched the pin out of the air. If he needed proof someone had been sneaking around, here it was. "The likes of you aren't welcome here."

"Well, now, I don't think your pappy would take kindly to hearing you talk to me like that. He ain't gonna like what you did with the place, either." Leaning slightly to shoot a leer at Twyla, Ludwig added, "For the most part, that is."

Forrest tossed the pin onto the couch before he stepped forward and grabbed Ludwig by the shirt front. "While you're telling my *pappy*," Forrest said, "tell him he's not welcome around here, either."

Nasty Nick struggled and tried to tug off Forrest's hands, but his hold merely tightened. Being half a foot taller than the thug, Forrest lifted Ludwig until his toes dangled above the floor.

"Remind him, too—my pappy, that is—that's he's not dealing with a scared little kid anymore." Tossing Ludwig against the wall, Forrest waited until the man had found his feet before he added, "Remind him of that, would you?"

Ludwig glared, but spun around. However, before he was all the way through the doorway, Nick turned around. "You're gonna be sorry you returned."

"I already am," Forrest snapped. Catching the surprise in Ludwig's eyes, he added, "And you just made it worse."

The man dashed down the hallway, and a moment later, the slam of the glass-paneled front door echoed over the noise of the people bowling on the other side of the dining room.

Forrest spun around, half expecting to see Twyla a shivering heap on the couch. She wasn't shivering. Or on the couch. Instead, she was standing right behind him, holding the bowling pin with one hand. Slapping the fat end of the pin against her other palm, she asked, "Ready to show me those bowling lanes? I suspect someone wants their pin back."

A mixture of shock, anger, pride and disgust swirled inside him. He'd never been oblivious to his home life, but he'd tried to keep the corruption hidden from the Nightingale sisters at all costs. Now was no different.

Twyla lifted an eyebrow in question. He didn't want her leaving right now, not with Nasty Nick hanging around, so Forrest said nothing as he once again gestured toward the door.

If her legs gave out on her now, Twyla swore she'd cut them off at the knees, or maybe even at the thighs, considering it was her knees that were shaking. They had been ever since that nasty thug had thrown open the door. If a fist-fight had come about, she was certain Forrest would have won. He was taller and beefier than the other man, but she'd collected the bowling pin and stood ready just in case. The pin was heavier than it looked, and she figured a couple of good clubs over the head would have sent the thug to the floor.

Questions swirled in her brain, but she knew Forrest wasn't prepared to answer any of them, so she wouldn't ask. There'd be time for that later. Once he realized he wasn't alone in this fight against Galen. Never would be again.

With a slight nod, she started for the door, and thanked her legs profusely for cooperating. Ludwig, as Forrest had called the man, had been at Palooka George's party last night. Twyla set the name deep in her head to ask Norma Rose about him. Right now, she was focused on Forrest, and would pretend to be amazed by his bowling alley.

And that notion turned out to be easier than expected. Her reaction was a surprise because it wasn't a nightclub. Speakeasies such as the resort—though it irritated everyone else in her family when she referred to Nightingale's as that—were her favorites. That was where fun was to be had.

Although she'd rarely been inside the Plantation, visiting only a few times when Forrest had lived there years ago, she did remember how impressive it had been. With its large white pillars and three stories, the building had always been the most magnificent for miles around. It might as well have had curtains made of dollar bills, it shouted money so clearly, and that, too, was what she loved above all else.

From Forrest's office they'd turned left and walked down the hallway to the front entrance, which held a coatroom on one side and a wide, curving staircase leading upstairs. A red velvet rope with gold ties was stretched across the staircase, discouraging people from going up.

Double doors leading from the entrance led to a dining room, one she barely recognized. She'd been in this room for Forrest's graduation party. Heavy drapes had hung from the windows then and dark carpet had covered the floor. Charcoal-colored linoleum with white specks now stretched from wall to wall, and several small round tables with two or four chairs were spread about. Sunlight filled the room from windows covered with nothing but short valances across their tops. The wooden bar, with a long mirror behind it, still lined the far wall, but the people sitting on the stools were drinking soda pop or slurping up ice-cream sodas. A short stage, one step up from the floor, was angled in the far corner and right now two young boys were pounding on the piano keys.

Twyla glanced up at Forrest, expecting him to yell at the boys, but he merely grinned and gestured to the other side of the room. Galen Reynolds would certainly have put a stop to those boys. Children were never allowed to touch anything in his presence.

At his side, Twyla walked with Forrest toward where the top half of a wall had been removed. A waist-high barricade had been left, and on the other side of it, what had once been the ballroom now held five long and shiny alleys that stretched clear to the other side. Several groups were gathered at each alley, rolling balls toward the pins. Two young boys ran back and forth, setting up or pulling pins out of the way before they rolled balls back down long open chutes that framed the alleyways.

Forrest led her through an opening in the waist-high wall and pointed out the back of the wall that held rows of bowling balls.

"Why do you need so many?" she asked.

"Because they weigh different amounts," he answered. "Women and children like lighter balls than men." After rolling over a few balls, he pointed at one. "Try that one."

She picked up the ball, taken aback by the weight. "I'm supposed to throw this at the pins?"

"No," he said, with a grin that showed his dimple. "You roll it." Picking up another ball, he gestured toward the one she held. "Put your fingers in the holes like this."

Copying his actions, she cringed. "Oh, yeah, that's real comfortable."

He shook his head, but chuckled. "Come on."

Twyla, carrying her ball with both hands, followed.

"That over there," he said, gesturing past all the lanes, "is the billiards room. There are three pool tables."

She nodded, seeing people through the arched opening holding cue sticks. Forrest led her to the last lane before he stopped. Twyla was a bit surprised when a black-haired man helping a young boy maneuver a ball out of the side chute turned out to be Scooter Wilson.

"Hey, Twyla," Scooter said, after the boy had rolled the ball down the lane and knocked over several pins.

"Hello, Scooter," she replied. "You come bowling?"

"Sure do. Brought my nephew, Jonas, over today. It's his birthday."

"Happy birthday, Jonas," she said to the boy, who had hair as black as his uncle's.

"Thanks," the boy said. "Tomorrow is my real birthday, but Uncle Scooter brought me today 'cause his fueling station will be open tomorrow and he'll have to work."

Twyla grinned at Jonas's explanation while Forrest stepped forward and ruffled the boy's hair.

"Happy birthday a day early," Forrest said. "Are you winning or is your uncle?"

"I got two strikes," Jonas said proudly. "He hasn't gotten any."

"So you're winning, then," Forrest said, laughing.

"What are strikes?" Twyla asked.

"When you knock down all ten pins in one shot," Jonas answered before sending his ball rolling.

Twyla lifted her gaze to the end of the alley, where the young boys were tossing pins over a short wall and rolling balls into the side chutes. Then the boys jumped over the wall, waved and disappeared. "Why'd they do that?" she asked Forrest.

"First they get the pins out of the way, then

they throw the balls back and hide so they don't get hit," he answered.

She watched a few other bowlers send their balls down the alleyway. The speed astounded her, and the clatter when the ball hit the pins made her glad those boys had a wall to protect them. "Oh, goodness."

"I'm going to be a pin boy for Forrest when I get old enough," Jonas said.

"Oh?" Twyla asked. "Does your mother know that?"

"Yes," Jonas answered. "But just like Forrest, she said I have to wait until I turn fourteen."

Forrest nodded as the boy looked his way questioningly.

"The boys have to be old enough to keep focused," Jonas told her seriously.

"Your ball's back," Forrest said, gesturing toward the ball rolling down the chute.

Scooter and Jonas went over to pick up the ball and Twyla asked, "Don't the balls just fall in those little chutes along the side?"

"Yes, then it's called a gutter ball. Those little chutes on each side of the lane are called gutters. Bowlers need to keep their ball out of the gutters and hit the pins. When all ten pins are knocked down in one shot it's called a strike, as Jonas said, and if it takes two balls, it's called a spare."

"How many times can you throw the ball?"

she asked, watching as Jonas once again sent the ball spinning down the lane.

"Roll the ball," he said. "Your turn consists of rolling the ball two times." Turning to Scooter, he asked, "Mind if Twyla takes a turn?"

"Of course not," Scooter said. "We just started a new game." Bowing, he gave a grand sweep with one arm. "Right this way, my lady."

Twyla grimaced at Scooter as she stepped up to the red line. He'd always been a teaser.

"Not so close," Forrest said, pulling her back a few steps. "There. Now, when it's time, you swing the ball behind you—" he swung her arm backward as he spoke "—and take three steps forward and let go of the ball."

It sounded easy enough, and having always enjoyed games, Twyla nodded. "Got it." She also gave him the thumbs-up sign before she stuck her fingers and a thumb into the holes in the ball. He grinned and though it was hard to pull her gaze off his dimple, she managed to turn her attention back to the game. While the boys at the other end set up the pins again, she watched the other bowlers. By the time her pins were in a perfect triangle, she was holding the ball before her face. The boy at the end of her lane waved before ducking down and she prepared to swing her arm backward.

This was going to be so simple, and once she

proved how easily she could master bowling, she would convince Forrest how much help she could be in his fight against Galen Reynolds.

To her utter surprise, the ball slipped off her fingers. A great crashing noise followed. Twyla spun about, opening only one eye, half-afraid to see who she'd hit. The chairs and little table sitting there had toppled, but Forrest, Jonas and Scooter were all still standing.

"Sorry," she said, rather sheepishly.

Jonas gathered her ball from where it landed and carried it back to her. "I did that once, too," he said. "You gotta keep your fingers curled until you let the ball go forward."

"Gotcha," she said, taking the ball he held out.

Her first ball rolled directly into the gutter. The second one managed to knock over one pin.

Forrest stepped up to the alley next and with the ease of Babe Ruth throwing a baseball, he sent the ball rolling straight into the pins. All ten toppled.

Her competitive nature kicked in. "There's something wrong with this ball," she told Forrest, holding up her ball.

"Is there?"

"Yes," she insisted. "I'm going to get a different one."

"Suit yourself," he said, laughing.

By the time Scooter and Jonas had thrown

their balls, she had a new one picked out and stepped up to the line. Then, very carefully, she took three steps backward and hoisted the ball before her face. Taking perfect aim, with her eyes glued to the center pin, she swung the ball back and then forward. It bounced once, but rolled straight down the lane and hit the front pin, scattering the other nine in all directions.

Jumping for joy, she spun around. "See? You'd given me a faulty ball. On purpose, most likely."

Forrest's grin widened.

She turned to where Scooter was writing on a piece of paper. "What's that?"

"I'm keeping score," Scooter said.

"Score?" she asked, turning her gaze to Forrest.

The gleam in his eyes was as bright as the sun. He nodded.

"No wonder people like this game," she said. Scorekeeping always made games more fun, and she was all about winning.

Chapter Nine

Forrest waited until Twyla was invested in the game before he snuck away. Once in his office, he picked up the receiver and waited for the line to be connected to the resort. When a voice came on, he paused slightly before asking, "Is Ty Bradshaw there?"

"Who's calling, please?"

"Forrest Reynolds."

"Hold, please."

The next few moments seemed to take hours while Forrest contemplated if he'd made the right choice. Ty seemed to have Norma Rose under control, and therefore, he would be the best one to come and get Twyla. Forrest kept one eye on the door. Though Twyla was focused on winning the bowling game, she'd question his absence and could burst into the room at any moment.

"Ty here."

"Ty, its Forrest. You need to come get Twyla."

"Why? Is she hurt?"

"No, she's fine. She's bowling right now. I just don't want her to drive back to the resort alone." Checking that the door was still shut tight, he added, "A man who'd been in jail with Galen, Nasty Nick Ludwig, was here a short time ago. I'm not sure where he went, but wouldn't put it past him to follow her."

"I'll be there shortly."

Forrest hung up and arrived back at the lanes just as Twyla was rolling her second ball. She jumped up and down and then spun around when the last three pins fell. "Where'd you go?" she asked. "Jonas bowled for you."

"I had something to see to," he answered, before thanking Jonas for rolling a spare for him. He played it up, saying the boy would soon be the Plantation's champion bowler, ultimately taking away Twyla's opportunity to ask more questions. Once the pins were set back up, he took his turn at bowling and then sat down on a chair beside Twyla.

She was all smiles and laughter right now, but two things could quickly change that—losing at bowling and discovering he'd called Ty to come and get her.

The latter of those two couldn't happen fast enough. Being next to her, watching her bowl and laugh, made everything else in his life fade into the shadows. If he wasn't careful, he'd soon be recalling the kiss from earlier today. In fact, he didn't need to recall it. He was already craving another one like there was no tomorrow. Her antics were drawing attention, too. Men on both sides of them were cheering each time she knocked over a pin, and when it was her turn to bowl, the rest of the alleys went quiet. Even the billiards room had spectators peering out the door.

Forrest couldn't help but wonder if any of these men had visited her kissing booth. Had they paid a dime to taste her sweetness and catch a feel of those perfect lips? That, too, had him feeling things he hadn't experienced for a long time. It had taken him a while to realize he was jealous, and once he did understand that, it didn't settle well.

He kept glancing toward the door, wishing Ty would hurry up and dreading his arrival at the same time. She'd be furious, and a furious Twyla could put on a show for the customers like they'd never seen before.

When Twyla came in last—even though he'd purposely thrown a couple of gutter balls to lower his score—Forrest was surprised that she didn't try to cajole Scooter and Jonas into bowling another game..

Her smile never faltered, and Forrest had an

eerie sensation he should be worried about that. After saying farewell to Scooter and Jonas, she turned that smile on him.

"I need to use the powder room."

He gestured toward the separate men's and women's bathroom doors near the billiards room.

"Thanks, I'll be right back."

Forrest couldn't stop from watching her walk away, even though he tried. His gaze scanned lower, all the way to her heels, which made him frown. She didn't appear to be favoring one foot over the other, but there was a large red blotch on the back of one ankle.

He positioned himself to keep one eye on the front door, and the other on the ladies' room. When Twyla exited, he walked back to meet her halfway and took her elbow. "Why didn't you tell me you hurt your foot? Was it on the plane?" He'd been racking his brain to remember if she'd tripped or stumbled while climbing up or down but couldn't recall such an event.

"No," she said. "I didn't hurt it on the plane."

"Here? Bowling?"

She shook her head.

"You must have," he insisted. "You're bleeding."

She stopped and lifted a foot, twisting it so she could examine the heel. "The blister must have burst."

"New shoes?" he asked.

A pink tinge covered her cheeks, yet she began walking again with her head up. "Yes."

"Doesn't it hurt?"

"Oh, yes," she said. "But I'm choosing to ignore it."

He kept one hand on her elbow and led her through the dining room. "How's that working for you?"

She made a cute little guffaw. "How do you think?"

In the front entranceway, he unhooked the velvet cord across the stairway. "I have bandages upstairs. Will that help?"

Grinning, she shrugged. "It can't hurt."

They encountered Jacob halfway up the stairs. While ignoring the man's raised eyebrows, Forrest told him they'd be upstairs if anyone asked. He had no doubt Jacob could read between the lines and would send up Ty as soon as he arrived. Jacob might add a bit more between the lines, too, but for now, Forrest wasn't going to worry about that. He did, however, wish he'd spent a bit of time repairing his apartment.

It wasn't shabby or messy, but it wasn't up to the standards Twyla was used to. At one time it had been a rather lavish living space with a full kitchen, living room and three bedrooms. It still had all the rooms, but the peeling wallpaper and the kitchen cupboard doors that had been ripped off their hinges detracted from what it once had been.

Arriving at the door, he turned the knob and gestured for her to enter, freezing slightly when a little voice in the back of his head reminded him how alone they'd be for a few minutes. There would be plenty of time for a repeat of the kiss they'd shared at the hangar.

"I've never been up here." Her stride slowed and she turned around, flashing those sparkling blue eyes his way. The shine dimmed slightly. "Did you have a party up here?"

"No," he said, closing the door behind him while thinking more about being alone with her than the apartment. "Someone broke into the place between the time when my mother and Galen left and I arrived." He wanted to bite off his tongue.

"Broke in? Goodness." She started across the room, to the wall between two windows that overlooked the parking lot. "What did they take?"

Concerned she might see Ty pulling in to the parking lot, Forrest followed. "They damaged more than they took. The bathroom's this way. That's where the bandages are."

She stopped before reaching the windows, but didn't follow him to the bathroom, the only door that hadn't been destroyed. Standing in the center of the room, with the colorful but worn Persian carpet beneath her feet, she asked, "What were they looking for?"

Forrest stomach dropped. Trust her to pick up on that immediately. Playing ignorant, he asked, "Looking for?"

Frowning while glancing around, she nodded.

Forrest wished he knew. It must have been something to do with printing money, or the printed money itself. He had yet to figure that out. He glanced around the large area that made up the all-in-one kitchen, dining and living room. Everything from the kitchen cupboards behind her had been tossed about helter-skelter and paintings had been torn down off the walls. He'd cleaned it all up and resurrected what could be saved. "Anything worth money, I suspect," he said, hoping she'd believe that.

She shook her head. "I don't think so."

He sighed, but then an eerie quiver coiled around his spine. "Why do you say that?"

"Because this rug I'm standing on, although it needs a good cleaning, is worth a goodly sum," she said. "So are those two vases on the mantel."

Leave it to Twyla to pinpoint the few things in the room that were original and worth money at one time. His grandfather had left several valuable items when he'd died, but they'd long ago been sold. Forrest stepped forward and held out one hand, which she readily took hold of. "The rug is heavy and bulky to carry, and the vases are cracked."

The warmth of her fingers against his skin ran up his arm and down his legs. The gleam was back in her blue eyes and challenging him in a secret and exciting way. She'd mastered that teasing glimmer years ago, and he had no doubt she'd used it on plenty of men since then.

"What about that ashtray on the table?"

His mind was not on the ashtray—he was too captivated by how perfectly her lips moved when she spoke. How delicate the fine line surrounding them was, and remembering how sweet they'd tasted.

"What about it?" he asked, before he completely lost his mind and kissed her again.

"It's jade, and I'd guess it's also rather priceless." Lifting one eyebrow, she added, "And not heavy or cracked."

She licked her lips and nibbled slightly on the bottom one, knowing full well what she was doing. Forrest would have liked to say it wasn't affecting him, but that was a lie. He was about to crack.

Stepping forward, Twyla used her free hand to tug at his collar. A fingertip slipped down to tap on one of the buttons of his shirt. "I could help you look for other valuables," she whispered.

There was no question what she was doing. Forrest, however, was questioning how many men she'd practiced her wiles on. "Girls who play with fire can get burned, Twyla. You know that."

"How could I?" she asked, saying far more with her eyes than her lips. "You never let me play with fire. Whenever we lit anything, even a candle, you were the only one to strike a match."

She was driving him crazy. He'd never wanted to kiss a pair of lips so badly. "I don't believe we're referring to the same type of fire," he said, close to her mouth, giving her back a bit of what she was dishing out.

She didn't back away. "I think we are."

Forrest drew in air, searching for a response that didn't include kissing, but failed. The moment her lips met his, he lost all comprehension. He'd kissed plenty of women over the years, dated some for months to get to know them. At least that's what he'd believed he'd been doing, whereas, in reality, he'd been comparing them all to her. To the way she'd made him feel way back when they'd been kids running barefoot through the grass and jumping off the rope swing hanging over the water.

Her body was far more mature than it had been back then. The delicate curves beneath the silk of her dress were as perfect as he'd imagined. This was the real reason he'd never come home. Seeing Twyla and not acting upon that reckless, rebellious and youthful love some never experienced was impossible. He'd known that years ago.

Forrest considered pulling away from the kiss, but her lips, her mouth, her tongue all teased and coaxed his into a competition of wills he couldn't lose. There was too much at stake.

The wild give-and-take of their kiss slowed and became far more intense, affecting other parts of his body. Namely his heart. His heart was Twyla's. It had been for years, and he felt as if it had just cracked open, preparing for his mind to agree and reveal his best-kept secret.

He managed to keep that from happening, just barely, and released her lips with a few small and delicate kisses. The kind of kisses she deserved. She may act the part of an experienced woman, but he sensed she was as innocent as she'd been when he'd left home.

Glorying in the way she fit perfectly against him—which was not so different from how he took the time to appreciate flying into a sunrise—Forrest tucked her head beneath his chin and simply relished holding her for a few minutes.

"You haven't changed a bit, Forrest," she whispered. "You're as gentle and kind and caring as ever."

Forrest opened his eyes and glanced around the room, at the shattered remnants of his past, and he, too, sighed. "Everything's changed, doll. Everything's changed."

She lifted her head and Forrest wasn't prepared to answer the questions in her eyes, so he released his hold and took her hand. "The bandages are this way."

Twyla cursed her blister silently, while following Forrest into the bathroom, where he let go of her hand to open a small cupboard door. He was right, everything had changed. Inside her, that is. Or maybe it hadn't changed. After all, she had been in love with him once before. He'd been her first true crush. Way back when he'd made her insides warm and her knees weak as if she'd lost all coordination. That had happened again, and she lowered herself onto the toilet.

"Do you need some help?"

She glanced at the hand he held out.

"I found some iodine," he said.

"That stuff burns."

"Yes, but it will make the wound heal faster."

She took the little brown bottle and the bandage tin. "Thanks."

"Do you need help taking off your shoe?"

For a moment she wondered if he would remove it and her stocking, if she asked, and how enticing that might be. The thought made her cheeks burn. She may act the part of a doxy to get her way now and again, but had always retreated or escaped before things went too far. Her motto had been to leave them wanting more, but it wasn't that way with Forrest. She was the one wanting more. Sighing, she shook her head. "No."

"I'll wait for you in the other room."

Twyla waited until he'd closed the door before looking up, and then she let out a long breath. Kissing him was something she could do all day, every day, but that wasn't any more likely to happen now than it had been way back when. The fact he'd been Norma Rose's boyfriend hadn't stopped Twyla from having a crush on him before. His leaving had stopped all that. That was bound to happen again, whether Galen Reynolds was released or not. Her father had told her Forrest was set on acquiring an airmail route from the government.

Twyla set the bottle of iodine and the tin on the edge of the sink and removed her shoe before tugging up her dress to unhook her stocking from the garter. Though her heel was still bleeding slightly, dried blood had stuck the stocking to her skin. She managed to get it off without tearing a hole in the silk and dropped it in the sink. The blood would stain if she didn't get it rinsed out. After applying the iodine, which stung as badly as she remembered, she covered the area with a bandage and then removed her other shoe and stocking. Going without any was better than wearing just one stocking.

After rinsing the stained one, she draped them both over the edge of the sink and picked up both shoes. The iodine made the blister sting too badly to be further irritated with shoes.

As she opened the bathroom door, a knock sounded on the apartment door. That annoyed her, but so did the wary look Forrest shot her way as he crossed the room. When he opened the door, the two people standing there made her give a moan of exasperation.

"Come in," Forrest said, waving toward the cluster of furniture that made up the living room.

Ty and Norma Rose walked in, offering greetings as if they'd just encountered her and Forrest on a street corner. Twyla returned their hellos as she made her way to Forrest's side. While Norma Rose and Ty proceeded all the way to the gold-colored velvet sofa in the center of the room, Twyla leaned over to complain, "Why'd you call them?"

"Who says I did?" Forrest asked.

"Norma Rose would never step foot in the Plantation and not even Ty could convince her to, unless it was to tell me it was time to go home."

Forrest grinned. "Must be past your curfew."

"I no longer have a curfew."

"Says who?"

"Me," she snapped, before smiling at her sister and Ty. "Forrest taught me how to bowl," she said. "You should try it."

Norma Rose frowned, but Ty grinned. "I haven't bowled in a long time, but I got a glimpse of the lanes.They look good."

"Where are your stockings?" Norma Rose asked, obviously more interested in the shoes in Twyla's hand than the bowling lanes.

The glare in her sister's eyes was colder than the water Twyla had used to rinse out her stockings. Evidently, her sister had forgotten the peace treaty they'd created back at the resort. Then again, Twyla wasn't feeling overly warm and friendly herself. Forrest had to have called for someone to come and get her. She hadn't told anyone where she was going. "In the bathroom," she said, lifting her foot to show her bandage. "I ended up with a blister that popped and bled. I had to rinse out the blood before it stained." She crossed the room and sat in an armchair situated diagonally from the sofa. Telling herself she'd get more bees with honey than vinegar, she added, "At least I didn't drop a ball on my foot. They're heavier than they look."

"But she did throw a ball behind her and almost took out Scooter and his nephew," Forrest said, stopping to stand behind her chair.

"He makes it sound much worse than it was," Twyla said.

Norma Rose's glare hadn't diminished, and her frown increased as she looked around the room.

"There was a break-in," Twyla said before her sister could comment. "Prior to Forrest's arrival."

"Did they steal anything?" Norma Rose asked, surveying the area again.

"I don't know," Forrest said, still standing behind her. "I hadn't lived here for years. I had no idea what might have been missing or not. Jacob wasn't sure, either, as he wasn't on the upper levels very often."

Ty was looking around, too, thoughtfully. "Looks to me like they were searching for something specific."

Twyla glanced up at Forrest.

"Hard to say," he said. "They could have just been vagrants."

He'd laid a hand on her shoulder that, as wonderful as it felt, also made a tiny quiver tickle her spine. She didn't need to love Forrest in order to help him. The creep from earlier, Nasty Nick Ludwig, knew Galen and could have been the one to break in. Thugs like him could never be trusted.

"I agree with Ty," Twyla persisted. "I think they were looking for something specific."

"Forrest, would you mind giving me a tour of the place?" Ty asked. "I used to bowl quite often back in New York and wouldn't mind getting a closer look at all you've done here."

Ty's attempt to change the subject said he knew more than he was willing to share. What Ty knew, Norma Rose knew. That much, Twyla was certain of.

"Sure," Forrest said.

As Norma Rose and Ty stood, Twyla glanced over her shoulder to ask Forrest, "Would you mind if I waited here? My heel still hurts and I don't want to put my shoes on without stockings."

"Your stockings won't be dry for hours," Norma Rose intoned.

"I know," Twyla snapped back. Forrest's hand was still on her shoulder and the pressure of his fingers increased, as if reminding her of what he'd said back in the coat closet at the resort. She didn't need a reminder. Norma Rose did. "When it's time to go home, I'll put my shoes on without them, but until then, I don't want to traipse up and down the stairs any more than I have to. Why don't you wait here with me, Norma Rose?" she asked, widening her eyes. "Let the men go on the tour by themselves."

"That sounds like a good plan," Ty said, placing a peck on Norma Rose's cheek. "We won't be long."

Norma Rose was clearly not impressed, and Twyla thought that if her teeth were clamped as tightly as her lips she probably would have bitten off the end of her tongue. Nonetheless, Norma Rose sat back down and Twyla waited until the men had left and closed the door behind them, before asking, "Why'd Forrest call you?"

"You knew he called?"

"It didn't take much to figure out," she said. "Why? What did he say?"

Norma Rose sat back and crossed her legs. "I don't know. He talked to Ty. Why'd you come here? I told you to wait until I learned more information."

"Have you found out more information?"

"No, not really."

Twyla wasn't sure how long the men would be gone and didn't have time to mess around. Crossing her arms, she gave her sister a glare that said she needed more of an answer.

"I haven't had time," Norma Rose pointed out. "Ty said Forrest didn't want you driving home alone. That Nick Ludwig had been here and he was afraid the thug might follow you."

"He was here, all right."

"We should leave," Norma Rose said. "Get your stockings."

"No," Twyla said, frustrated. "I know you claim to hate Forrest, but do you? Or are you still in love with him?"

Norma Rose pinched her lips together before she hissed, "Of course I'm not in love with him. I love Ty."

When Twyla shook her head, Norma Rose sighed.

"I am in love with Ty," she insisted.

Twyla did believe her, but still pointed out, "Not so long ago you loved Forrest. When he returned last fall you told us all to stay away from him. Why? Did you still love him then?"

Norma Rose remained quiet for a few long moments, and the solemn look that formed on her sister's face left Twyla wondering if she wanted to hear what Norma Rose was about to say.

"The only person I've told is Ty."

Twyla's stomach gurgled.

"I may have thought I loved Forrest at one time, but he never loved me." Uncrossing her legs, Norma Rose leaned forward. "Galen Reynolds didn't catch us kissing that night. Forrest had told me he was going to Harvard and that he'd probably never be back. He said I should forget all about him and find someone else to marry."

Twyla couldn't come up with a response. All she'd truly heard was the fact that Forrest had planned on leaving and never coming back.

Her sister stood and crossed the room to stare out the window for a minute before turning around. "Galen said we were necking and I let everyone believe it, even Father, thinking maybe he might make Forrest return."

"Why?"

"You remember what it was like back then," Norma Rose said. "We were so poor we didn't even have mice in our house because there wasn't anything for them to eat. Father worked at the brewery, but the money didn't go far when there were so many to feed and clothe. Besides all of us, Grandma and Grandpa lived there, and Uncle Dave until he went to the war. Mother depended upon the baskets of food Karen Reynolds used to bring over when she'd drop Forrest off. You remember them, don't you? They held things we never got otherwise. Bananas and oranges, candies and cookies and other store-bought treats."

The baskets must not have meant as much to her as they had to Norma Rose because Twyla really couldn't remember them. Everyone had been poor back then, except for Forrest. It hadn't been until Forrest had left that she realized how poor they were. Perhaps because that was when the days started to drag on. One was just like the last, with nothing to look forward to. Or perhaps she'd realized because Galen, and Norma Rose, had shouted how poor they were from the rooftops and pointed it out daily.

Norma Rose sighed heavily. "I remember them as if it was yesterday, and I remember thinking that would be me someday, bringing baskets of food home so none of you would be hungry." She glanced around the room. "I remember dreaming about living here, too, and wearing fashionable clothes and never, ever, worrying about money." She shrugged. "When Forrest told me he was leaving and never coming back, he stole that dream. I had nowhere else to look for it. No hope."

Twyla could relate to Forrest's departure stealing dreams. He'd certainly left her without any. Or at least changed the ones she'd once had.

"I was furious with Forrest," Norma Rose said, "but eventually, I transferred that energy into thinking of ways I could make money instead of marry it. Father had started his business and I suggested we could offer the men he was dealing with places to stay at the cabins. It worked."

It had worked. That was also when Norma Rose had become a slave driver. Twyla had been the one who'd had to clean the cabins, make the beds and wash the sheets every day before and after school. That was when she'd formed new dreams. Dreams of money, enough to hire people to make beds and wash sheets. Even when their father's business had started to make money, her dreams had continued. The money he made all went back into the resort. The parties had started at the pavilion, too, but Norma Rose had been the only sister allowed to attend.

"You see now?" Norma Rose asked. "I never was in love with Forrest. Just his money." She sat back down on the sofa. "And now I—we— have our own money, which is a lot more than Forrest has. He's broke."

"What?" Twyla asked, questioning her hearing, before her mind reacted. "Forrest isn't broke. He has the Plantation and his airplane, and all the money his grandfather left him."

Norma Rose shook her head. "Galen spent it all."

"That can't be," Twyla insisted. "Galen went to jail for money laundering."

"Exactly," Norma Rose said. "Laundering counterfeit money. After he spent everything else, he got involved in making it, but no one knows exactly how or where the counterfeit money came from."

A strange sensation made the hair on Twyla's arms stand on end. She glanced around the room before saying, "Someone else is looking for where it came from, too."

Chapter Ten

Forrest couldn't believe Twyla hadn't put up more of a fight. As meek and polite as any schoolgirl, she'd thanked him for the bowling game and readily climbed into the backseat of Norma Rose's Cadillac.

And that had him worried. She was a fighter, but also a conniver. He had to wonder what was going on inside her pretty little head, and he was worried it involved him and his situation. Ty had confirmed Ludwig had been recently paroled, and said he'd look into the thug's connections. As much as Forrest didn't want the Nightingales involved, he was grateful for their affiliations. Being a former federal agent, Ty had acquaintances across the nation who had information they'd only share with other agents.

The front door opened behind Forrest and Jacob stepped out. The man said one word as his gaze wandered toward the car pulling out of the parking lot. "Telephone."

Forrest pulled his gaze away from Norma Rose's Cadillac and asked, "Mother?"

Jacob shook his head. "Your aunt Shirley."

Instantly concerned, Forrest pulled open the door and went directly to his office. Shirley rarely called. He picked up the receiver lying on his desk. "This is Forrest. Aunt Shirley, are you there?"

"Yes, Forrest," she said, quiet as a whisper even through the phone lines. "It's good to hear your voice."

"Yours, too," he replied, sitting down. "Is something wrong? Is Uncle Silas all right?"

"He's fine, we both are. Looking forward to a visit from you when you have time."

"I'll make it down there before long," he said. "I promise."

"I'm sure you will, but I didn't call to press you into a visit," she said softly. "I'm calling because your mother asked me to."

"My mother?" Forrest stopped at that revelation. His mother and aunt hadn't spoken in years.

"I was as surprised as you by the call," Shirley said. "She's tried to call you, but you're never home."

"I've been busy," he responded, "and have tried calling her back."

"I'm sure you have, darling. I thought about not calling, but felt I had to. She wants you to come and get her. In your plane."

Forrest had no intention of leaving, but if push came to shove, he would make the flight to California. "I'll give her a call, and I'll be down to see you soon. Tell Uncle Silas hello from me."

The silence on the other end of the phone said his aunt wasn't ready to end the conversation, but he was. If his mother called her sister, things were happening in California. Things he needed to know about.

"You two take care," he said into the receiver.

"We will," his aunt said. "And you be careful, Forrest. You know how we felt about you coming home."

"I know," he said. "But it's something I had to do."

He said goodbye and hung up before the conversation went any further. He had no idea if his mother had told Shirley about Galen's pending release, but he hoped not. His aunt and uncle didn't need more worries on their plate. They'd questioned his mother's choices for years and had tried several times to make her leave Galen.

Sitting back, Forrest glanced around the room. When he'd arrived, it had been completely torn apart. He'd assumed, since it had been Galen's office, that people had been looking for anything of value, or opium. Now he knew it had to do with those counterfeit California banknotes. While showing Ty the bowling alley, they'd discussed how Galen had been forced out of the opium business long ago. His arrest records documented human trafficking in connection with money laundering, but trafficking didn't hold much weight. An act had been put in place last year by the League of Nations. Ty claimed the government was only upholding the trafficking law in order to combat the influx of immigrants. Therefore, he felt the counterfeiting was the direction they had to stay focused on. Ty also said there wasn't enough evidence to charge Galen with counterfeiting, which was why he was petitioning for release and might get it.

Slapping a hand down on his desk, Forrest fought the guilt surging inside him. If he had paid more attention when he was a kid, he'd know more now. The main thing he remembered was how the Plantation had always been full of young women. They'd filled the third floor and he'd heard them crying through the ceiling in his bedroom. He spun around in his chair, to the wall of shelves filled with various books. He'd never given the books much thought before, but now he scanned the titles. A lower shelf contained a volume that leaped out at him. *The History of Money.*

Forrest grabbed the book and contemplated calling his mother. He'd come to understand she was his greatest weakness, and he also knew she wouldn't give him any answers. He knew his second greatest weakness, too. She'd just climbed into her sister's Cadillac. Twyla hadn't even questioned where her car had gone. Perhaps Norma Rose had told her they'd given Bronco a ride into town and he'd taken it back to the resort.

Still, Twyla—the Twyla he knew—would have questioned that.

"Blast it," he growled. She was trying to throw the wool over his eyes. Grabbing the phone, he concluded he was blind enough.

When a voice on the other end answered, knowing the drill, Forrest said, "Roger Nightingale, please. It's Forrest Reynolds, I'll hold."

Roger wasted no time on greetings. "Bronco just delivered Twyla's car."

"Was he followed?" Forrest wanted to know. "No."

"Twyla, Ty and Norma Rose should be there shortly." Drawing in a breath, Forrest said, "I need a favor, Roger."

"You name it."

"I need a couple of men. Maybe Bronco and someone else. I'll pay you for their time."

"Like hell you will," Roger said. "We're in

this together. Bronco and Tuck will be there in ten minutes. What did you discover?"

"Nothing, really," Forrest admitted. "But Nick Ludwig was out at your place last night and he was here today. He'd been in jail with Galen."

"Ty told me that before he and Norma Rose left," Roger said. "I can't say I know Ludwig, but if he was here last night, Palooka George knows him. Ninety percent of what happens around here goes through Chicago."

"Maybe," Forrest said, "but Galen alienated himself from that stream long ago, which is why he had to go through California."

"That's true," Roger said, "but someone knows something."

"Ludwig knows something," Forrest said. "I need Bronco and Tuck to help search for him."

"They'll find him," Roger said. "I'll talk to George right now. I'll let you know if I find out anything."

"Thanks, Roger," Forrest said.

"I know it hasn't been easy for you, Forrest, and calling me for help wasn't easy, either. But I'm glad you did. We're in this together, son, and this time, I have your back. You can be sure of that."

Roger was right. It hadn't been easy to ask for help. If not for Twyla, and fearing what she might do, he might not have called Roger. Disconnecting that call, Forrest dialed another number and flipped open the book while waiting. After three rings a voice answered.

"Hello, Mother," he said.

Hours later, the ringing of the phone woke Forrest. It was a moment before he realized he'd fallen asleep on the couch in the office. The book tumbled off his chest as he swung his feet onto the floor. He crossed the room, and the faint light of dawn entering the window made his heart skip a beat as he wondered who could be calling this early.

He grabbed the phone. "Hello?"

"Forrest, it's Scooter. I thought you might like to know I just saw Dave Sutton's Chevy drive by."

Rubbing his head, trying to wake up and make sense of Scooter's call, Forrest asked, "So?" The whereabouts of Twyla's uncle was no concern of his.

"Dave wasn't driving the car," Scooter said. "Twyla was."

Forrest was suddenly wide-awake. "What direction?"

"Toward town."

"Thanks, Scooter." Forrest hung up and headed for the door.

He cursed all the way to the back door and across the parking lot. This was exactly what he didn't want happening. Twyla had no idea of the danger she was in. Ludwig was out there somewhere. With Bronco and Tuck looking for him, that left fewer men at the resort to keep an eye on her. Why hadn't he realized that?

He jumped in the roadster and fired up the engine. Gravel sprayed as he floored the gas pedal and shot around the building, his mind trying to fathom where she'd be going at this time of the morning.

Half questioning his vision when he recognized a blue car coming up the road, Forrest hit the gas harder. The Chevy turned into the nightclub's parking lot. Forrest slammed on the brake pedal, blocking the car in. He cut the roadster's engine and jumped out over the door. "What are you doing?"

"What are you doing?" Twyla shouted, climbing out of the Chevy. "Skipping town?"

Forrest was torn between hugging and shaking her. Opting to do neither, he grabbed her arm as they met near the front of the Chevy. "Get in my car."

"Why? Where are we going?"

"I'm taking you home."

She dug her heels into the gravel. "Not until you answer a few questions."

Grasping her waist with both hands, he hoisted her off the ground and flipped her over his shoulder.

"Put me down," she shouted, while pounding his back. "I mean it, Forrest."

"I mean it, too." Thankful he'd never put the top back on his car, he plunked her into the roadster's passenger seat. "I'm taking you home."

"Oh, no, you're not."

She'd popped up like a child's toy. Forrest grabbed her shoulders to push her back onto the seat. "Oh, yes, I am."

"No, you're not." Her fingers grabbed hold of the frame of the windshield.

He couldn't push her back down, not without hurting her. "Let go and sit down, Twyla."

"No."

She was as stubborn as a mule. He'd always known that. Forcing her to do something had never worked, so he let go of her shoulders and took a step back. "Fine." He started walking toward the Chevy.

"Where are you going?"

Forrest didn't bother answering. He climbed into the Chevy, which was still running, and pulled it to the side of the parking lot. Pocketing the keys, he climbed out.

She was still standing in his car, with her arms crossed, glaring at him over the windshield. "Did I interrupt your escape?"

"I'd like to escape, all right," he said ruefully. "From you."

Her glare turned even more bitter.

He walked to the roadster, opened the driver's door and climbed in while clamping his teeth together to keep his curse silent. He should have known better. The key no longer hung in the ignition. Instead, Twyla dangled it between her finger and thumb.

"I will go home after we talk," she said smartly.

Forrest leaned back and crossed his arms. "About what?" There was no way he would tell her about the counterfeiting, and he prayed neither Roger nor Ty had.

She plopped onto the passenger seat and splayed her pink skirt over her knees. "Where were you going this early in the morning?"

"I heard you'd stolen your uncle's car and was on my way to find you," he answered honestly.

"I didn't steal—"

"Does Dave know you have his Chevy?"

"No, but—"

"Does anyone know you left?"

"No." Her eyes snapped to meet his. "No one does. How did you know?"

"I have my ways."

She glared at him harder for a short time and then turned to look straight ahead. "Norma Rose says you were planning on leaving town." Her lip quivered slightly. "The night of your graduation. Even before everything else happened, you were planning on leaving. Were you?"

Not about to admit all that had happened that day, Forrest simply answered, "Yes."

"Why?"

"I'd graduated. It was time I headed out on my own."

"Without telling anyone?" she asked quietly.

"I'd told Norma Rose."

"And she was the only one that mattered."

Forrest's stomach fell. Twyla had said that so softly he'd barely heard it. He couldn't tell her she was wrong. That he'd discovered the only way to assure her and her sisters would be safe from Galen was to leave. The protection he'd thought he'd been providing them all those years had in fact put them in more danger. After that day, he was certain Galen would harm them, just to get back at him.

Anger stiffened his spine. That wouldn't happen again. Never again. "It doesn't matter now, does it?"

She turned his way slowly, and the glistening in her eyes, that of unshed tears, almost ripped him in two. "Yes, Forrest, it does." Handing him the roadster's key with one hand, she reached for the door handle with the other.

Stretching his arm in front of her, he stopped her from opening the car door. "I'll drive you home."

"There's no need."

"Yes, there is."

"Dave will need his car," she said, rather submissively.

He didn't like that. Twyla rarely gave in. Not without a much more gallant effort. "I'll give him a ride back to get it."

She let go of the door handle and slumped against the car seat. "Fine."

The ride to the resort was cold, but the chill had nothing to do with the cool early morning temperature or the open top car. Twyla didn't say a word, not even when he parked the roadster in front of Dave Sutton's bungalow—one of the many cabins surrounding the resort building. As she clasped the door handle, he laid a hand on her knee.

"Your father's leaving for Chicago today, to go get Ginger, and I'd appreciate it if you'd stay close to home while he's gone." It was the most he could say.

She closed her eyes for a brief moment before pushing the door all the way open. "There are several things I'd appreciate, Forrest."

"Twyla—"

"Thanks for the ride home," she interrupted, climbing out.

He knew better than to go after her.

Chapter Eleven

On Tuesday morning, Twyla sat in the office, not doing much of anything, just as she had the day before. She couldn't concentrate, not on her duties. The fact Forrest had planned on leaving years before was front and center in her mind. He'd never planned on telling her about it.

It shouldn't surprise her. It didn't, really. But it did have a profound effect on her. It was almost as if her heart was breaking all over again.

She hated that feeling. His disappearance had changed so many things in her life. She was not willing to experience that again.

The doorknob clicked and Twyla grabbed a pen to hold over the paper lying on the desk. The paper was blank, but she wanted it to appear as if she'd been working.

Norma Rose walked in, and after closing the door she laid a glossy magazine, open to a specific page, on the desk. "What do you think of that one?"

Twyla laid down the pen to lift up the magazine so the sun shining through the window didn't distort the picture. The gown was gorgeous, white with a dropped waistline and covered with lace, but Twyla pointed out, "It's a wedding a dress."

"I know it's a wedding dress," Norma Rose said. "Ty and I have decided to get married on the eighteenth of July."

"That's only a month away," Twyla said, setting down the magazine. Marriage was not something she'd see. Not in this lifetime.

"I know it will go fast," Norma Rose said, "but it seems like forever to me."

Twyla had admitted, more than once, that Norma Rose had changed lately. The transformation had amazed her. Right now, in her state, her sister's starry eyes and dreamy expression filled her with the ugliest jealousy she'd ever experienced.

Norma Rose picked up the snow globe that sat prominently on the desk. "Ty's taking me to Niagara Falls for our honeymoon and I can hardly wait."

Twyla examined Norma Rose more closely, including the way her sister stared at the globe.

How had her sister found such happiness? "You're really in love with Ty, aren't you?"

"Yes." Norma Rose set down the globe and sighed as she sat down in one of the chairs beside the table near the window. "I am."

Loving a man wasn't what Twyla didn't understand. "How'd you make him love you in return?"

The smile on Norma Rose's face was serene. "That's the wonderful part. I didn't. He just does." She sighed dreamily. "I wake up every morning thinking about him, and I go to bed every night thinking about him. And I know he does the same."

Twyla refrained from pointing out that was because Norma Rose was in Ty's cabin most every night and morning. Her sister thought no one knew that, and as it was Norma Rose, no one was about to admit otherwise. Besides, that theory held no creditability. Twyla had spent half her life or more thinking about Forrest every morning and every night. He, on the other hand, hadn't even planned on telling her he was leaving.

Norma Rose giggled slightly. "It's like knowing the sun will come up in the morning. I can't explain it." Norma Rose folded her hands over her heart. "It's like his heart talks to mine. I can look at him and know what he's thinking." Shaking her head, she continued, "It's hard to explain, but I know Ty will always be there for me. Like we know Father will always be there for us. But this is different. It's stronger. I know Ty needs me as much as I need him."

Her sister giggled again, and Twyla's stomach clenched as if she wanted to throw up.

"I didn't feel that way at first," Norma Rose said. "I didn't even like him."

"Because he is—was—a federal agent?"

"I didn't know that then." Norma Rose stood up. "But now I know we'll work out whatever comes about together. I've never been more sure of anything in my life."

This entire conversation seemed a bit far-fetched to Twyla. "And you just woke up one morning knowing that?" she asked, a bit sourly.

"Yes, I guess I did," Norma Rose replied. "Now, what do you think of the dress?"

Twyla picked up the magazine again. Talking to someone who was so love-struck she was crazy wouldn't get anyone anywhere. "It's lovely, but there's not enough time to order it, if that's what you're thinking."

"I won't order it. I'll go into Minneapolis and buy one like it." She took the magazine back. "Want to go with me?"

"Sure," Twyla agreed—she'd say anything to be left alone again. "But I can't today. Josie is at a Ladies Aid meeting all day."

"I know," Norma Rose said. "We'll find a

day all three of us can go together. It'll be fun, and you two will need to pick out bridesmaid dresses. I have to write out all the invitations first. I thought I'd do that today, while you're working on the Fourth of July party. The Fourth is on a Saturday this year, so people will be expecting a huge bash from us."

The Fourth of July party was the next big event for the resort and she should be excited. Josie had already ordered a large supply of fireworks and hired Scooter to light them. Twyla was supposed to secure a musician for the night.

"I thought we'd ask Slim again," she said off the top of her head. "He did a good job the last two weeks."

"He's also Forrest's musician. I only asked to hire him for two weeks."

The mention of Forrest did several things to Twyla. Mostly, it brought back a bit of her spirit. If he could just up and leave town whenever he wanted, she could do whatever she wanted, too. Like throw the best parties for miles around. "I'll ask him," Twyla said.

Norma Rose shook her head. "No, Forrest needs Slim. He's likely planning an event for the Plantation that night."

"Ours will be better," Twyla said out of spite.

Norma Rose frowned. "We aren't in competition with Forrest. The crowd he pulls in is of the younger set, and he's sticking with the law, doesn't offer alcohol of any kind. He could make more money if he did, but he doesn't want the place to resemble anything from the past."

"You sure seem awfully forgiving all of a sudden," Twyla said, feeling no mercy toward Forrest whatsoever.

"I don't hate Forrest," Norma Rose said, "if that's what you're thinking. I never have, and the Plantation isn't competition for us. No place can rival Nightingale's. Really, the two of us should work together. Our guests would enjoy bowling and billiards, especially in the winter, and I'm sure plenty of Forrest's guests would enjoy the amenities we offer. His older guests, that is. We don't want teenagers out here drinking. A partnership could help Forrest with his dire financial situation."

Twyla had to get one thing straight. "You want to partner up with Forrest?"

Norma Rose shrugged. "Maybe not me, but the two of you were always close. He might listen if you suggested it."

Twyla couldn't even form a comeback to that suggestion. Not right now.

"Think about it," Norma Rose said. "In the meantime, who else is there for our party? And don't say Wayne Sears."

Despite everything, the way Norma Rose

cringed made a tiny giggle tickle Twyla's throat. Wayne had performed at the resort right after Brock had left, and wasn't the best musician on earth, to say the least. However, the night had been successful, and Twyla decided to remind Norma Rose of that. "He did a great job with our impromptu dance-off."

Norma Rose grinned. "People sure did love that. They'd probably love it again. But you made that event a success, not Wayne."

"My feet were killing me the next morning."

"Mine, too," Norma Rose said, her smile growing. "Let's do it again. Call Wayne and book him for the fourth and we'll advertise a dance-off!"

"All right," Twyla agreed. Planning the event would certainly take her mind off other things. "But you and Ty can't win this time. People will think it's rigged."

"True enough." Norma Rose clapped her hands together. "We could build an outdoor dance floor and light fireworks at the end of the competition. Josie already has that all set up."

"And we could hang Chinese lanterns from wires," Twyla suggested, growing excited. This was exactly what she wanted, to plan and participate in fun and fascinating parties. "Josie's already ordered several dozen of those."

"Let's go outside," Norma Rose said. "Figure

out where we want the dance floor so the ground-skeepers can start building it."

They deduced the large area from the balcony to the water fountain would serve perfectly. After the fountain, the hill started sloping toward the lake, but gradually enough that a few tables could still be set up around the floor. They were standing next to the fountain, and Norma Rose was talking about whether lights could be installed in the fountain when a familiar buzz sounded.

Twyla's heart started thumping before she looked skyward, and increased when she recognized the tiny yellow plane in the distance. It looked smaller than a bird from where she stood. She knew Forrest couldn't see her, but she clearly remembered what it was like. Flying. Looking down on the earth below. Once again she was reminded of Norma Rose's snow globe and the miniature waterfall it held. "I bet Niagara Falls is going to be beautiful in person."

"Ty promises it will be," Norma Rose said. "You enjoyed flying with Forrest, didn't you?"

The trees now obscured her view, but she could still faintly hear the buzz of the plane and imagined Forrest gliding toward the ground near his hangar. "It was amazing," Twyla admitted.

"Ty hasn't learned anything new," Norma Rose said. "About Galen."

Chagrin balled in Twyla's stomach. She'd forgotten all that Forrest had going on in his life. All he'd always had going on. "You're sure Ty would tell you if he did?"

"I'm sure," Norma Rose answered.

Forrest may not love her, but he was her friend. Always had been. "I, uh—" Digging deep, she tried to come up with an excuse to leave. If she hurried, she could catch him at his hangar. "I need to put gas in my car," she said. "I didn't think I'd get a chance to today, with Josie being gone, but since you're here, would you mind if I drove up to Scooter's station?"

"Ask one of the men to put gas in for you," Norma Rose said.

"I normally would," Twyla admitted. "But this way I can ask Scooter about the fireworks and if he knows if we can have lights put in the fountain."

"Call him."

"You know he's always too busy to talk on the phone." Twyla curled her toes, excitement zipping up and down her insides at the prospect of seeing Forrest, if just for a minute.

Shaking her head, Norma Rose said, "Fine, go, but don't be gone long."

"I won't be," Twyla assured, turning around. Over her shoulder, she added, "I'll call Wayne as soon as I get back."

She took a shortcut through the ballroom and

out the front door, as close to sprinting as one could get without actually running. Walter, the main groundskeeper, was at the garage where the family cars were kept.

"Going somewhere?" he asked.

"Just up to Scooter's station," she said. Walter most likely knew her car had a full tank of gas. "I have to talk to him about our Fourth of July party."

"Does Norma Rose know you're leaving?"

With their father in Chicago, his men were extra cautious of any and all comings and goings. Furthermore, old habits died hard; Walter had stopped her from leaving when she hadn't had permission more than once over the years. "Yes, she does," Twyla said. Every minute wasted put Forrest that much closer to his hangar. "I won't be gone long."

Walter's look was skeptical, but he moved to open the large swinging door. Twyla scurried to her car and started the engine, ready to back out when Walter swung open the second door.

She considered taking the back road, as it was faster than the main one, but Walter was sure to question that, so she turned and made her way through the parking lot, driving so slowly her teeth clenched. As soon as she was out of sight, she gunned the car and tightened her hold on the steering wheel when the back of her coupe fishtailed.

She fought the wheel, and eventually won the battle of keeping the car on the road. Slowing a bit, she maneuvered the rest of the curves without any trouble and bounced over the railroad tracks a short while later.

Forrest had been angry with her yesterday morning, and might be again, but so be it. He needed help in assuring his father remained behind bars, and that's what friends did. They helped each other. She could live with the fact he'd never planned on telling her he was leaving, but she couldn't live with the thought of Galen hurting him again.

The highway was clear both ways, and she hit the gas harder after taking a left toward Lester's farm. A second later, it hit her that someone might call Scooter to double-check she put gas in her car.

Flustered, she hit the brake and cranked the wheel. The car spun so fast she grew dizzy, but once again she kept it on the road. Now facing the other direction, she laid her foot hard on the gas. A mile later she cranked the wheel again, to pull into the fueling station.

To her utmost astonishment a large Closed sign hung on the door. Dang. She'd wasted valuable time for nothing.

Gravel sprayed from beneath her tires as she rounded the gas pump and headed toward the highway again. A couple of miles later, she slowed her speed, watching the side roads to make out the exact one she and Forrest had used on Sunday. When her heart skipped a beat, she turned, knowing it had to be the one.

This road was as rough as a washboard, but Twyla had to drive slowly anyway, watching carefully for the field road that led to Forrest's hangar. It seemed as if she went a hundred miles, and was just about to turn around, figuring she'd missed the turn, when she saw it.

Little more than two tire trails in the grass, the field road wasn't very long. In no time she pulled up next to Forrest's roadster.

Climbing out of her car, she examined his. How could a man have a car that nice, and an airplane, and a bowling alley, and be broke? Perhaps that was why. All those things cost money.

The hangar doors were open, and no doubt having heard her pull in, Forrest, dressed in his flyboy jacket, hat and boots, was leaning against one of them. "What are you doing here?"

"Aren't you a little bit excited to see me?" she asked. Considering the way her insides were leaping, she was a lot more than a little happy to see him.

He shook his head. "Your father should keep you handcuffed."

She ignored his jibe. His grin said more. He was happy. He just didn't want to admit it. Maybe hearts could talk to each other, just like Norma Rose had said.

"I heard your plane," she said, arriving at the hangar. He'd gone back inside and was hooking the fuel nozzle back onto the barrel. "And thought I'd come to see where you'd gone."

"Just for a short flight," he said.

"Where to? Why?" Twyla couldn't help but wish he'd asked her to accompany him. She'd have gone, even though her father had said she couldn't go flying until after he returned from Chicago.

"North a ways," Forrest said, pulling the barrel toward the door. "For a friend."

"For a friend? Who?"

He shook his head.

Walking beside him, she shook her head too, and wished she'd taken the time to reapply her lipstick or run a comb through her hair. "Fine, don't tell me."

"I have no intention of telling you anything," he said.

She rolled her eyes, but wasn't surprised. There had to be a way to show him she was more than a pretty face. That she had a mind and could help him in all situations. Noticing one of the concrete blocks the barrel sat on was tipped slightly upward, she hurried ahead to push it back in place. Stomping on it didn't work, so she kneeled down, but couldn't budge it with her hands, either. When Forrest crouched down beside her, she said, "There must be something under it."

"I noticed that one was loose the other day. Here, let me see. A root might have pushed a rock up."

She scooted over, but when Forrest lifted the edge of the block, she leaned closer. "What is that?"

"What's what?" Forrest asked.

"That," she said, pointing and moving aside so he could peer under the block.

"I don't know." He shoved the block aside and then scraped at the dirt. "It looks like a handle." Forrest lifted up another block. "There wasn't anything here when I dug out this area."

"Why do you put your gas tank here?" she asked.

"Because it would get too hot inside. Here it has some shade, and is far enough away that if any fuel leaked out, it wouldn't be under the plane, where it could catch fire."

He'd removed three other blocks while talking, and was now digging with his hands.

"It's a suitcase," he said.

For the first time in years, Twyla didn't consider the damage she might do to her freshly painted nails, and dug beside him. "It's like buried treasure."

"Hardly anyone knows about this place," Forrest said. "And I know nothing was here when I laid the blocks."

"Maybe the tree roots pushed it up," she said.

"Tree roots wouldn't have pushed this up."

They'd dug all along the edges and were now digging down. "It's huge," Twyla said. "I didn't know they made suitcases this big."

"That's because you're used to the little one your uncle Dave carries samples of whiskey in," Forrest said teasingly. "This is the size people pack clothes in for trips."

She scrunched her nose at him. "I've seen other suitcases. People bring them to the resort all the time."

"Then you'll see," he said, still digging. "They're about the size of this one. You've just never had to dig one out of the ground before."

"You're right," she said, "as usual."

He laughed, and so did she, her heart overflowing. Finding a suitcase like this was fitting. Everything with Forrest was an adventure.

Once they had dug all the way around it, she

leaned back while Forrest pulled the suitcase upward. "I don't know what's in it, but it's heavy."

Twyla grabbed the bottom of the suitcase, pushing for all her worth. The last bit of ground seizing the suitcase crumbled and she and the case tumbled against Forrest. The suitcase landed on his lap as he grabbed her arms, keeping her from falling on top of it.

"You all right?" he asked.

She couldn't even nod, not when she was close enough to see the dark centers of his eyes. Her gaze wandered down to his mouth, and her entire being wanted to lean forward and taste his lips all over again. If only she could make him love her.

"Twyla?"

"Fine," she said, her mind snapping to attention. She couldn't make him love her years ago, and couldn't now. "I'm fine. What's in the case?"

"I don't know yet."

The look in his eyes stole her breath away. He still had a hold of her arms, but it was an invisible connection she felt more. Something strong and powerful, and as old as time. Accepting she'd never be able to fight it—the love she felt for Forrest—she closed her eyes.

The kiss didn't startle her. It was exactly what she wanted. A slow, tender merging of their lips. But it was short. Much too short.

"Let's see what's in it," Forrest said as his lips left hers.

Convinced nothing in that case could be as amazing as kissing him, Twyla almost said it could wait, but didn't. Instead she reminded herself that nothing was forever. Even Forrest. He was only here for a short time again. However, rather than moping about it, she was going to take it for what it was. Enjoy every moment to the fullest, and treasure those memories when he disappeared again.

"What are you grinning about?" He let go of her arms, after easing her backward, to where she sat on her knees again.

Gravel dug into her shins and she glanced down. Dirt covered the front of her white-and-pink-striped dress, enough that it was sure to be stained forever. Not even that mattered. "Because I want to know what's in the suitcase," she said. "Open it."

Forrest shook his head, but then let out a low whistle as he lifted the lid.

Twyla crawled around to peer in the case. "What are those?" She gestured to what looked like a box of metal bricks.

Forrest held one up. "They're engraved printing plates." Turning it slightly, he added, "From the American National Bank of Los Angeles."

Excitement laced his words. She picked up a

block, but couldn't read it. Everything was backward. "They're what?"

Forrest was looking through the case. "Printing plates," he said. "To print money."

Twyla surveyed the piece she held more closely. "Money?"

"Before the *Federal Reserve Act* was enacted in 1913, banks printed their own money. All their plates were to have been turned in, so I doubt these are originals, but I'd bet they're exact copies."

"How do you know all that?"

He grinned. "You, the girl who claims to love money, doesn't know the history of it?"

She shook her head.

"Money became a necessity when trading commodities, fish for corn, or bread for meat, became too cumbersome to keep up," Forrest said. "First there were coins, and then paper money. Local banks would print notes for people to exchange based on the collateral they gave the bank, but a lot of the bank notes were only good in specific regions. During the Civil War, Congress created demand notes. They were different from banknotes, because they were backed by the government and payable upon demand in coin at certain treasury locations, and legal tender across the entire United States, no matter where they were printed or spent. Later those became U.S. notes and the National Currency Bureau was formed to oversee national banks across the nation, who printed national banknotes."

She was listening, but in truth, was a bit lost. "So these aren't any good?"

"Yes, and no," Forrest said, placing both the bar she held and his into the suitcase and shutting the lid. "Bills are made of paper, which eventually wears out, making a need for new ones to be printed. However, old bills show up all the time. You could have some and spend them as easily as new ones. It's when a bank gets them that they are finally destroyed and replaced by the Federal Reserve. So if someone had these, and the right machinery, and the right paper and ink, they could print bills and easily pass them off as real."

"Counterfeiting," Twyla said, now understanding things, at least in part. She'd always been amazed by how smart Forrest was, but this time his intelligence had gone beyond her.

"Yes, counterfeiting." He stood and helped her to her feet before he picked up the suitcase. "Come on. I have to get these to town."

They had yet to turn around when a voice proclaimed, "Not so fast."

Chapter Twelve

Forrest knew without turning around who was behind him and Twyla. Nasty Nick Ludwig. Bronco and Tuck had searched far and wide but hadn't found hide nor hair of the thug. As far as he knew, Bronco and Tuck were still looking. Forrest would have been looking, too, if Scooter hadn't shown up at the Plantation earlier today, needing a fast ride to Duluth to fetch Josie from the jail.

He glanced down at Twyla, and as crazy as it seemed in his own mind, he wished she'd been locked up with her sister today. Then they would both be on their way home with Scooter right now.

"Go ahead and turn around there, flyboy," Ludwig said. "But put down the suitcase."

Without much choice, considering he didn't know if Ludwig was armed, or alone, Forrest set down the suitcase. He put an arm around

Twyla before spinning them both around at the same time. She was shivering and he tugged her a bit closer, settling his gaze on Ludwig and the three thugs at his side. All four men had firearms drawn. Not small pistols, but long Tommy guns.

Though the other three didn't have a distinguishing scar like Nasty Nick, their scowls gave them the overall appearance of bottom-barrel boys. As slimy as an eelpout and with fewer morals, they were just the type Galen would latch on to.

Twyla shifted slightly, and Forrest glanced at her face, which was turned up to his. Despite the fear in her eyes, and her quivering lips, she whispered, "I can take the two on the left if you can take the two on the right."

She really was something. Everything except keeping her safe escaped from his mind. "Don't move. Those are machine guns," he whispered.

"I know."

"Stop talking," Ludwig shouted. "And step away from the suitcase."

The tree behind them was the only one for several yards, and the gas barrel beside it was one more reason he didn't want guns to start firing. Keeping his arm around Twyla, he took a step, but paused when Ludwig shouted again.

"Not that way." Waving his gun in the opposite direction from the hangar, Nick added, "That way."

Forrest guided Twyla sideways several steps, stopping when Ludwig said that was far enough. The man then instructed two of his thugs to get the suitcase.

"I figured you'd lead me to it sooner or later," Ludwig said. "Once I ditched those torpedoes you put on my tail."

Forrest could only hope Bronco or Tuck hadn't been ditched and would show up soon. Only Jacob knew he was out here, and he suspected even fewer knew Twyla was here. "Take the suitcase, Ludwig, and get out of here."

"Oh, I'll take it all right, and leave, but you and your little tomato are coming with me." He winked at Twyla. "Without her, I wouldn't have found you. Thanks, doll."

"I'm not your doll," Twyla snapped. The fire disappeared from her eyes as she turned and whispered, "I didn't lead…no one followed… I didn't think—"

"Shh," Forrest said, tugging her closer. "You wouldn't have known."

"But I should have," she said despondently. "I knew he was the reason you had Bronco come and get my car on Sunday."

"It's all right," Forrest offered. "Just do as they say. We'll think of something."

"I told you two to stop talking," Ludwig snarled.

"You know who she is, Ludwig," Forrest said. "You harm a hair on her head, and The Night will see your days are ended."

"The Night is in Chicago," Nick said.

"You think that will stop him from seeing you're killed?" Forrest wished he had more to threaten the man with, but he wasn't carrying any iron and with four machine guns pointed at them, their overall outlook was bleak.

"The Night doesn't scare me any more than your pappy did," Ludwig said, looking at Forrest. "He talked big, but when it came down to it, Reynolds didn't have enough guts to smear a windshield."

"You killed him?" Twyla asked.

Ludwig laughed. "I wish, doll, but I couldn't. Not before knowing if he was lying to me. Turns out he wasn't just singing." Gesturing toward the grassy field road, he demanded, "Start walking."

"To where?" Forrest asked.

"You'll see soon enough," Ludwig said.

Keeping one arm around Twyla and her tucked closely to his side, Forrest started walking. He knew this area down to the last stick, having seen it from the air, and that was more disconcerting than comforting. The few clumps of trees offered little protection and the wide open pastures were too big to run across.

Ludwig, swollen with pride at having the upper hand, started yakking. "Your pappy and I shared a jail cell for a time. When he first started yapping, I didn't pay him much mind, but then he told me about this one-time banker who stockpiled up a bunch of paper and ink the government issued for printing the bank's money and had a copy of the printing plates made for his private use." He laughed loudly. "That there was information I could use."

Forrest wished the man would shut up, but at the same time he wanted to know more. Alone he would have had more options. With Twyla by his side, he had to stay in a position to keep her safe.

"While the banker printed money, your pappy sent it overseas, buying girls and claiming he'd make them film stars. It was a good game. American money is good worldwide. Even old money."

"What happened?" Twyla asked.

Forrest cringed at the same time he felt pride swelling. She wasn't whimpering or begging to be released as some girls might. Not Twyla. Head up, she was marching forward and, just like him, scanning the area for a possible escape route.

Ludwig laughed again. "Your pappy happened, doll. The Night set the hounds on Reynolds. The banker got scared and Reynolds got greedy. He didn't tell me that. I figured it out, and no old bootlegger scares me."

Twyla stiffened, and Forrest whispered, "Just keep walking. He's trying to get to you."

"I know," she said quietly. "And you."

Forrest squeezed her shoulder. "Just don't let it show."

She nodded slightly.

"I'm smarter than both of your pappies," Ludwig continued. "I had Reynolds's arrest record checked out. No one ever learned of the money-making. He was arrested for human trafficking and money laundering. He was exchanging too much Mexican money into American bills for all those little girls he liked to buy and sell. He'd sold a boatload of whores and shouldn't have tried to exchange the currency so fast."

Ludwig's laugh fit his name—it was as nasty as anything could sound. "I told your old pappy I had a mouthpiece who could get his charges dropped, the same one who got me out." After another laugh, he said, "I didn't kill those men I was accused of killing. They just got tangled up in more chain than they could swim with."

Ludwig was just the kind Galen would take up with and promise a piece of the action to. Forrest bit his lip as he glanced around. The field road curved around a line of trees and he saw two cars parked on the road and backed up to head straight for the highway. Older models with no back doors.

Twyla hissed and leaned a bit closer. "I thought I recognized the man beside Nasty Nick," she said. "That blue one is his car. He tried selling Norma Rose a vacuum cleaner yesterday."

Forrest internally kicked himself. He'd sent Bronco and Tuck out searching when the thugs had been right under their noses. "Was he alone?"

She nodded slightly. "He stayed overnight in one of the cabins."

"A traveling salesman who could afford to stay at the resort?"

"That's why I remember him."

Pain shot up Forrest's spine as the barrel of a gun rammed into his back.

"You two don't listen very well," Ludwig barked. "I told you to shut up. I was telling you about your pappy."

Twyla attempted to spin around, but Forrest stopped her. He, too, wanted to turn around and grab Nasty Nick by his shirt as he'd done at the Plantation a couple of days ago, but he willed his patience to remain intact.

Side by side, they continued forward as he attempted to form a plan. All of his combat training had taught him that when outnumbered, do as you were told. Which was useless. Soldiers normally didn't have a woman at their side.

"Don't you want to know how my story ends?" Ludwig asked as they neared the car. Chortling again, he said, "I've got a partner looking for the banker, but whether we find him or not, now that we have these plates, I don't need your pappy. One phone call and my mouthpiece will drop the case."

Galen's case was the least of Forrest's worries. Once he and Twyla were inside the cars, their chance of escape dimmed. Not that it had ever shone brightly.

Jabbing another hard nudge in the center of Forrest's back, Ludwig instructed, "Stand over there. You," he said, gesturing toward the man carrying the suitcase, "put that in the backseat of my car, and you," he said to the second one, "open the trunk."

The third man, the one Twyla recognized, curled his lips into a wicked smile. Forrest, clenching one hand into a fist, could almost feel it driving into the man's jaw.

As if he sensed that, the thug turned his smile to Forrest while raising the barrel of his gun.

"You two take that car." Ludwig was still talking to the other men. "Leave it at the train station. We'll meet at the rendezvous spot tomorrow."

Frowning, the two men glanced at each other.

"That way, if anyone asks, you won't know what happened to these two," Ludwig explained.

The men nodded.

Forrest was encouraged to know the two men were as stupid as they looked, and optimism rose at the thought of taking out two men instead of four. That was far more doable.

"Don't be spouting off to anyone, either," Ludwig barked.

The two goons nodded their heads again and scrambled into the blue car.

The car roared to life and the tires sprayed pebbles as it took off. Nasty Nick and the other man laughed. "Idiots," Ludwig said before turning his full attention on Forrest and Twyla.

"You two get in the trunk," he said, waving his gun. "Hurry up, unless you need a bullet to help you."

Forrest, buying an ounce of time, waved toward the tree line up the road. "Dac Lester will hear the gunfire. He's in the field on the other side of those trees." He hadn't seen anyone in the field from the air, but needed to get a glance inside the trunk. As the men took their eyes off him for a moment, he scanned the trunk. Elation bubbled. Just as he'd hoped, an iron rim tool lay next to a spare inner tube.

"It won't bother me to take out one more person," Ludwig growled. "Now, get in the trunk."

With no intention of climbing in, Forrest stepped forward. Twyla grabbed his arm, but before she could speak, he shook his head and hoped she read more from his expression. This was it, their one and only chance. If they climbed in that trunk, it was all over.

As if following instructions, Forrest leaned into the trunk, placing both hands on the floor and twisting as if he needed to climb in sideways. Glancing up at Twyla, he silently told her to get ready to run. She didn't so much as blink an eye, yet he knew she understood him.

Ludwig and his partner stepped closer, ready to give him a helping shove, which was also exactly what Forrest had wanted to happen.

Every muscle she had was trembling, but Twyla willed herself to remain still. Forrest had a plan. Exactly what that might be, she had no clue, but she trusted him.

However, when both Nasty Nick and his thug lunged forward to push Forrest into the trunk, she couldn't help but scream.

Forrest bounded upward, swinging something that hit first the fake vacuum cleaner salesman and then Nasty Nick on the head. As the men stumbled, she sprang into action, scrambling for the gun Ludwig had dropped. A second blow from Forrest with whatever he'd grabbed out of the trunk sent Ludwig to the ground. Twyla grabbed the gun, but having no idea how to fire the thing, she started kicking dirt in Ludwig's face, flinching slightly when her toe met his nose and blood sprayed onto the white leather of her shoe.

Forrest had knocked down the second man and was holding his machine gun. "Get in the car," he shouted.

Twyla ran, and because she was on that side, jumped in the driver's door. As Forrest climbed in beside her, she froze momentarily and asked, "Do you want to drive?"

"Do you know how to shoot a gun?" he asked.

"No."

"Then drive."

He hit a button on the dash and the engine whirled to life, thankfully, for she'd been looking for a key.

"Drive, Twyla," Forrest said. "You can do it."

"I know I can do it," she said, stomping on the gas pedal. "It's just different than mine." Not chancing a look backward, she asked, "Are they dead?"

"No, they're climbing to their feet."

She pushed harder on the gas. "What did you hit them with?"

He'd thrown the weapon in the backseat, where she'd put the gun. "The rim tool," he said, watching the thugs through the rear window. "It's what you change tires with."

A popping noise made her screech. "They're shooting at us!"

Forrest had spun around and, holding the gun out the window, he fired. She screamed as a tremendous noise filled the car, making her ears ring.

"Just keep driving," Forrest shouted. "They only have a pistol, the bullets can't travel this far."

"Dac will hear the gunfire," she reminded him. "What if they shoot him?"

"Dac wasn't in the field."

"But you said—"

Forrest had turned around and was once again looking out of the rear window instead of hanging out the side. "I know what I said. Just keep driving."

"I am driving," she told him. Her hands were already cramping up from holding on to the wheel as the car jostled over the washboard road. Her teeth were rattling together and her entire body bounced against the seat. "Oh, no, Forrest!" she shouted as another car, coming toward them, appeared before her.

"It's the other thugs," Forrest said. "They must have heard the gunshots."

"What do I do?" With no intention of slowing down, she really didn't need an answer. It was just her nerves talking.

"Just keep driving, honey," he said.

Focused, she kept the car in the center of the road, making the other one swerve as they met. Both men, the driver and the passenger, looked baffled as she passed them.

She kept the gas pedal against the floor and the jarring ride continued. No matter how hard she attempted to tighten every muscle in her body, she bounced and shook.

As if leaping out of nowhere, the highway appeared before them. She stomped both feet on the brake, but nothing happened. "Forrest, I'm hitting the brake, but we're not slowing down. I'm not going to make the corner, I know I'm not."

"We're going too fast for the brakes," he said. "Just go straight across the highway. That road leads to the north side of the lake. We can catch the bootlegger's road back to the resort."

Twyla swore all four tires left the ground when they crossed the highway. They had to have, because for a split second the ride had turned smooth, like when she'd been in Forrest's airplane. Her landing, though, was nothing like Forrest's had been. The top of her head bumped the car's roof and her backside hit the seat so hard it stung all the way up her back.

"You're doing great, honey," Forrest said. "Just keep driving."

"Should I slow down?" she asked. "Where's the bootlegger's road?"

"It's a ways yet. And no, don't slow down."

Before she could ask why, the popping of gunfire started again.

She screamed. "I guess the other thugs are chasing us."

She didn't expect Forrest to answer. She couldn't have heard him if he had. He was hanging out of the window, shooting the gun.

When there was a moment of silence, she asked, "Did you hit them?"

"It's a little hard to hit anything, bouncing around like this," Forrest answered as he pulled the gun she'd thrown in the car over the seat. In an instant, he was back to hanging out of the window, firing again.

The thugs seemed to be having the same issue. None of their bullets were hitting the car, at least none that she knew of. Although Forrest's gun was so loud, she couldn't have heard a cow hitting the car. When the noise stopped her ears were ringing louder than the resort's phone. "Now what?" she yelled.

Forrest sat down in the seat. "There's a road to the left coming up."

Remembering the highway, she said, "The brakes don't work."

"You have to pump them," he said. "Don't

just stomp on them. Pump them like you would a tire pump."

They were both shouting in order to hear, and the thugs were still on their tail. "I've never used a tire pump."

"Step on the pedal several times, short and fast."

Following his directions, she was relieved to feel pressure build beneath her feet and the car starting to slow. "That road?" she asked, noting a break in the long grassy field ahead.

"Yes, that one, but don't slow down too much," Forrest said. "They're still coming."

Having never taken a corner at such speed, Twyla closed one eye, not wanting to witness what might happen as she wrenched the wheel. Her arms trembled from her efforts, but the steering wheel wouldn't turn as far as she needed it to. Just when she thought they'd end up in the field, the car made the corner.

Opening her other eye, she knew why. Forrest's hand was on the steering wheel between hers.

"Good job, doll," he said. "You can drive my getaway car anytime."

Stomping her foot hard against the gas pedal once more, she admitted, "I'm thinking we might not want to do this again."

"You wanted more adventure than a kissing booth."

She grinned, enjoying his teasing despite the fact they were being chased by gangsters. "Yeah, well, this might be a bit more than I wanted."

He chuckled. "You're doing great, Twyla."

"They're still back there, aren't they?"

"Yeah, they are."

Just then a fresh bout of gunfire started up. "They have more bullets," she shouted. "What are we going to do?"

Forrest was silent for a moment, but then asked, "You still know how to swim, don't you?"

"Like a fish," she said. "You taught me."

"Good, because we're about to go swimming, doll."

Twyla held her breath as if she'd just jumped in the water. No one had to tell her a fast-moving car and swimming didn't go hand in hand.

"There's going to be a sharp corner to the left about a mile up the road," Forrest said. "A very sharp corner."

"All right."

"You aren't going to take it."

"I'm not?"

"No. You're going to drive over the bank."

"Bank, as in water below?"

"Yes."

Twyla let the idea settle and pushed harder on

the gas, even though the pedal was flush against the floor.

"I've seen it a dozen times from the air," Forrest said. "The water's deep there. As soon as the car goes airborne, you have to open your door and dive. Dive as far away as you can. You don't want to get sucked in by the car sinking."

For a split second her nerves got the better of her. They may have overwhelmed her, if not for Forrest's hand rubbing the back of her neck.

"Did you hear me, Twyla?"

"Yes," she said. "Airborne, door open, dive."

"You can do it, Twyla," he said. "I know you can."

"I know I can, too," she answered. "I'm just worried if you can."

"I'll be right beside you, doll," he said. "Right beside you."

She believed that as strongly as she knew the sun would rise tomorrow, whether she and Forrest were alive to see it or not. That thought brought tears to her eyes.

"You can do this, Twyla," he said. "We can do this."

The corner was straight ahead, and she knew no amount of pumping the brakes would slow the car down enough to make the turn. She chanced taking her eyes off the road for a split second, just long enough to glance at Forrest and shout, "Here we go!"

After a brief moment of jostling when they hit the tall grass, the car launched off the ground. Twyla let go of the wheel and grabbed the door handle with both hands.

"Dive, Twyla! Dive!" Forrest shouted.

His voice faded as she fought to push open the door. The force of the car nose-diving downward made the door heavy and awkward. Finally, she had enough room, but not enough time to get in position for a dive. She leaped, but the car hit the water about the same time and she instantly found herself fighting the undertow Forrest spoke of.

For the first time since this whole escapade had started, real terror she could die overtook her. The dark and murky water blinded her, and no matter how hard she kicked and paddled with her arms, she was tugged backward instead of moving forward.

Something snagged her arm and she flailed against it, but when the hold tightened, an inner calm told her it was Forrest. A profound strength appeared inside her, too. Whether it was him pulling her on, or her will to live, Twyla wasn't sure, but the force tugging her backward disappeared and she surged forward.

Her lungs were on fire when her head finally

broke the surface. Gulping for air, she saw Forrest before her. Her heart pounded so hard in her ears, she couldn't hear him, but instinctively knew he'd told her to dive again.

This time she went down like a fish, just as Forrest had taught her all those summers ago. Gliding through the water at full speed, she sensed him beside her, challenging her to swim faster, stay under longer. Letting the air out of her lungs slowly little by little to utilize every last bit, she kept swimming, and swimming.

It was his tug on her waist that brought her to the surface again, and this time they both spun around, treading water and keeping their heads as low as possible to prevent being seen.

The thugs were no longer looking for them, or firing their guns. All four were standing on the hill, their car's front tires hanging treacherously over the edge. She and Forrest watched as two of the men jumped in the lake. Forrest nodded then, and in unison, they dove under the water once more.

When they resurfaced, the hill was far behind them, to the point she could barely make out the car. Treading water with one hand, she wiped at her eyes. "Now what?"

Forrest grinned and kissed her. Twice. And then twice more, letting her go only when their kissing caused them both to sink beneath the water.

Popping up beside her, he shook the water out of his hair. "Well, doll, we have two choices."

She wiped her eyes with one hand while treading water with the other. "And they are?"

"Swim to the shore and follow the road back to the resort, or swim from island to island, which is less than half the distance of walking."

"Considering I've lost my shoes, I vote for swimming," she said.

"Then swimming it is."

Though their efforts were much more lax than when they'd first hit the water, as time went on, the islands seemed to get farther away rather than closer. Twyla couldn't combat the way her movements grew sluggish. She relished each short break Forrest offered when they stumbled onto the smaller islands. He asked if she needed to rest longer at each stop, but she refused. Her mind was reliving the car chase and she feared Nasty Nick showing up at the resort with his machine gun.

"No, I can make it," she kept saying.

However, when they were almost at the big island, pain gripped her right leg. For a millisecond she thought Ludwig had caught up with them and grabbed hold of her. She screamed and momentarily dropped beneath the surface. Forrest instantly had her head above water again, and flipped her onto her back. By then, the pain had left her with no control over her leg.

"Cramps?" Forrest asked.

She could barely nod. The constant, fiery pain threatened her ability to breathe.

"Relax as much as you can," Forrest said. "I've got you."

Holding onto the thick forearm he wrapped around her, she tried to let her body go limp, so it wouldn't take too much of his energy to tug her to shore. He was swimming backward, with one arm. Keeping his head close to hers, he kept whispering that they were getting closer to the island.

When he stopped and lifted her into his arms, Twyla couldn't even wrap her arms around his neck. Everything about her felt heavy and useless. Even lifting her head was impossible.

"You're going to be fine, honey," Forrest said as he maneuvered her head to rest on his shoulder. "I promise, you'll be fine."

Her eyes didn't want to stay open. It was as if she was slipping away. To someplace where there were no fears, no worries, just wonderful peacefulness. As her thoughts faded, she whispered what was in her heart. "I love you, Forrest. I've always loved you."

Chapter Thirteen

Forrest removed his shirt and spread it out before shifting Twyla from his lap onto the sandy ground. Positioning her head on his shirt, he examined every inch of her body. A bit frantically the first time, slower the next. So many bullets had been fired, one could easily have hit her. He found nothing. No torn flesh, scrapes or scratches. Not a single blemish marred her delicate skin. He was thankful, so very thankful, but his heart had twisted into a hard knot and tightened again when he felt for the pulse in her neck. It was so weak he barely detected it.

Fury, intense and hot, rose up inside him. This was exactly what he'd known would happen. Deep down he'd known she'd be hurt, just like everyone else who ever became involved with his family. Even locked behind bars, Galen's actions were still hurting people. It was inevitable. Forrest had wanted to stop it for years, but he hadn't been able to, and now his greatest fear had come to be. Because of him, Twyla was hurt.

Forrest growled and cursed and then laid a hand on her chest to assure there was a slow rise and fall. The faint movement gave him hope. It was up to him to make sure the hurting was over. As soon as he got Twyla to safety, he'd get those printing plates back and see that neither Galen nor Ludwig ever saw the light of day again.

Ironically, he could see the resort, but unless someone was looking directly at this particular spot, no one could see him, or Twyla. The sun was still out, but evening was settling in, and the air was getting cooler with each second.

He could make the swim, although it would be the longest one of the journey, and his main concern was that if he left the island, Twyla might wake up and try swimming the distance, too. Checking her pulse one last time, he scanned the woods behind him. He'd carried Twyla across the island, to this side, where they used to play, because this was, at least he hoped, where he'd find what he needed and where they'd be seen.

It had been a very long time, but he was certain he knew where things were, as long as no one had disturbed them over the years.

Pressing his lips to her forehead, he whispered, "I love you, too, Twyla. I have for a long, long time."

She made no move, no indication that she'd heard him. Yet, because it was Twyla, he firmly said, "Stay right here, sweetheart. Don't move. I'll be right back."

Forrest kissed her forehead again before he jumped to his feet and jogged toward the woods. He'd thrown off his jacket and kicked off his boots before they'd jumped from the car, but the sticks and stones beneath his soles didn't bother him. His entire body had grown numb. Twyla wasn't injured, not physically, as she very well could have been. She was exhausted. The swim had used up all her vibrant energy. That's what he kept telling himself. Being held at gunpoint, driving a getaway car over a cliff and into the lake, swimming for miles. She had a right to be exhausted. And had more guts and courage than most men he knew.

He had to find the building materials they'd hauled over here years ago, and hope the rest of the supplies were there, too. Gloria Kasper lived at the resort. She was the best doctor for miles and would examine Twyla as soon as he got her home and confirm she was just exhausted. He wouldn't venture any other belief.

The brush had grown considerably over the years, but it was there, their pile of lumber. Forrest rushed forward, tossing aside gray, weathered wood, and felt a jolt of excitement when he uncovered the tin can. Prying off the lid, he found the contents still intact.

Quickly gathering several boards, he sprinted back to the sandy beach, where he checked on Twyla again. She hadn't moved, and he quickly went to work. After he assembled the wood, he gathered a handful of leaves and dried grass.

The matches in the tin can were old. Several merely hissed when he struck them, but one flared. He held it to the pile he'd assembled. First the grass caught, then the leaves and eventually the wood he'd broken into small chunks. Once they started burning, he threw on more, and then gathered a few dried branches. The fire was soon as large as he needed, and then he tossed on more leaves and moist moss, to make as much smoke as possible.

That would do the trick—someone at the resort was sure to smell and see the fire.

A cough had him spinning around.

Twyla smiled as her eyes fluttered shut again.

Arriving at her side, Forrest crouched down. "How are you feeling?"

"You built a fire."

Relief washed over him. "Yes, I did."

"Good. I'm cold," she whispered.

Gathering her onto his lap, he whispered, "I'll warm you."

She giggled.

He rubbed her arms before wrapping both of his around her, holding her against him. "You sound almost drunk."

"I feel almost drunk." She snuggled her head beneath his chin. "Or maybe I'm dreaming that I'm on a deserted island with a handsome man."

"You aren't dreaming," he said, kissing the top of her head. "But I'm hoping the island won't be deserted for long. That's why I built the fire, to signal to someone at the resort."

"Aw," she said with a long sigh. "But that'll ruin my dream."

As much as he wanted her to stay awake, he knew she wasn't truly conscious. Just somewhere in between. In that comforting place between dreams and reality. "Shh," he said softly. "Go back to sleep, love. No one will ruin your dream."

"This is nice," she said groggily.

"Yes, it is." Lifting his head to gaze toward the resort, for a brief instant Forrest wished he was dreaming. But knowing reality was what he needed, he was happy to see people climbing into a boat.

Twyla opened her eyes and stared at the sunlit ceiling of her bedroom for an extended length of time. A plethora of visions danced in her head. It wasn't until she attempted to raise an arm in order to rub her forehead that she realized they weren't just visions, but memories. Her arm, her entire body for that fact, felt weighed down with lead.

"Wow," she muttered, in response to both her body and memories of gunfire, fast driving and that long swim.

"Hello."

She twisted, but flinched at the way even her neck muscles burned. Slowly, with painful effort, she forced her arm to obey so she could rub her neck. Even her fingers hurt. "Hi," she said with a gasp.

"How are you feeling?" Norma Rose asked.

"Like I'm a hundred," she mumbled. "No one my age should hurt this bad."

Her attempt to sit up was too excruciating and she gave in, sinking slowly back into the softness of her mattress and pillow.

"I brought you something to eat," Norma Rose said.

"That was nice of you," Twyla answered, seriously considering going back to sleep.

"You have to be hungry by now."

Turning just enough to see the clock on the table beside her bed, Twyla closed her eyes again to let the numbers sink in and make sense. "Does that say three in the afternoon?"

"Yes."

"Oh." She huffed out a breath. Some adventurer she was—one day and she was completely worn out. "That swim exhausted me."

"I'd say. You slept for over a day. Gloria said you would."

Twyla opened one eye to peer up at Norma Rose. She was tired and sore, but being treated by the resident doctor seemed a bit unnecessary. "I've been asleep since Forrest built the fire on the island yesterday?"

"Yes and no."

Confused, Twyla frowned.

"Today's Thursday," Norma Rose explained.

"Thurs— What happened to Wednesday?"

"You slept through it."

Despite the pain, Twyla pushed herself up and closed her eyes as the room spun. The mint-green walls, a color she loved, didn't look so wonderful when zipping by. "Slept through it?" Flashes of memory assaulted her mind, before she was able to cry, "We have to call Sheriff Withers, and Father, and—"

"Hush," Norma Rose said, with both hands on Twyla's shoulders. "Sheriff Withers has already arrested Nick Ludwig and his three accomplices. Although they'll never get the car out of the lake, divers did get the suitcase out. Ludwig and his cronies were still trying to do that when the sheriff arrived at the scene. And Father is on his way home."

"How's Forrest?" Twyla asked. "Is he still sleeping, too? Is he here? At the resort?"

Norma Rose rubbed her shoulders gently. "Forrest is fine. But, no, he's not here."

"He's at the Plantation?" Twyla asked, with a distinct gut feeling she was wrong.

"No," Norma Rose said. "He's not at the Plantation. He left for California yesterday."

"California?" Twyla's mouth tasted rotten all of a sudden. It had happened again. Just as she'd known it would. "Without even saying goodbye."

"He said goodbye," Norma Rose assured her. "You slept through it. He had to get there before tomorrow. That's when Galen's hearing is. He wanted to deliver the evidence himself."

"The printing plates?"

"Yes," Norma Rose answered. "Are you ready for something to eat?"

Twyla didn't think her stomach could manage that right now. "No, thank you. Did Forrest say how long he'd be gone?"

"No."

"I'd have gone with him," Twyla said, mainly to herself, "if he'd asked."

"I'm sure you would have," Norma Rose answered.

Twyla glanced at her sister as Norma Rose sat down on the edge of the bed, but said no more.

"I do have some other news for you," Norma Rose said.

"What?"

"Father is on his way home, but Ginger isn't."

"She's not?"

Norma Rose grinned. "Nope. She and Brock got married."

At least someone was happy. Twyla pulled up a smile. It was weak, but heartfelt. "I knew that would happen. Good for her."

"I have some other news, too."

"Great, does everything happen while I'm sleeping?" Twyla asked jokingly. She was attempting not to think about Forrest. That he'd left again. "What is it?"

"Josie was arrested."

"What?"

Norma Rose nodded.

"For what?"

"I don't know. She's being tight-lipped about it. So is Scooter."

"Scooter?" Twyla shook her head. "You know what, yester—Tuesday, when I went to get my car filled with gas, Scooter's station was closed."

"So you drove out to Forrest's hangar instead?"

"Yeah," she said. Even worn out, her mind attempted to cover her tracks. "Scooter fills a barrel of gas out there for Forrest and I thought maybe Scooter was there."

"He had been," Norma Rose said. "Forrest had flown him to Duluth. Scooter had called him, told him Josie had got arrested and he had to go and bail her out."

"Why'd she call Scooter instead of one of us?" Twyla asked. "At least I'm assuming that's how Scooter knew she'd been arrested."

"It is," Norma Rose said, "but that's all I know."

Twyla let out a whistle. "Ginger's married, Josie was arrested, I was almost kidnapped— but I'm fine." Shaking her head, she finished her thought. "Daddy's not going to be happy."

"Probably not." Norma Rose stood and picked up the tray of food sitting on the floor. "You know, it wasn't me."

"You?" Twyla asked, lost.

"I wasn't the one locking you girls upstairs. Father was afraid Galen would try to kidnap one of you." Norma Rose indicated the tray in her hand. "Are you going to eat this, or should I take it back to the kitchen?"

"Thank you, but take it back to the kitchen," Twyla said, feeling a deep understanding for her sister. "I'll eat after I take a long bath. I ache from head to toe and a tub of hot water will feel good."

"You had quite the harrowing day."

"Forrest must have told you all about it."

"He told Ty, who told me."

"You and Ty don't have any secrets, do you?"

"No, we don't." Norma Rose headed for the door. "I'll go start a bath for you."

"Thank you," Twyla said, while noting the red dress Norma Rose wore. She'd worn black for years, but that, too, had changed since Ty had arrived. Love had changed her sister, and Ginger, too. Love was the reason Ginger had run away with Brock.

Norma Rose pulled open the door. "I'll start your bath before taking this downstairs, so hurry up or it'll overflow."

Twyla nodded, but a bath was no longer her focus. Resting her head on the pillow, she whispered, "I'm in love, too." Glancing at the door Norma Rose had closed, she added, "I'm just not loved in return."

She and Forrest could read each other's minds, like Norma Rose had said her and Ty could—Tuesday had shown that, but Tuesday also proved that Forrest didn't tell her everything. He'd never once mentioned he'd flown to Duluth so Scooter could get Josie out of jail. As a matter of fact, he'd said he had no intention of telling her anything.

Twyla threw back the covers and gritted her teeth at the pain crawling out of bed caused.

She'd expected Forrest to leave again. Had told herself she'd go right on living when he did. No broken heart for her this time.

Pushing up off the bed, she wobbled. Nothing would be the same this time. She'd make sure of it.

The bath helped, and while soaking in it, Twyla confirmed in her mind that things wouldn't be the same. Phone lines went clear to California.

After getting dressed and eating, she obtained a phone number for Karen Reynolds in Los Angeles. Her numerous calls that afternoon went unanswered. Norma Rose kindly pointed out that the *Standard Time Act* of seven years ago put California two hours behind Minnesota, meaning Forrest could still be conversing with law enforcement officials, or, Norma Rose also suggested, he might not even be there yet, depending on how many times he'd had to stop to refuel his airplane.

Twyla accepted her sister's knowledge and started to question if she'd learned anything during all her years of schooling. Evidently, not much. Not as much as Forrest had known about money or Norma Rose about time.

While still contemplating that, Twyla chose to visit Josie, who from what Norma Rose said had sequestered herself in her bedroom, leaving only to visit the bathroom. The door wasn't locked, so after knocking, Twyla let herself into Josie's room. Her sister was sitting on the built-in bench in front of her window, knees drawn up to her chest, and only acknowledged Twyla's entrance with a brief glance.

"Want to talk about it?" Twyla asked, shutting the door. There was no sense in hiding the reason she was here, and as she well knew, Josie rarely offered anything unless asked.

"No," Josie answered.

"All right, want to hear about my adventure?"

Josie grinned slightly. "I already have. The entire resort is buzzing with it."

Twyla sat down on the floor and leaned her back against Josie's cushioned bench. "I thought I wanted adventure, Josie, but that was too much for me."

"That wasn't adventure," Josie said. "That was danger."

Twyla sighed. "The only time I was scared— really, really scared—was when I jumped in the water. The suction of the car sinking was pulling me down and for a minute I thought my life was over. But then Forrest grabbed my hand, and I was no longer scared."

"I'm sorry he had to fly Scooter to Duluth," Josie said. "If that hadn't happened, Forrest wouldn't have been at the hangar and you two wouldn't have been kidnapped."

Glancing up at her sister, Twyla said, "But if that hadn't happened, Forrest and I would never have found those printing plates. They were what Ludwig was after. That's the only reason he tried kidnapping us. He never got a chance. Forrest hit him over the head with a rim tool—that's what you use to take off tires—before he could actually kidnap us. Then we stole his car, and the chase was on."

Twyla folded up her legs and twisted, about to tell her sister more. "That was amazing, Josie. I jumped in the driver's side and Forrest jumped in the passenger side." Excitement raced through her veins, this time from enthusiasm instead of fear. "I asked Forrest if he wanted to drive, and he asked me if I knew how to shoot a gun. I said no, so he said I had to drive. And I did! I had that car going as fast as it could, and bullets were flying at us, Forrest was shooting back." She sighed and closed her eyes. "If I live for another hundred years, I'll never forget it."

"And the only time you were scared was when you jumped in the lake?" Josie asked.

"Yeah," Twyla said, meaning it. "Sure, I was nervous, especially driving, but that was because I didn't want to crash the car. We both could have been hurt or worse. As it was, I knew we'd make it out alive. Forrest was with me." Propping one elbow on the bench, she rested her cheek in her palm. "I knew he wouldn't let me get hurt. Even when my legs cramped while swimming, he just took hold of me and swam to shore."

Josie was once again staring out of the window, and Twyla felt a bit guilty, going on about her adventure while Josie was so clearly upset. She let her gaze wander around the room. The walls were painted white, Josie's choice, to match the furniture, curtains, and bed coverings. The only color in the room came from the pictures of flowers on the walls and a few knickknacks on the shelves.

"What's your favorite color, Josie?" Twyla asked, just to put the focus on her sister.

"I don't have one. I like all colors."

"But if you had to choose, what would it be?"

"I don't know if I could choose just one." Softly, Josie added, "They all have a purpose."

Twyla let her gaze land on her sister again. Josie was dressed as usual, in blue cotton trousers and a white blouse. The only time she put on a dress was for the evening parties, so up until a couple of weeks ago, she'd rarely worn dresses or skirts. She claimed to like the comfort of pants and that they were easier to work in. Besides now helping in the office, Josie still cleaned rooms on a daily basis, a chore Twyla had readily given up when Norma Rose asked for help. Josie, though, didn't seem to mind.

"You heard about Ginger, didn't you?" Twyla asked.

"Yes. I figured that would happen."

"Me, too," Twyla said. "Still, it's rather amazing. Ginger married. Norma Rose getting married."

"You getting married."

Twyla's heart nearly stopped dead. "Me?"

Josie nodded. "Don't act surprised. You've been in love with Forrest since we were kids. All that's left now is to tie the knot."

"That will never happen," Twyla muttered.

"Yes, it will. That's the reason you and Norma Rose never got along," Josie said, then added, "until she fell in love with Ty."

Twyla couldn't deny the truth of that, even if she hadn't realized it until this very moment. Letting out a sigh, she said, "Forrest doesn't love me back."

Josie sighed, too, loudly. "I just pointed out that's why Norma Rose was always so grumpy. She knew Forrest liked you more than her years ago. She was always afraid you'd be the one marrying him, living in his big house with all that money while she remained poor." Josie turned back to the window. "Forrest loves you, he just doesn't want to."

Although what her sister said made sense, Twyla couldn't quite believe it, or understand. "Why?"

Josie sighed again. "Forrest couldn't love you years ago because you were too young, and he was too old. Not to mention that he was rich and we were poor. Now, when age doesn't matter, he can't love you because you're rich and he's poor. It's obvious."

"I don't care if he's poor," Twyla said.

"Since when? You love money more than Norma Rose."

Irked that her sister knew her so well—too well—and that she didn't have an answer for that, Twyla chose to stare at the ceiling. "Forrest will leave again. Start his airmail service."

"Maybe, maybe not."

Not up to arguing that point, Twyla said, "Fine, smarty-pants, if you're so smart, why did you get arrested?"

Josie didn't answer. Twyla didn't glance her way, but said, "I've known for a long time that there is more to your Ladies Aid meetings than meets the eye. You have cases of rubbers in your closet. So what happened?"

"I can't tell you," Josie said. "I can't tell anyone."

Rabid dogs couldn't get a secret out of Josie. "You were right about Galen Reynolds," Twyla said. "He was buying and selling girls. Nasty Nick Ludwig babbled on like a baby just learning to talk."

"Norma Rose told me that."

"Were you scared when you were arrested?"

"Partly."

Twyla stood and squeezed herself onto the bench near Josie's drawn-up legs. She took Josie's hands, holding them tightly between her own. "Is there anything I can do to help?"

Josie shook her head and closed her eyes.

"Are you scared now?" Twyla asked.

Josie nodded and a single tear slipped out beneath one closed lid.

Twyla let go of Josie's hands to wrap her arms around her sister's shoulders. She couldn't think of the right words, so she went with what was in her heart. "I wish someone like Forrest had been with you, Josie, someone who can erase fears even when you're being shot at."

Chapter Fourteen

Forrest paced the well-worn painted floor in the hovel his mother called an apartment. Over the years he'd lived in many places, but few could compare to this. Yet she refused to leave it.

"You heard the authorities, Mother," he said. Two days with little to no sleep was enough to make him testy, but she was making him angry. "There is no reason for us to remain here. The evidence the authorities now have will put Galen in federal prison for life, with no chance of parole."

"I have to talk to him one last time," she insisted from where she sat on a lumpy and tattered sofa. "In person."

"Why?" Forrest demanded. "You tried today, he refused. He's going to go on refusing just to keep you here." Running both hands through his hair, Forrest tried to calm his temper. "It makes no sense, Mother. I don't understand—" Taking a breath, he said, "I've never understood the control Galen has over you."

She bowed her head.

"Mother," he said, then stopped, having no idea what to say next. He'd tried everything.

She looked up at him then, her brown eyes welling with tears that slowly escaped. "Your father's not dead."

"Galen's not my—"

"Not Galen," she said. "Your real father."

So taken aback that his lungs locked, Forrest had to force out the air. "What?"

He couldn't help but notice how gray her blond hair had become as she hooked it behind both ears. Then she wiped her nose on the back of her hand and sniffed. "I lied to you." She pulled a handkerchief from her sleeve and wiped her nose again. "I've been lying to you for twenty-seven years."

Forrest sat down beside her and tugged her head onto his shoulder, giving her and himself a moment to collect their thoughts.

"I'm sorry, Forrest, very sorry."

A twinge of guilt flared inside him for not being as upset as she thought he should be. "Well," he said, "why don't you start over? Tell me the truth this time, from the beginning."

She nodded and sat up, but still leaned against him. "I was young, and fell in love with your father so swiftly. I'd gone to New York to attend finishing school. Back then there weren't colleges like there are now. It was more of a prep school to prepare a girl for marriage. A well-to-do marriage. Which is what my father, your grandfather, wanted. It was the same school where Aunt Shirley met Uncle Silas. A few of us girls snuck out one night to attend a party at the home of one of the local girls. Her family was extremely wealthy and there was an enormous number of people there. I got scared that I might get caught, or…I don't know— But I left the party."

She sat forward and wiped her eyes with both hands. "There was another girl with me, from the school, and your father was one of the young men parking coaches. There were very few cars back then. Anyway, he offered us a ride home. It was a long walk, and dark, so we agreed, but we gave him false names and an address a block away from the school. A couple of weeks later, quite by accident, I bumped into him again."

Pushing off the couch, she rose and walked to the kitchen, where she poured herself a glass of water. "All the minor details aren't important," she said. "Suffice to say, I snuck out to meet him several times, but never once told him my real name or where I lived. He was very poor, and I knew my father would never approve of him."

"So what happened?" Forrest asked, feeling more than a bit detached. Or maybe he wanted to be detached because he remembered his mother telling him many times as a young man that money didn't matter when it came to love, yet she'd always acted as if it did.

"When the school discovered I was pregnant, they sent me home, and my father demanded they find the boy responsible."

She crossed the room and sat back down beside him. The couch was the only piece of furniture in the apartment, aside from the kitchen table—which had no chairs with it—and a bed in the one other room.

"Galen arrived." She shook her head. "The school had contacted the gang Galen was affiliated with back in New York to try to find your father, maybe alongside the police, I don't know. But Galen convinced your grandfather I was pregnant with his child. I denied it and refused to marry him, but in the end, I had no choice."

His grandfather forcing her to marry Galen must have been what Jacob had referred to. The thing his grandfather had wished he hadn't done. "Why didn't you try to contact my real father?" Forrest asked.

"I did. I still am."

"You still are?"

"Yes, I've been trying for years. I even used

Rose Nightingale's name to search for him, knowing Galen would intercept any mail sent to me. In the beginning, Galen promised to help me find your father, said he'd grant me a divorce when it happened. I soon learned he was lying. You see, your father knew I'd given him a false name, and he gave me one, too, as a joke." She laughed slightly. "We called each other crazy, silly names, but never our real names. Galen, however, knows your father's real name. Over the years he's shown me pictures of him. Real pictures. I know it's him."

"That's why you want to stay here?" Forrest asked. "So Galen will reveal where my father is? What makes you think he will after all these years?"

"Because I was the one who buried the printing plates under your fuel tank."

He shook his head, knowing it was useless to explain how that implied she knew everything that had transpired. "They've been found, Mother. It'll make no difference to him to know who buried them."

"He knows I buried them," she said. "He knows I have other evidence, too, that I'll take to the authorities if he doesn't tell me what I want to know."

"They don't need any more evidence," Forrest said.

"They might." She closed her eyes for a moment and then opened them. "I know where the banker is buried. Galen killed him."

Forrest stood and walked across the room and wished there was more than water to drink. Letting that bit of new, yet not surprising, information settle, he said, "So for twenty-seven years, he's been holding out on you, and you've been gathering evidence on him. Battling."

"Yes." She looked at him as if he didn't understand. "I loved your father, Forrest. I still do. I won't ever stop looking for him."

"Isn't twenty-seven years long enough for you to understand Galen is never going to tell you?"

"I just want to know where the pictures are. Then I'll have the clues to find him myself."

Forrest shook his head, until another question sprung to his mind. One that Nasty Nick's arrest hadn't answered. He realized he now knew the answer and voiced it. "You paid someone to break into the Plantation, to search for those pictures."

Without demonstrating a hint of regret, she answered, "Yes, but they didn't find anything. I told them they could take whatever they wanted. Thought the idea of things being stolen might make Galen reveal his hiding spot. It didn't, of course. Nothing I've tried has worked."

There was another question rambling around

in Forrest's head. "If you've been searching for a lost love all these years, why did you tell me to leave Norma Rose alone? To not dredge up the past."

"Because you never loved Norma Rose," she said.

That couldn't be denied. "Maybe not, but—"

"Roger Nightingale would have killed Galen, given the opportunity, and then I'd never—" She leaped to her feet. "That's the phone."

It wasn't until she opened the door that he heard a faint and faraway ringing.

He'd seen the pay phone upon entering the building, two flights down, in a small booth in the narrow entranceway.

Her running footfalls had barely stopped, when his mother shouted up the stairwell, "Forrest, it's for you."

No one had this number except Jacob. Forrest's heart skipped several beats as he ran for the door. *Please, don't let Twyla have taken a turn for the worse. Please,* he prayed while running down the stairs.

Forrest met his mother halfway up the stairs. She was smiling brightly, which confused him. Minutes ago she'd still been crying. Crying over a love twenty-seven years old.

He entered the booth and picked up the phone dangling by its cord. There was no room to sit, so he leaned back against the wall for support. "Hello."

"Hello."

Warmth and relief raced through his system. Leaning his head back, he grinned at the heavens far above the ratty old building. "How did you get this number?"

"Well, let's see." Twyla's voice came through the line with as much charm as ever. "On this piece of paper next to the model airplane on your desk, it says, 'Mother' and this number is printed right beside it. You have nice penmanship."

His grin grew so wide it pulled on his cheeks. "My desk?"

"Yes."

He closed his eyes, imagining her sitting there. "How are you feeling?"

"Fine. How are you?"

"Fine."

"Why didn't you tell me about Josie being arrested?"

Forrest laughed. "That explains the phone call."

"Why didn't you?" she asked again.

"Because it wasn't for me to tell. Scooter asked for a ride to Duluth and I gave him one."

"But you knew he was going up there to get Josie out of jail?"

"Yes," he admitted. "He told me that was the reason."

"And you didn't tell me."

He sighed. "No, I didn't tell you."

"Why?"

"Because that was—is—Josie's business," he said. "Now, on the other hand, if that had been you…"

"If that had been me, you wouldn't have had to tell me because I'd already have known."

He was too tired for any more twisted tales. "Twyla."

"Yes."

"You are the only Nightingale girl I care about."

Her silence made him question if he should have admitted that or not.

"I am?" she finally asked quietly.

"You are," he answered. "Now please tell me you didn't drive to the Plantation this late at night by yourself."

"Father wouldn't let me. Bronco drove me."

"That's the first good news I've had all day."

"It is?" she asked. "What's happened with Galen?"

"There will be a new trial," he said, "but this one against him is for the actual counterfeiting. The officials say he'll never get out." Once his mother told the officials where they'd find the banker's body, that would be even more of a certainty. Forrest would see that happened.

"How's your mother?" Twyla asked softly.

Forrest closed his mouth before the word *fine* could exit. "She's doing all right," he said. "I'm trying to convince her to come home with me."

"That's nice," she said, after a lengthy pause. "You'll like having her home. When might that be?"

There was an undertone to her voice, and a double meaning there somewhere, he just couldn't grasp it right now. Probably due to lack of sleep, among other things. "I don't know yet," he said. Not wanting to wear her out, he added, "I'd better hang up now, and you'd better get on home." Recalling the thank-you she'd slept through, he added, "And Twyla, thank you. If not for you finding that suitcase, Galen would be getting out."

"You're welcome, but if not for Josie getting arrested, we wouldn't have found the suitcase."

"I'm not going down that road again," he said, although he was grinning. "Bronco's there to drive you home, right?"

"Yes, he is. Goodbye, Forrest."

"Bye." He hung up and stared at the phone.

Miles away from California, sitting at Forrest's desk, Twyla stared at the phone she'd just hung up. Reaching over, she spun the little propeller on his model plane, as she had done several times during their conversation. She folded her arms across her chest and leaned back to survey the room as the propeller made a clicking sound. Hearing Forrest's voice made her miss him all the more and that certainly didn't settle anything inside her.

She was the only Nightingale sister he cared about. That was fine and dandy, but he was still keeping secrets from her. Sort of. It was Josie's tale to tell, and she hadn't told anyone, except perhaps their father. He'd arrived at the resort just as Twyla had been leaving.

Was she making more out of this secret than need be? Yes. Because the real problem lay within her. She might love Forrest, he might even love her, but that didn't solve anything. Could she live with the fear of him leaving all the time?

No, and he would leave. Being an airmail pilot was still in his future. Where would that leave her? An old woman sitting alone. A poor lonely wife. She had money—plenty of it. But Forrest hadn't wanted help from her family in solving the mystery behind his father's parole, so he'd never accept money. Not even from her. Airmail pilots couldn't make the kind of money she could bring in running the resort.

Giving the plane propeller one last flick, she said, "Love or money, Twyla, which will it be?"

There was no one to answer that, so she stood and walked around the desk to go find Bronco. He said he'd be at the bar, talking to his uncle. At the door, taking one last look around, Twyla's gaze landed on the pictures on the wall, namely the one of Babe Ruth.

For a man with no money, Forrest had some influential friends.

Twyla clicked off the light and went to find Bronco. It wasn't until hours later, while lying in her bed, staring at the shadows of the trees cast by the moon dancing around like dark fairies on her ceiling, that the picture entered her mind again.

Babe Ruth.

As the idea formed she grew giddy. Forrest wanted to become an airmail pilot to make money—money the Plantation wasn't making right now. If the Plantation all of a sudden became successful, there would be no need for him to leave. He could fly his plane anytime he wanted. With her as a passenger.

Her idea grew until she laughed out loud, convinced it would work.

From then on, time barely ticked by. She looked at the clock so many times she had to check to make sure it was working properly.

When dawn peeked in through her window, she leaped out of bed, threw on a comfortable yellow dress and matching shoes, combed her hair and headed for the office. She made notes of everything, and then lists of people to call—once it was of an appropriate time—and then, unable to keep it to herself any longer, she ran upstairs.

She reached Josie's room first, throwing open the door. "Did you talk to Father?"

Rolling over and rubbing the sleep from her eyes, Josie answered, "Yes."

"Is everything all right?"

"For now."

"Good. I need you downstairs in the office in ten minutes." Closing the door, she ran to Norma Rose's room and shoved that door open. "Good, you're here."

Standing before her closet, Norma Rose frowned. "Where else would I be?"

Ty's cabin, that was where. Twyla didn't say that, but then, determining it might give her a bit of playing power, she pointed out, "There's wet grass on your feet."

Norma Rose's cheeks flushed and Twyla chuckled. "Wear red again. You look good in it, and meet me and Josie in the office in ten minutes."

"Why?"

"Because I say so," Twyla answered, shutting

the door. She went back downstairs and into the kitchen, knowing full well it would take at least twenty minutes before either sister arrived. She ate a cinnamon roll straight from the oven, along with a glass of freshly squeezed orange juice, and chatted with the cooks about a Fourth of July barbecue. Though people had been cooking outside for years, calling it a barbecue was a fairly new idea, and not something upscale resorts did. She was going to change that.

Twyla was sitting at the office desk when her sisters arrived. "Good morning," she greeted. "Take a seat."

Norma Rose and Josie glanced at each other. Twyla grinned and handed each of them a sheet of paper.

"What's this?" Norma Rose queried.

"Your job duties."

"My what?"

"Your job duties for the Fourth of July celebration," Twyla explained.

"We already planned this," Norma Rose said.

"We planned what we are doing here," Twyla pointed out. "At the resort. This will explain what we are doing in town."

"In town?" Josie asked.

"Yes, we are going to have an entire community celebration." Waggling a finger at their papers, she said, "Read those. You'll see we are going to need a parade, a sailboat race, games for kids at the city park, a scavenger hunt—I really like that idea—and airplane rides. That will all happen throughout the day, and that night, people will come to the resort for a barbecue, dance-off and fireworks."

"We can't do all this," Norma Rose said.

"Yes, we can," Twyla insisted. "There are three of us." She turned to Josie. "Your Ladies Aid Society can help. They can take care of the parade, the games for the kids and the scavenger hunt."

Josie opened her mouth, but Twyla said, "They owe you after your little incident."

Josie merely looked down at her paper.

"Airplane rides?" Norma Rose asked. "Does Forrest know about this?"

"No, but he will," Twyla said. "I'll tell him when I tell him about Babe Ruth."

"Babe Ruth? The baseball player?" Norma Rose asked. "What about him?"

"He'll be here, too," Twyla said. "That's why we need a parade."

"Does Babe Ruth know that?" Josie asked.

"He will," Twyla said. "As soon as I call him."

Norma Rose dropped her paper on the desk. "Stop right there. You can't just call Babe Ruth and tell him to be in White Bear Lake, Minnesota on the Fourth of July. That's not even two weeks away."

Twyla tossed one of the daily newspapers the resort received across the desk. Seeing that article this morning had confirmed that everything was going to work. "He's already going to be in Minnesota. On the third. I'll just ask him to stay one more day."

"Why?" Norma Rose then asked. "Why would we want to do all of this?"

Twyla bit her bottom lip while determining just how much to say. "Because the Plantation needs to start earning money again, and Forrest is in California with his mother. I want to do this for him. You're my sisters, and I need your help to make it happen."

She knew her eyes were full of pleading, and for the first time in years it was genuine.

"I'm in," Josie said. "I'll call a special meeting for the society today."

"Thank you," Twyla said before she turned to Norma Rose.

"Of course I'm in," Norma Rose said. "I'm the one who said Nightingale's and the Plantation should partner up."

"Yes, you did," Twyla said. "And thank you for the idea."

"Now you just have to get Forrest to agree," Josie said.

Twyla nodded even as a lump formed in her stomach.

Chapter Fifteen

It had become one of the longest weeks of his life, and seeing the hangar below lifted Forrest's spirits considerably. Alone, he'd have been home yesterday, but with his mother as passenger, he'd put the plane down overnight. A good thing, too. Flying over the mountains in Montana had left her rather queasy.

The landing was smooth. Taxiing along the runway, he waved at Jacob standing next to his trusty old Model T, ready to take them to the Plantation.

This hadn't been his home for years, but lately, for the first time in Forrest's life, it had started to feel like home.

With Jacob's help, his postflight chores took half the time. Before he knew it, Forrest was in the backseat of Jacob's Model T as the man drove toward town. His mother was full of questions, and Jacob was busy answering them, which gave

Forrest time to watch the scenery—especially the road to Nightingale's—as they rolled along.

At the Plantation, the rumble of bowling balls and laughter echoed through the air as he carried his mother's luggage up the stairway. He glanced over his shoulder at Jacob, who was carrying two more suitcases—his plane had never been packed so full.

Jacob grinned. "Busy place today."

"I'd say so," his mother replied, carrying two small bags. "I can't wait for a tour."

"I'll give you one as soon as we put your luggage in the apartment," Forrest said, opening the door. He stopped in his tracks. And only moved inside when Jacob gave him a little shove.

The cupboard doors had all been rehung and painted. The walls had been painted, too, and the rug looked almost new. He turned to Jacob.

"I'll give your mother a tour of the place," Jacob said. "You're needed in the office."

Forrest didn't ask why. He might not want to know.

The door had been closed when he'd walked past, but that wasn't unusual when no one was in it. At least no one should be in it. By the time he'd run down the stairs, he had a feeling he knew who was behind the door.

He thrust it open and let loose the smile that instantly tugged at his lips.

"Hello," Twyla said, leaning against the corner of his desk.

She had to have more dresses than a midnight sky had stars. Today her outfit was green and sparkly and fit her as snugly as his flying helmet. She was also the most beautiful sight he'd ever seen.

"I saw you drive in," she said.

He closed the door. "You did?"

She nodded. "I thought it might take you a little longer to get your mother settled."

"She wants a tour."

"Oh, well, go ahead, I can wait."

He started walking forward, slowly, which was torturous. Every part of him wanted to fly across the room, grab her, kiss her, tell her how much he'd missed her. "You can?"

"Yes."

"Liar."

"What?"

He arrived in front of her. "You're lying. You can't wait. No more than I can."

A frown tugged at her expression. "What can't you wait for?"

Forrest grabbed her shoulders and pulled her close. "This." He kissed her like a man would eat his last meal. Savoring every tiny morsel. His hands couldn't get enough of her. Her back, her sides, her cheeks, her hair.

When his hands cupped the sides of her hips and he felt the way her legs trembled, he picked her up. Setting her on his desk, he stepped between her legs, all the while never releasing her lips.

Her heels hooked him behind the knees, bringing them flush together, and a blazing inferno let loose inside him. The kiss could have lasted one, ten, or even thirty minutes—he lost track of time. All he knew for certain was that he wanted Twyla more than he wanted to fly.

Their kissing slowed, but the mood was just as heartfelt and intense, even when they parted by some sort of mutual agreement. Her blue eyes were twinkling and her soft palms rubbed his cheeks.

"I take it you're happy to see me?"

"No, not really," he teased.

She laughed and kissed his chin. "Liar."

"We're even," he said.

"Yes, we are," she said. "You were right. I couldn't wait."

He kept her sitting where she was, with him between her knees, massaging her hips with his thumbs. "Are you the one who fixed up the apartment?"

"I wanted your mother to have a nice homecoming."

"What about me?"

"Oh, darn it," she said, playfully slapping his shoulder.

"What? Don't I deserve a nice homecoming?"

"Yes, but you made me forget something."

"What?"

She reached behind her and then tugged a slip of paper between them. Holding it beneath her chin, she grinned. "Interested?"

Written with red lipstick, the words on the paper said, *Kisses, Flyboys Free*.

"I might be."

It took some serious willpower not to lock the door and have his way with her on the lime-green sofa. It was several kisses later before Forrest released Twyla completely and walked around to sit behind the desk. A bit of separation was what he needed to cool down.

"The apartment looks great. Who do I owe?"

She'd spun around to sit sideways on his desk and swung her feet back and forth. "You don't owe anyone. I found the paint in the basement, left over from remodeling the bowling lanes, and the hinges were all there for the cupboards. They just needed to be straightened, and the carpet just needed a good cleaning." Rolling her eyes, she added, "Someone had nailed it to the floor, of all things. The hardest part was taking off the wallpaper."

"You did all that?"

She laughed. "Don't be silly. But I did oversee your employees and made sure they did it right."

"My employees?"

"Yes, you have maintenance workers, cleaners. The apartment is part of the Plantation." Resting one palm on his desk she leaned toward him. "Trust me, Forrest, your employees are not overworked. Other than the pin boys, of course— they run their tails off. Did you notice the ladies bowling?"

"I didn't pay much attention."

"They're the women from Josie's Ladies Aid Society," she said.

"They are?"

She nodded, but it was the way she nibbled on her bottom lip that snagged his full attention.

He laid a hand on top of hers. "What is it?"

"Nothing bad," she said.

"Then tell me. You've never been afraid of telling me anything."

"I know, and this is good, I—I just—"

"Tell me, Twyla."

"I set up a partnership between the resort and the Plantation," she said.

His skin tingled eerily. "What kind of partnership?"

"For the Fourth of July. It'll be beneficial to both of us, or both businesses. The whole town, really."

Nodding his head as she nodded hers, he asked, "What's the partnership?"

She jumped off the desk and crossed the room to where the pictures hung on the wall. "The day starts out with you flying Babe Ruth in from New Ulm. He was already going to be there on the third for a charity baseball game, all I had to do was ask him to come here on the fourth. He remembered you and said he'd do it if you flew him up here in the morning and back to New Ulm the next morning." Scrunching her nose, she added, "I said you would."

That didn't sound bad. Unable to resist taking advantage of the opportunity, he leaned back in his chair and crossed his arms, as if thinking for a few moments. "All right, then what?"

She sighed, before her excitement started up again. "Then the entire town is having a parade, a huge one with Babe Ruth in your roadster—Josie's Ladies Aid Society is taking care of that—and games for the kids in the park across the street. Jacob has set up a sailing contest, and people can bowl, and play pool, and eat, and go to the amusement park, and then that evening, everyone can come out to the resort. We're having a barbecue and a dance-off on an outside dance floor with Chinese lanterns and fireworks." She took a deep breath and asked, "What do you think?"

Before he could answer, she said, "Oh, there's one more thing. I've already put ads in the Minneapolis and St. Paul newspapers. The resort is already full, so are most of the other resorts and hotels around town, so I have your employees working on a few rooms upstairs, so you can have overnight guests here, too." Scrunching up her shoulders, she held up one hand, with her index finger and thumb an inch apart. "There's just one other little thing. I don't have anyone giving airplane rides yet. And I've advertised them. It won't be all day, just short rides in the afternoon. People have to buy tickets for everything, so there's lots of money to be made."

Her last statement struck a chord.

"What do you think?" she asked.

"I think it sounds like something the entire town can benefit from, but I want to know one thing."

"What's that?"

Eyeing her, he asked, "Why?"

She opened her mouth, but then clamped it shut and closed her eyes. As much as he wanted to cross the room to her, he wanted to know her answer more.

"Why are you doing all that? For the town? For the resort? For the Plantation?"

She nodded. "Yes, to all of them."

"Why?"

* * *

Twyla wished an answer would form, one other than the one in her head. But it was to no avail. Perhaps that was for the best. The truth was always best.

"Because I love you, Forrest. Years ago you couldn't love me because I was poor and you were rich, and now you can't love me because I'm rich and you're poor. I want you to be successful again. The Plantation to be successful again."

"You want to make me rich again so I can love you?" He lifted an eyebrow. "Or so you can love me?"

Why did the way he said it sound so awful? Her mouth went dry, and she couldn't spit out either a yes or a no.

"Which is it?"

Twyla's mind couldn't come up with a way to make him understand.

When she didn't answer, he continued. "What if I told you I don't want to be rich again? What if I told you I don't want to run the Plantation? What if I told you my mother's here so she can run the Plantation and I can fly my airmail route?"

After licking her lips to moisten them, Twyla asked, "You don't want—"

"No," he interrupted. "I don't. I saw how money hurt people. How it's still hurting people."

"Forrest, I—"

Standing, he held up one hand. "I'll go and get Babe Ruth, I'll give airplane rides and I'll do whatever else you need me to do that day, but Twyla, next time you want to form a partnership, leave me out of it."

"Forrest—" Biting her lips together, Twyla stopped before she started begging him to listen. It wouldn't do any good. Her plan had failed. Nothing would ever keep Forrest here.

She stopped herself from following him to the door, too. The tears were the hardest thing to stop, but she did it, with painful, sheer will. It hurt, too, to walk over to his desk and retrieve her purse from the floor, and to walk to the door. But she did it. She walked all the way to her car and drove all the way home. Then she walked up the stairs to her bedroom, where she threw her purse against the wall, not caring about the contents that scattered on the floor or the picture that fell.

Yes, she did all that. And she'd done one other thing.

She'd chosen money over love. At least that's what Forrest thought she'd done. In truth, it didn't matter what she did or what she wanted. Forrest was bound to climb in his plane and fly away. He was a bird that couldn't be caged. Nothing would ever change that.

Twyla was about to throw herself upon her bed when a knock sounded on her door.

It opened without her response.

"Twyla?" Josie asked. "Are you all right?"

Staring out the window, at the blue water of the lake shimmering in the sunshine, she shook her head. "No, but I will be."

"Anything I can do?" her sister asked.

"No, there's nothing anyone can do."

Twyla spun around and walked past her sister. "Excuse me. I need to be alone."

Josie didn't follow, and for that Twyla was thankful. She took the back stairway and used the room off the hall where all the supplies were held to make her way outside. Barely thinking and too numb to feel, she made her way to the dock, and then, without a second thought, she kicked off her shoes and made a swan dive into the lake.

It had taken Forrest all of a minute to realize what a fool he'd been. How he'd twisted and distorted everything Twyla had said. Was he some sort of martyr? Or was he trying to follow in his mother's footsteps, loving someone for years and years, and never doing a solid, tangible thing about it?

He spun around and dashed back down the

steps. His office was empty. Out the window, he saw her car leave the parking lot.

Getting his roadster out of the garage was yet another fiasco. Three ladies from Josie's society had to be found so their automobiles could be moved, and then to top it off, he had to wait for a train to pass at the Bald Eagle crossing.

At least all that gave him time to really regret his actions. As if he needed that.

Sundays were quiet at the resort. Walking through the front door was like entering a tomb, it was so still and silent. He headed for the stairway, but paused when he noticed someone on the deck outside of the ballroom doors.

It turned out to be Josie.

"Where's Twyla?"

Josie gave him a silent and rather frosty stare before she pointed toward the lake. Forrest scanned the area but couldn't see anything or anyone.

Pointing again, this time Josie spoke. "The island. She just walked ashore. Swam all the way there."

Forrest cursed.

"You can say that again," Josie said. "What did you say to her? That you didn't like the Babe Ruth idea? She's been working on it night and day. She did it all for you. So the Plantation would be a success again and you wouldn't leave."

Forrest held up both hands. "I know. I think it's a great idea." His mind caught then. "Leave?"

"Yes. Leave. You broke her heart when you left years ago."

He cursed again. "I'm borrowing a boat."

Josie grabbed his arm. "Wait. Just wait. Give me five minutes." She held on even tighter when he took a step. "Five minutes isn't going to matter. Twyla has to catch her breath, and you need to calm down. Figure out what you're going to say to her."

Josie had always been the wisest sister. "Five minutes for what?" he asked.

"You'll see, and you'll like it," Josie said. "I promise."

"Five minutes," Forrest said, his eyes on the island. "No more."

As Josie suggested, he used the five minutes to calm down, and to figure out what he wanted to say. If Twyla wanted him to be rich again, that was what he'd do. He'd work twenty-four hours a day, seven days a week.

Forrest slapped the balcony railing. "You're an idiot," he growled, seething.

"Maybe just a man in love," Josie said, walking through the doors. "Here, this is your surprise."

He took the handle she held out. "It looks like a picnic basket."

"It is," Josie said. "What better place to have a picnic than on a deserted island?"

Twyla had always loved the deserted-island idea. On impulse, he kissed Josie's cheek. "Thanks, you're the best."

"No, I just figured I owed you one for flying Scooter to Duluth to get me out of the hoosegow."

He hadn't given that a thought for several days. "How'd that turn out for you?" he asked.

"I'll let you know, when I know," she said. "Go. Take the boat out of the first boathouse, it has a motor."

He gave her a thumbs-up as he ran down the steps, and in no time, had the boat skimming across the water.

It wasn't as if he could camouflage his arrival, so Twyla definitely saw him. When she didn't move, just sat with her knees tucked beneath her chin, Forrest experienced a moment of panic. What if she'd cramped up again? That was a long swim.

He shot the boat far up onto the sand before jumping out. Her gaze, though solemn, let him know she hadn't cramped up, at least not in her muscles. He had probably put a hard cramp in her heart, though, if it felt anything like his.

He left the picnic basket in the boat and approached slowly, as one would if they came upon something they didn't want to frighten away. Sitting down beside her, he remained silent, thinking about the Twyla he'd known and loved what seemed like a million years ago. She'd matured, grown into a beautiful, vibrant woman, but deep down, she was still the same girl he'd fallen in love with.

She made the first move, as she'd always done when they were young. It was little more than a shift, where she bumped her shoulder with his. "What are you doing here?"

He bumped her back. "Came to apologize."

"Really?"

"Yep."

"What if I don't want to hear it?"

"Then I'll wait until you do."

"That could take hours."

"I know. I've got a picnic basket in the boat if I get hungry."

He could tell she tried not to smile, but a small one appeared. "You do?"

He reminded himself to thank Josie again. "Yep, I do."

"What's in it?"

"I'm not telling." That sounded better than telling her he didn't know.

She reached forward and shoved aside a pair of wet silk stockings and garters before she stretched her legs out. Long shapely legs he sincerely admired. There wasn't a single thing he didn't admire about her. Didn't adore.

"I'm sorry, Forrest, I—"

He twisted and pressed a finger to her lips. "I'm the one who came to apologize." Removing his finger so he could hold her chin with his thumb and knuckle, he said, "I'm so sorry, Twyla. I have no idea why I said what I did."

"Because it's how you really feel."

"No, it's not. I love you, I have for years. I loved you when you were poor and I was rich, and I love you now, when you're rich and I'm poor."

Her smile was gentle and sweet, but she shook her head. "Oh, Forrest, I love you, too, rich or poor, young or old, but that's not the problem."

"Then what is?"

"The conversation we had earlier wasn't about love. It was about what you want and what I want." She pulled his hand away from her chin and held it between both of hers. "Wanting something and loving someone are two separate things."

"That's true," he said, "and you want to be rich."

Her face fell and her eyes filled with sorrow. "I know that's what you think, and at one time I honestly thought that, too. I thought that was the answer."

"The answer to what?"

"The emptiness inside me. It didn't use to be there. But then things happened, and I attributed it to how poor we were. How boring our lives were." She shook her head. "But even after we became rich, I was still empty inside. No matter what I tried." A becoming blush covered her cheeks. "And you know I tried almost everything." She sighed. "But nothing filled that void."

He rubbed her cheek, knowing she was referring to all her antics with Mitsy.

"Everyone looks at things differently, Forrest, but I, because I wanted to follow in her footsteps, thought I had to think like Norma Rose. That money was at the core of everyone's happiness."

"It can be the core of everyone's evilness, too," Forrest warned, having seen that first-hand.

"I've seen that, too, for years, but I didn't comprehend it." Tears welled in her eyes. "Because I'd only been thinking about myself. I only thought about what I wanted, and ironically, when that became clear to me, I realized I hadn't known what that truly meant."

Forrest was trying hard, but he wasn't grasping what she was saying. However, he was determined to make this work; whatever she wanted, he'd find a way to get it. "Adventures?" he asked. "The night of Palooka George's party you told me you wanted more adventure than a kissing booth." He kissed her fingertips. "I liked your booth today."

Her mood lightened slightly and she giggled. Leaning her head back, she looked up at the sky. "I only said that because it was you. The adventures in my life stopped when you left. That's when the emptiness formed inside me. When my world became lonely and cold." She sighed. "I thought money would solve it all. Today, I realized I was wrong."

"Twyla—"

"I've been jealous, Forrest, for years. Of Norma Rose. Of..." She shook her head. "There's even a part of me that's jealous of your airplane. You see, Forrest, what I want isn't money or adventures. All I've ever wanted is to be what you want."

He grasped her face with both hands. "You are exactly what I want. Who I want." Wanting her to understand, he explained, "You always were, even when we were kids, but you scared me."

"I scared you?"

"Yes, you scared me," he admitted. "You were so fun, so adventurous and outgoing and determined. I can't say I knew what love was back then. No one in my family loved one another. The only place I ever saw affection was out here, at your house, and when I realized that's what I felt for you, I tried to convince myself otherwise, because I knew eventually you'd get hurt because of me. I didn't want you to become a part of my family because it was an ugly place to be. Yet I couldn't stay away, so I pretended to be in love with Norma Rose. The night I left, when Galen supposedly caught us kissing, I was breaking up with Norma Rose."

"But you were already planning on leaving that night."

Forrest nodded, and closed his eyes for a moment, pulling forth a memory he'd suppressed long ago. "When I came home from college, the day of my graduation party, Galen had a graduation gift for me. A young Asian girl. She was in my room, naked. Her body was bruised and her face stained with tears. I'd seen girls like her before, the third floor was full of them, and for years Galen had goaded me to sample them. I'd refused, said I'd never fall to his level. I told the girl in my room to leave, but she said she couldn't. That they'd kill her. I told her that wouldn't happen, but when I opened my bedroom door, one of Galen's men entered, with a gun."

Twyla gasped.

It was such an ugly tale, one he'd tried to completely erase from his memory, yet he knew it played a significant role in making Twyla understand how he'd always loved her, but had to leave—for her sake. "I told the man to go ahead and shoot me because I wasn't going to touch her. Eventually he yelled for Galen. When Galen came in the room, he held the gun on the girl and said he'd kill her before my eyes if I didn't take her. I was afraid he might, but I still refused. And then I grabbed her hand, threw a blanket over her shoulders and walked her out the door. I took her to Gloria Kasper's house. I have no idea what became of her." Forrest took her hand and squeezed it. "I didn't want to return, but I had to, when my party started. I remember watching you walk through the door. You were wearing a blue dress, the same color as your eyes, and your hair was long, past your shoulders. I remember that very moment, because that's when I knew I had to leave. Not even stay the summer as I'd planned. You'd grown up that year, and I knew if I stayed, something would happen between you and me, and you'd be hurt. Galen would find a way to hurt you. When Norma Rose asked me to drive her home, I agreed because it would give me time to tell her I was leaving." Forrest withheld the part about how Galen had threatened to kidnap the Nightingale girls.

Twyla lifted his hand and kissed his palm. "I knew Galen was evil, but I had no idea."

"I didn't want you to know. I didn't want anyone to know," he said. "But your father did, and I knew he'd never let Galen harm you girls. Years before, when I was little and you might just have been a baby, my mother and I were at your house and Galen came and forced us to go home. That night your father literally kicked the front door of the Plantation in. That's all I remember, but from then on, Galen never refused to let my mother visit yours. I held that memory close the entire time I was gone. Hoping and praying your father would keep you girls protected."

"Of course he kept us safe," Twyla said. "Daddy's a force to reckon with. He'd never have let your father harm us." She kissed his chin. "Just like you never let him harm us. And now he's in jail. Forever."

Forrest caught her under the chin with a knuckle. "Thanks to you. For finding that suitcase and driving the getaway car. I have no doubt that if I'd been on the driver's side of that car, I'd have been driving and you shooting—whether you knew how to or not."

"That's how it always was between us, wasn't it?"

"Still is," he said.

She nodded, but then glanced out to the lake before gazing up at him again. "So, where do we go from here? Now that Galen's locked up forever, you'll start your airmail business, and I'll…" She shook her head.

He knew whatever else they had to work out

would happen naturally, as it always had between him and her, but needed to reassure her of that. "Well." He attempted to sound thoughtful. "I know this gorgeous, vivacious woman who throws spectacular parties."

Her frown was immense. "You do?"

Smoothing out the little point between her brows with his fingertip, he said, "Yes, I do, and she has planned quite an extravagant Fourth of July party. The entire town will be in attendance, probably half the state and beyond. There's going to be a pilot there, too."

She laughed, now following his line of teasing. "A flyboy, you mean."

"Yes, a flyboy, and I probably could convince him to give that gorgeous woman a night flight."

"What's a night flight?"

"Flying at night, of course."

"Isn't that dangerous?"

"Not if the pi—flyboy knows what he's doing."

Her eyes were twinkling and Twyla, showing enthusiasm in a way only she could, scooted closer to him. "And why would that gorgeous woman want to go flying at night?"

"Well, you see," he said, flicking the end of her nose, "that flyboy is thinking as long as there is already a party going on, he might invite a reverend to say a few words before the barbecue starts. And then, after a few dances, that flyboy would take his new bride, that gorgeous woman, on a night flight, so that when the fireworks started they'd be high in the sky, looking down at all those fiery sparks filling the air."

Her frown was not what he expected. "What about your airmail route?"

"What about it?"

"Won't you be flying across the nation all the time?"

"No," he said. "If I get the contract, I'll be flying from Minneapolis to Iowa five days a week. I'd be home every night."

"You would?"

"Could you deal with that?" he asked. "Me being home every night?"

Smiling, she nodded. "Yes, I could, but…"

"But?"

"This is where it gets complicated again," she said woefully. "I need to be busy, too. I don't want to sound—"

"You're going to busy all right," he said, rubbing his nose against hers. "You'll be running the Plantation."

"Your mother—"

"Doesn't want any more to do with it now than she did years ago." Regret swelled inside him. "I have no idea why I said what I did. Jealousy,

I guess. Thinking you wanted to be rich more than you wanted to be with me."

"I've been rich," she whispered. "I am rich. But it's nothing compared to how much I love you."

"I love you, too, Twyla Nightingale. The best hostess in the country. This town isn't going to know what has hit it on the Fourth of July."

She giggled. "I hope so."

He kissed her nose. "And I hope you say yes, that you'll marry me."

She squealed and leaped forward, pushing him onto his back. Wiggling until her body rested perfectly atop his, she asked, "You mean it, Forrest? You really, truly want to marry me?"

He framed her cheek with a hand and relished the way her breath merged with his as he whispered, "Yes, I mean it. You are, and forever will be, exactly what I want. If you marry me, I promise to never go anywhere again without telling you or taking you with me."

Her smile was so bold, so beautiful, its glow spread across her entire face. "Oh, Forrest," she whispered. "You make me so happy. It's like my heart is so full it's singing. I love you so very, very much."

"So," he said, running a hand down her back to press her hips deeper against him. "Will you marry me or not?"

"Of course I'll marry you."

Their kiss started with a few slow gentle pecks, which quickly escalated into a passionate exchange that should have scalded them both. When it ended, knowing he couldn't wait much longer, he asked, "On the Fourth of July?"

Unexpectedly, she crawled off him and jumped to her feet. "I'd marry you right now if there was a preacher handy." She grabbed his hands to tug him upright. "But since there's not, get up."

To say he was disappointed was putting it mildly. Lying on the hot sand with her, married or not, had instantly become a favorite pastime. Forrest stood and shook the sand off his pants and shirt, trying to also shake away a small portion of the desire still blazing through his veins. He could wait. It might kill him. But he could wait.

"Grab the picnic basket and follow me," she said.

The flame in his blood flared again, so strong his breath caught. "To where?"

"The other side of the island," she said even more saucily than usual. "Where there are no houses and no balconies where someone is standing with a pair of binoculars."

He laughed. "Josie?"

"That would be my guess."

"She packed the picnic basket."

The twinkle in her eyes said she knew something he didn't.

"That's what I hoped," she said, giggling.

Chapter Sixteen

Twyla wasn't blindsided by love. That would have been impossible. She'd been in love with Forrest forever. However, the freedom of being able to admit her love was spectacular. And knowing wholly, inside out, that he loved her in return was the best thing of all. Who said a girl couldn't have her cake and eat it, too?

They ran hand in hand to the other side of the island. Past the spot Forrest had carried her ashore several days ago to where a large cluster of boulders made a tiny, enchantingly private alcove. He set down the basket, and she wound her arms around his neck, kissing him freely, openly, and laughing to the heavens above when it ended. The happiness inside her was so great, so phenomenal.

She was full again. No emptiness, no longing.

Trailing kisses down his neck, she started unbuttoning his shirt. "Let's go for a swim."

"A swim? You just swam across the lake."

His hands roamed up and down her back, creating a swirling and wondrous storm inside her. An energy she only felt when he touched her formed, and she wanted to experience it all the way to a thunderous end. "Not just swimming," she whispered against his neck. "Skinny-dipping."

"Skinny-dipping?"

She stepped back to pull his shirt out of the waistband of his pants. "Yes. You have heard of skinny-dipping, haven't you?"

"I've heard of it, all right," he said, grabbing the hem of her dress.

Twyla lifted her arms, aiding in the swiftness of the green material's departure from her body. As Forrest dropped the dress, she pushed his shirt off his shoulders, running her hands over his fascinating bare skin. She kissed the center of his chest, where a cluster of hair tickled her nose.

Laughing, and more delighted than a robin in spring, she stepped back. "Last one in's a rotten egg!" Swiftly, she pulled off her camisole, stepped out of her tap pants and ran toward the water.

"Hey, hold up!" he shouted. "I have on more clothes than you."

A glance over her shoulder showed him struggling with his britches, and she laughed, loving how the sound echoed over the water. She ran until the water was deep enough and then arched her arms over her head to dive in.

The water here was crystal clear. The sandy bottom whizzed past and sunfish darted out of her way as Twyla glided forward, arms at her sides and paddling her feet leisurely. She didn't see him, but sensed Forrest's arrival and held out one hand, which he clasped. Together, as one, they swam forward a measurable distance before a silent, mutual consent made them surface at the same time.

He kissed her, and Twyla knew she'd never tire of it. She wrapped her arms around him, and then her legs. The awareness of his flesh merging with hers caused such pleasure, a gravelly moan rumbled inside her throat. They sank beneath the water, and the lack of air finally forced them to separate in order to swim back up to the surface.

Forrest grabbed her waist and gave her a playful shove back toward the beach. She swam a few strokes, and then went under. After a few strokes, she flipped around to swim behind him, where she jumped on his back.

They sank again, and came up kissing and laughing. They dunked each other, kissed and frolicked in the water until they were almost back to shore. Forrest was ahead of her and dropped his legs to stand in the water that was chest-high. Twyla swam right into his arms, and, knowing they wouldn't sink this time, she once again wrapped her legs and arms around him.

"I haven't gone swimming in years," she said. He held her with both arms, so she used her hands to wipe the water off her face and comb back her hair, and then his.

"Why not? You live on the lake."

"Because you weren't here," she said. "Nothing was fun without you."

It seemed so natural, and so easy, for her to rub the tips of her breasts against his chest. The connection caused the muscles down low in her body to flex and quiver, and a hungry need inside her tripled.

Forrest lifted her higher, until her thighs were around his waist, her center flush against his stomach, and her breasts no longer beneath the water. He kissed her shoulder first, then her collarbone.

A craving, as unique and wild as she'd ever known, had her leaning back just enough so that her nipple brushed his chin. The simple contact was so spectacular tiny shivers of delight spread over her.

He kissed her nipple and licked it, leaving Twyla too enthralled to speak—or think. But she was anxious, so very anxious, for more. And

Forrest provided more, just as she'd known he would.

Twirling his tongue around her nipple, he closed his mouth and sucked. The pleasure was so grand, if he hadn't been holding her she'd have sunk beneath the water and probably drowned. For she certainly wouldn't have wanted him to stop. Not even in order to breathe.

"Goodness, Forrest," she said, almost whimpering. "Whatever you do, don't stop." She dug her hands into his hair, holding him where he was as her leg muscles tightened around him and her center throbbed.

Forrest released that nipple, but only because he turned slightly to lick the other one. "But I don't want this one to get jealous," he said.

"You're right," she said, arching against his mouth. "You must be fair."

He provided the same pleasure to that nipple, and the other one again, and that one again in turn, until Twyla was in such a state of frenzy she lost track of whose turn it was. She was burning with an agonizing yet pleasurable tension she couldn't describe.

"Forrest. Forrest." She grabbed his head and pulled his lips away, not sure she could take much more. Her toes were curling and little, very distinct jolts sped through her, making her arch against him. "I—I—" She had no idea what she wanted to say. It was all too splendid.

Forrest kissed her, over and over, and when he started to lay her down, she panicked for a brief moment, believing they were still in the water.

They weren't. Her fingers found warm sand, as did her back. She spread her arms out at her sides and dropped the back of her head into the sand. Those crazy, wonderful little jolts were still making her squeeze her thigh muscles.

Forrest unhooked her legs from his waist one by one, and lowered them onto the sand. Water washed over her feet and ankles. As it dawned on her that her eyes were closed, Twyla opened them and smiled as Forrest leaned over her. She wrapped her arms around his neck and luxuriated in a long kiss.

When he broke away, he whispered, "I'll be right back."

"No," she whimpered, but he was gone.

However, true to his word, he was back a moment later.

She held up her arms to wrap around his neck again, but as she tried to pull him down, he lifted her off the ground by sliding both arms beneath her.

"Where are we going?" she asked, when he stepped into the water.

"I'm just going to rinse the sand off you," he said. "I laid out the blanket from the basket."

Holding her in his arms, he glided into the water and swam a small circle. Then he stood and carried her onto the beach. The little jolts had lessened, and were no longer stealing all of her attention, so this time when Forrest laid her down, she was able to fully appreciate the view. Him, in all his naked glory.

Unabashed and unashamed, she let her gaze roam over him, knowing he was doing the same to her. In silent communication, their eyes met and their smiles grew.

"You are so beautiful," he said, his voice a bit raspy as he lay down beside her.

Knowing he'd never find fault in her, she admitted, "My boobs aren't very big."

Propped on one elbow, he chuckled and cupped one breast with his free hand. His hand and thumb had almost the same effect on her as his mouth had.

"I think they're perfect." He kissed one peak, and then the other. "More than a mouthful is a waste."

Twyla had no response because he'd started to taste one nipple, and all those sensuous and wonderful sensations he'd created had leaped to life all over again. She grappled for some sort of control, but it was useless, and suddenly, for the first time that she could ever remember, she realized she didn't want to control anything.

Forrest stroked the length of her side and her stomach, which sent those fiery little jolts into such chaos she released a pleasure-filled moan and arched her hips. His hand slid lower, igniting turmoil inside her like she'd never have believed.

Twyla gave herself complete freedom to experience each nuance of the pleasure Forrest brought forth. Legs spread, arms stretched at her sides, she encouraged him to caress and kiss her at will.

Her eyes were closed, soaking up the sweet agony of those toe-curling jolts, when the heat of his breath blew across the juncture of her thighs. She opened her eyes, let her smile assure him of her consent and lifted her hips off the blanket.

The first brush of his tongue sent a zip of sweetness clear to her toes. She'd had no idea this was part of lovemaking, but trusted Forrest completely. She bent her knees, giving him more room, but then she lost all train of thought.

Forrest took her to uncharted regions, licking her, kissing her, until she hooked her legs around his shoulders and arched her back as a cry of pure gratification left her throat.

The jolts were huge now, swirling and growing bigger, and multiplying by the thousands. Her breath was uneven, her heart racing, and the strain inside her was massive. She was sure she couldn't take any more, but Forrest continued. He was a flyboy, and it was as if she was his plane, soaring higher and higher until there was nowhere else to go.

Then it happened, an inner explosion that released all the pressure within. It was as if she floated there for a moment, on some majestic cloud that cradled her in its softness as it slowly started to descend.

Just like his airplane, she returned to earth as smoothly as she'd left, and there was nothing to compare to the satisfaction swimming in her veins.

Too weak to lift an arm, she sighed heavily. "Forrest, if I didn't know better, I'd say you lit a firecracker inside me."

He didn't answer right away, and she opened her eyes, wondering why. Another bout of excitement shot through her as she watched him roll on a rubber.

A second later, he poised himself over her. "That firecracker is you."

"Well, come on, flyboy," she said, hooking her heels to the backs of his knees. "I'm ready to take off again."

His entrance was a single long stroke that stole her breath. Not because of the tiny snap of pain; that was nothing compared to the long, gratifying rapture of being completely connected to him. Mind, body and soul.

Knowing what to expect this time, Twyla participated for all she was worth. Every thrust Forrest gave, she welcomed, and lifted her hips to prepare for the next one. This flight was more fulfilling than her first one, more rewarding knowing that Forrest was enjoying it just as much as she, and when she found herself skyward, she rejoiced by shouting his name.

His body was rock-hard, driving into her with stamina and precision, and she cherished every second of climbing higher and higher with him. Together they flew past all their dreams and fantasies.

Twyla was at the point she could go no further, but wanted him at her side, and asked, "Now, Forrest?"

"Now, Twyla," he growled in response.

Their joint completion left her speechless, and satisfied, and happy, and, most of all, full. There was no emptiness inside her heart now, and she knew there never would be again.

With the sun shining upon them, they lay there for some time, doing nothing more than holding hands and watching the clouds roll by. Forrest then pulled the picnic basket closer and they fed each other strawberries and bits of cheese. Afterward they took another swim to rinse away the sand and put their clothes back on.

Twyla couldn't imagine a more perfect afternoon.

While Forrest shook out the blanket and folded it, Twyla dug to the bottom of the picnic basket. "What are you looking for?" he asked.

"I want to make sure there aren't any more rubbers in here," she explained. "I wouldn't want the kitchen staff to find them."

"There was only one," he said.

"Leave it to Josie to only give us one," she said, brushing the sand from her knees.

Forrest put the blanket in the basket and closed the lid. "Let me preface by saying I was happy to see it, because I hadn't thought that far ahead when I left town, but does your father know Josie has rubbers?"

Twyla grinned at the way his cheeks turned faintly pink. "Of course he doesn't. She keeps them hidden in her closet." Stepping closer, she kissed him. "Cases of them."

He grabbed her shoulders. "Cases?"

Twyla nodded. "I'll get a supply from her."

His eyes widened, and then he closed them for a minute, as if to catch a thought. "Why would Josie have cases of rubbers in her closet?"

"From her Ladies Aid Society."

"Her what?" He looked shocked. "Those little

old ladies bowling today? The ones I had to ask to move their cars so that I could leave?"

Twyla hooked her arm with his and gestured for him to pick up the basket. Once they started walking, she said, "I don't know all the ins and outs of it, but I know that group does more than grow flowers, watch birds and throw birthday parties for eighty-year-olds."

"Like what?"

"I don't know. Josie never talks about it."

"Do they have anything to do with her arrest?"

"I believe so," Twyla said. "But Josie said she can't talk about it, and she won't. She's always been the quiet one. I think that's why the group let her in. She is the youngest member by ten or more years. Maybe twenty. Gloria recommended she join."

"Gloria Kasper, the doctor?"

"Yes. That's where the rubbers come from." Growing tired of the conversation, Twyla hugged his arm. "Have you ever flown over fireworks before?"

"Not directly over them," he answered. "That would be dangerous. But close enough. It's an amazing sight."

"I can't wait." A dreamy sigh escaped her as she leaned her head against his shoulder. "It's going to be fabulous."

"Is that enough time for you to plan a wedding?" he asked. "If not—"

"Don't think you're getting out of this one, Forrest Reynolds," she said sternly. "You said the Fourth of July and I'm not letting you change your mind."

He swung her around in front of him. "I'm not changing my mind. But I know you. You'll want a new dress and shoes."

"Yes, I will," she agreed. "I'll buy them tomorrow. The only other thing we'll have to do is call the preacher. We can do that today. Nothing else matters."

"Except for the fact I haven't asked your father's permission."

She stretched on her toes to plant a brief kiss on Forrest's lips. "He'll say yes. He likes you. He always has." A flutter happened in her belly, and she bit down on her bottom lip.

"What?" Forrest asked, frowning.

"What about your mother?"

He kissed her forehead and then took her hand. Once they started walking again, he said, "My mother already knows. I told her in California that I was in love with you, and now that Galen is once and for all behind bars, I was going to ask you to marry me."

Twyla stopped in her tracks. "You did?"

"Yes, I did."

"Why am I the last to know?"

"The last to know?"

"Yes." They'd arrived at the beach facing the resort, and she waved a hand. "Josie knew you were in love with me, your mother knew you were in love with—" Forrest's kiss stopped her short.

"You knew I was in love with you," he said before kissing her again.

She pushed at his chest, but only after accepting another full kiss. "No, I didn't." He was kissing her neck now and she was growing a little fuzzy-headed. "I'd hoped, but I didn't know."

"Now you do." He lifted her chin. "But I think, if you think really hard, you'll realize you always knew. You just wanted something to be mad at Norma Rose about. You two have always needed something to argue about."

Twyla tried to be mad, but it was impossible. "You may be right. But you never had to live with her. From the time you left until Ty arrived, she was gnarly."

He flicked her nose. "And you were a brat."

She spun around and started walking to where she'd left her stockings.

Laughter followed her. "Not going to admit that one?"

"There's nothing to admit," she said.

He caught her around the waist and pulled her

back against him. "You were always a brat, but I loved you anyway."

She leaned her head back against him and folded her arms around the ones holding her tight. Her world was so perfect nothing mattered. Gazing up at the clear blue sky, she said, "Tell me about your airmail route. When will it start?"

"I don't have the contract yet," he said.

"You will," she said, believing in him fully. "You will."

He kissed her temple. "With you at my side, everything's possible."

"You'd better believe it," she said.

* * * * *

MILLS & BOON®

& HISTORICAL

AWAKEN THE ROMANCE OF THE PAST

A sneak peek at next month's titles...

In stores from 2nd October 2015:

- **Christian Seaton: Duke of Danger** – Carole Mortimer
- **The Soldier's Rebel Lover** – Marguerite Kaye
- **Return of Scandal's Son** – Janice Preston
- **The Forgotten Daughter** – Lauri Robinson
- **No Conventional Miss** – Eleanor Webster
- **Dreaming of a Western Christmas** – Lynna Banning, Kelly Boyce & Carol Arens

---